MW01048390

TO JACQUES

THANKS FOR
DOING AN
INSPIRATION
ALWAYS?!
MUCH LOVE

PORTER

MARCUS MATHIAS

BOOK I

N. M. BOBOK

ISBN-13 9781539051794 ISBN-10: 153905179X

This book is dedicated to my grandpa,
Nelson Miranda, the first person
to ever show me the stars.

Te amo, Vô.

CHAPTERS

I

THE LION AND ME

There aren't many places like this.

I have only been here about a couple of times before, and yet I have never been to any other beach like this one. This beach, unlike the ones in my hometown of Boston, Massachusetts, has crystal clear waters, pearly white, warm sand very well adorned by all the different types, colors and sizes of seashells.

This place is the very well-known Copacabana Beach.

The Copacabana Beach is located in Rio de Janeiro, Brazil, the place that birthed my dad many years ago. When my mom used to be her adventurous self, she would travel all over the world. It was on one of those adventures that she went to Rio de Janeiro for the carnival and met my dad.

Though their relationship was on-again, off-again, they would visit each other when they could; Mom would vacation in Brazil and Dad would make visits to Boston.

And then my sister Daniella happened.

After they found out they were expecting their first child, he decided to transfer his job to Boston and move in with my mom. It wasn't until after my third birthday that they decided to get married and spend their honeymoon in Brazil. That was the first time that I've been to this beach, the Copacabana Beach.

I remember sitting on the warm white sand and looking at all of those people just laying down on the beach, sunbathing; the kids building sandcastles, shirtless guys walking around selling coconuts or popsicles; people jumping in and out of the water. Everyone is just having a great time.

One of the things that caught my eye was the statue of Christ, the Redeemer. The massive statue of Jesus Christ with his arms wide open sitting atop the Corcovado Mountain stood at more than one-hundred feet tall; like I said before, massive. It stands as a symbol of Brazil's Christianity as well as a beautiful piece of art.

And that is where I am right now. Sitting at the warm white sand facing the ocean with the statue right behind me, to my right, on the top of the mountain just how I remembered it. Except that this time, I was by myself. No kids were playing in the sand, no women sunbathing in little swimsuits and no guys walking around selling fresh coconuts or popsicles.

Just me.

"It's beautiful, isn't it?" A woman's voice spoke right behind me, making me jump to my feet. "It's okay, Marcus. It's only me."

I saw it, but I couldn't believe it. There, standing less than a couple of feet away from me, was a huge white lion with bright-white eyes. If it weren't for its naturally frightening look, I would think the lion was actually smiling at me. Not to mention that the lion had addressed me by my own name.

"Don't be afraid, *querido*[1]. I want to talk to you," the lion spoke again.

"You can speak?" I managed to ask.

"There's more to it than meets the eye, Marcus,"

"But your voice is?"

"That of an old woman?" She finished my sentence, making her mane disappear around and inside her neck, in less than a couple of seconds, looking completely like a lioness now, "Is this better?"

"Whoa, how did you do that?"

I hesitantly approached the lioness only to realize how tall the animal was. My face reached the neck of the lioness barely. It was the biggest lioness I had ever seen, and I'm 5'8" tall on a good day.

"I don't have much time, but I need you to know that many people will try to grow closer to you to gain your trust. Many of them you cannot trust, and they will do whatever they can to destroy you. There

---

[1] *Querido:* Dear (Portuguese)

will be a time when you'll have no one but yourself, and only then you'll have the strength to become who you are meant to be," the lioness stated worriedly.

'Marcus Mathias, where are you?
I know you're here somewhere.
I bring you wondrous news,
News to tell you that no one dares.
Where are you, Marcus, where?'

A melodic boyish voice came singing from the ocean right behind me, interrupting the conversation between myself and the lioness. I turned and saw a little boat that couldn't possibly fit more than five people; in it was only a boy playing a stringed instrument of some sort, like a small harp. He had rich midnight-blue hair that contrasted against his pale skin which appeared to have been untouched by the Sun; he seemed to be older than me but not by much.

"I take it you were talking about him, huh?" I asked the lioness, while I stared at the boy wondering how the boat could be moving without him rowing it.

"He's here!" the lioness spoke sounding a bit disturbed by the boy.

"Who is he, and what does he want with me?" His melody wouldn't stop playing as he was growing closer and closer to the beach.

"Listen, my dear, I have to go before he sees me, remember what I told you, you're not alone. Find within yourself the strength you need, and you'll be amazed at all the things you can do. We'll talk soon,"

"Hey, wait a min—" I turned around to face the lioness again, but with a roar she shut me up, jumping right through me, making me fall backward on the sand.

I opened my eyes again only to find myself laying in my bed, in my house all the way back in Boston.

KNOCK-KNOCK

"*Bom-dia²*, sleepyhead." That would be my mom, knocking on my door first thing in the morning. Usually, I get quite annoyed by it, but I was actually kind of relieved to see her leaning against the door frame, hearing her voice. Besides, it was a special day for me. Today is May 8th, my birthday, not just any birthday but my sixteenth birthday.

"Happy birthday, honey," she said making her way into my room.

"I made your favorite, scrambled eggs with toast and chocolate chip pancakes, and I brought some O.J. as well.

"Aww, thanks, Mom," I said, sitting up to enjoy my birthday breakfast.

"Are you okay, honey?" She asked putting down the tray in front of me.

"Yeah, I just had a weird dream, that's all," I said, trying to shake it off.

"Well, today is your birthday. Don't let any bad dreams keep you from having a great day," she said kissing my forehead, "enjoy your breakfast and get ready. Jacques should be here soon so we can head

---

² *Bom dia:* Good Morning (Portuguese)

out to the mall. Take a shower. You'll feel better."

"Thanks, Mom."

"*Feliz aniversário, filho[3],*"

"Mom, your Portuguese is..."

"Hey, my Portuguese is pretty good, young man,"

"I know, but your accent destroys it," I laughed, mocking her.

"Well, it worked on your dad,"

"MOM!"

"You sure you're okay?" she asked before leaving the room.

"Yeah, it's just that, you know, I wish Dad was here for my birthday,"

"Marcus, honey, you know your dad is taking care of some family issues down in Brazil, he should be back soon. If he could, he would be here with you, but Nana needs him right now. She is very ill, and he is doing everything he can to help her through this difficult time," she reminded me.

"I know, I know. I just miss him a lot. It's been such a long time since I've seen dad, and it's the first time I'm spending my birthday without him."

"I'm sure he misses you too, plus he should give you a call later. You'll be able to see him on cam. We both love you very much, don't you ever forget that,"

"Thanks, Mom."

"Alright, now go brush off those teeth of yours, it seems like something has died in there," she said by the door, before leaving the room.

---

[3] *Feliz aniversário, filho:* Happy birthday, son. (Portuguese)

"Mom?"

"Yes, son?"

"You're the best,"

I sat there, looking at my plate thinking about what the lioness had said to me in my dream: "You're not alone, find within yourself the strength you need, and you'll be amazed at the things you can do." What did she mean by that? Who was she? Her voice was so familiar, yet I couldn't figure out who it belonged to. And who was that midnight-blue haired boy? What did he want with me? I have no idea who he was, and I barely saw his face. I only remember his midnight-blue hair, falling over his forehead allowing his matching midnight-blue eyes to glimmer right through it as if a dark-blue veil was holding a star trapped in the place where his eyes should be.

I got out of bed and reached for one of my rocks out of my collection.

I had always collected rocks. I had shelves full of stones of all kinds, types, colors, and sizes. To me, they were not just rocks; they have this particular thing about them, and every time I saw a different rock, I had to have it for myself. It always gave me the feeling of being well- grounded, focused, and even re-laxed at times. As weird as it may sound, I really liked having them around. I lost count of how many times I'd fallen asleep with one of them in my hand.

I ate my breakfast, turned on some music and took a shower. Mom was right; it definitely made me feel better. I grabbed this dark-green t-shirt that had always brought me luck. The last time that I wore it was underneath my jersey when my dad and I went to a football game, New England Patriots against the New York Giants at the Gillette Stadium. Final score: 28 - 24, Patriots. I put on some jeans and matched sneakers and headed downstairs.

"Hey, you finally made it! I thought you had gotten yourself lost on the way down to the kitchen from your bedroom," Mom mocked me as I made my way to the kitchen with my breakfast tray in my hands.

"Ha! Funny, very funny," I smiled at her.

"Just leave the dishes by the sink, I'll put them in the dishwasher in a moment before we head to the mall."

"Has Jacques called?" I asked.

"No, not yet. I can't wait to get you your new cell phone. Next time, please try to be careful with it when you're near a swimming pool."

"Mom, I told you, Jacques dropped it in the pool by accident."

DING-DONG - The doorbell.

"Speaking of him," I said as I made my way to the front door.

"*Joyeux Anniversaire*⁴, Marks!" Jacques exclaimed excitedly as I allowed him in.

"Wow, you guys must be psychically connected," my mom said. Her sense of humor never ceases to amaze me.

Jacques DüMicahellis and I have been friends since kindergarten. We are about the same age with

---

⁴ *Joyeux anniversaire:* Happy birthday (French)

a lot of things in common, besides one thing: Jacques is from a very wealthy family, me, not so much. However, Jacques never let money shape who he is as a person. Sometimes, he would even borrow money from me just to make me feel equal. I would find it back in my backpack the next day. His father was a very successful soccer player in France who retired when Jacques was only five years old. Jean-Luc, his father, had always traveled to America whenever he was on vacation, and on one of those trips, he met Jacques' mom, Alexia. Does that sound familiar?

They got married, and it hadn't been much of a struggle for Mr. DüMicahellis to retire in the United States. He soon found out that this was a country where paparazzi weren't too excited about retired soccer players, and this was everything he ever wanted.

Physically, Jacques and I are entirely different from each other. He has white skin, which is even paler in comparison to my olive skin. He has blue eyes just like his dad; I have green eyes, which I got from my mom. His hair is so naturally blonde that sometimes it would blind me in the sun, just like his mom's. Mine is dark-brown, almost black, similar to, well, both of my parents. I, however, am built slightly more prominent than him. My love of football had helped me in that department and Jacques is more into soccer, providing him with a slimmer, but equally toned, body. Soccer is huge in France and Brazil, and Jacques wanted to be a professional soccer player, just like his dad. I, on the other hand, have no clue what I want to be when I grow up; maybe a football player or a geologist.

Jacques and I would always play soccer on Sundays with our dads. My mom and Jacques' mom were also very good friends. They would spend afternoons together whenever they could, sipping coffee, talking about all the other kids' moms from school. Our families were very close.

"I got something for you that I truly hope you like. After all, I have been talking about this for way too long, and you just keep ignoring it, and this is the coolest sh—"

"What is it, Jacques?" I interrupted him before he could say any bad words in front of my mom, she would simply not have it.

"Oh, yeah. Here," he handed me this little box, and I knew exactly what it was.

"Mirabilis?" I asked before I even open the box.

"YES! How did you know?" Jacques asked disappointed for not being able to surprise me.

"As you said, you've been talking about it for too long now; I figured it had to be it."

"Well, what are you waiting for? Open it!" He demanded in excitement.

I untied the purple ribbon, opened the box wrapped in silver, as we made our way to the living room. Just as I thought, there it was, wrapped in a royal purple silk cloth: a titanium bracelet no more than an inch thick with the word MIRABILIS engraved on the inside. It was so beautiful to look at it. I couldn't believe he actually bought me one of the most expensive games out there.

"PUT IT ON!" Jacques' excitement almost made me drop the box and the bracelet on the floor with it.

I put it on my right wrist, and **BOOM** this beam of light came out of the bracelet projecting a silver screen onto the wall covering my mom's favorite painting of Van Gogh with the word MIRABILIS in bright-royal-purple letters.

MIRABILIS. STATE YOUR NAME A computerized female voice spoke it out from the bracelet.

"Marcus Mathias," I said a bit skeptical.

WELCOME, MARCUS MATHIAS. ARE YOU READY TO SAVE THE HUMAN RACE FROM THE FLESH-EATERS? The same voice asked the question, revealing beautiful graphics of a world destroyed by the Flesh-Eaters, that Jacques loved so much.

"Is this another zombie apocalypse video-game?" My mom asked as she entered the living room.

"THEY ARE NOT ZOMBIES!" Shouted a very aggravated Jacques, "*Je suis désolé*[5]," Jacques apologized, "their bodies are being held by a virus that makes them eat human flesh, but they are not dead, just prisoners inside of their own bodies," he explained to us both.

"It sounds pretty cool," I said removing the bracelet out of my arm, turning it off.

DING-DONG

"It sounds like a zombie apocalypse to me," Mom

---

[5] *Je suis désolé:* I'm sorry (French)

said opening the door.

"Hello, Mrs. Mathias. Hi, birthday boy." Mileena walked in with a small gift bag in her hands. "Hope you don't mind me stopping by before everyone else."

"Oh no, not all. Besides, Jacques is here too,"

"He doesn't count," she walked in the living room barely glancing at him from the corner of her eyes.

Mileena Watson is a seventeen-year-old girl from Tennessee; her almond-shaped and colored eyes matching her light brown wavy hair, flowing down to her elbows. Ever since she transferred to our school a few years back, the three of us have been the best of friends. She didn't know anyone else in town at that time. Her mom was from Boston but had moved to Tennessee way before Mileena was born. A few years ago, Mrs. Martha Watson divorced her husband, Mr. Joseph Watson, deciding then to move back to her hometown.

Jacques and I took turns showing Mileena around. She liked Boston a lot. In one of our recent trips to the North End, in between cannoli, pizza, and gelato, Jacques developed a crush on her, and none of us really knew about it until one particular day in school when she asked him to partner for a science project. He reacted with a blank stare and a whole lot of blabbing and slurred words until he was finally able to say 'yes'. That entire week he was referred to as Jacques, the Daydreamer. It was the highlight of the year. Now, Jacques had already professed his immense love for her, to which she just replied 'thanks'. But, according to him, Miles, her nickname, was also madly in love with him and was just afraid to express it out loud.

"Well, I am very happy to see you, *ma belle princesse*[6]," flirted Jacques.

"So, I got this for you. I hope you like it," Miles said, completely ignoring Jacques' comment, handing me a gift bag. As I opened the bag, I recognized the same small silver box that Jacques had handed me a few moments ago.

"Is something wrong?" She asked noticing the awkwardness in my face.

"No, no, not at all. It's, it's just that..." I took the box out of the bag showing it to Jacques the same game he had just given me a couple of minutes ago: Mirabilis.

"MILES! You were supposed to get him the book!" Jacques spoke a bit louder than usual to Mileena.

"The book? What book? You told me to get the game because you were going to get a book," she replied to him.

"No, I told you I was going to get him the game and you, the book. I don't read books; how would I know where to buy him a book?"

"What book are you talking about, Jax?" she asked a bit angry at him.

"I don't know, it was your idea," Jacques replied thoughtlessly.

"Alright kids, how about we go to the mall and re-

---

[6] *Ma belle princesse:* My pretty princess (French)

turn one of the games and get him the book? Whatever this book is. And besides, we have to go get your new phone anyway," my mom stepped out of her room suggesting it to us.

"YES! That's a great idea, right guys?" I, who don't like confrontation, agreed.

"Fine," they both spoke in unison with a slightly defeated voice.

"Let me go to my room to drop this game off and grab my jacket so we can head out." I wanted to go upstairs to play just for a bit my new game before we went to the mall.

Those graphics were amazing, and I had to see it just one more time before leaving the house. It was my birthday, after all, I'm sure Jax and Miles wouldn't mind waiting downstairs for just a little bit.

WELCOME BACK, MARCUS MATHIAS

The familiar computerized voice spoke again as soon as I put the bracelet back on my wrist, revealing the same beautiful graphics that I saw downstairs in the living room.

"Marcus, we need to talk," a different voice, computerized voice spoke making me jump and look around my room. "I'm here, right in front of you," the same boyish voice spoke again.

I turned my face back to the front where my bracelet was projecting the screen and right under Mirabilis I saw a guy standing about a foot taller than me in his late teens/early twenties staring at me.

"Whoa, this game is really good. He looks very real." I approached him as if to touch him. His midnight-blue hair and matching eyes gazing into my own eyes, I was looking for any pixels or any resolution that would give him away as a game projected character but couldn't find any. He was that real.

"Marcus, I can assure you that I am real," he spoke and walked my way passing through the projection and right in front of me, grabbing my arms. I fell backward onto my bed, forcing the game to turn itself off.

"Who are you? How did you get in here?" I panicked.

"Listen to me, your friends will be missing you soon so let me explain it before you panic any further," he tried to calm me down, his hands were pale, and his slim but toned figure made it almost impossible to succeed it.

"Panic? I'm not panicking! Who are you?" I lied, obviously panicking.

"Hey, Marks, is everything okay up there? Why are you taking so long?" Jacques shouted from downstairs.

"Marcus don't tell him I'm here. I'll come back later to talk to you. Please, Marcus, don't!"

"Marcus let's go. Your mom is calling you." Jacques' voice was getting closer.

"Happy birthday, Marks," the boy smiled at me.

"Hey, only my friends call me—," before I could finish my sentence, I saw something that made no sense at all. The boy stretched his two arms, and they were instantly transformed into two beautiful midnight-blue feathered wings just like his hair and eyes, his legs popped back inward taking the shape of bird legs, two times smaller than his own. Where his mouth was, now was a beak, also dark-blue. All of his head and body were now covered in the same matching midnight-blue colored feathers just like his eyes were, now, they were all white, shining as if a star had taken the place of where his eyes used to be. He winked at me and flew away through the window.

"MARCUS!" Shouted Jacques from the other side of the door almost breaking it down.

"Sorry," I unlocked the door, allowing him in.

"Couldn't find a jacket, *pote*⁷?" He made his away inside my bedroom, "Hey, are you okay?" Jacques asked, noticing my pale face.

"Yeah, no, I'm okay. Let's go," I grabbed a jacket nearby, heading out of the room.

"Marcus, the bracelet," Jacques pointed to it still on my wrist.

"Oh, right," I removed the bracelet and tossed it on my bed, walking out of the room and downstairs without glancing back at Jacques.

"Finally!" Mileena exclaimed by the door, "Your mom is already waiting for us in the car, Marks. Hey, are you guys alright?" She asked once noticing our blank expressions.

"Yeah, we're fine," answered Jacques before I could come up with an excuse, making me feel even

---

⁷ *Pote:* Buddy (French)

more guilty for lying to him. Jacques knew I wasn't good with lies. But then again what was I supposed to say? 'A boy walked into my room and wanted to talk to me, but before he could, he transformed himself into a huge blue bird and flew away.' I don't think so. I decided to keep it to myself, and as a matter of fact, I didn't speak much on the trip to the mall.

***

We got to the mall, and I spotted one of my favorite stores: Frontiers.

Frontiers is a store that sells music, electronics, comics, and books. They have all the major games and all the books you can think of, so it would somewhat be easy for me to choose what I would exchange my game for.

"Alright you guys, I'm gonna go to the scented candles store and be back in an hour. Please behave, okay?" Mom told us as she made her way to the store that seemed like the least fun place to be.

"Okay Marcus, go to the other side of the store, over by the manga and comics section while we go exchange your game for a book," Mileena dictated.

"Wait, what?" I asked.

"What? You thought we would let you see the book we are getting for you?" She laughed.

"Yeah…" I said kind of objectively but made my way to the comics section anyways.

From afar I could see Jacques' concerned face. I smiled and nodded at him as to assure that I was okay. But I wasn't sure if I was okay.

First was my dream this morning with the lioness that could speak and the creepy singing boy in the boat. Then there was this boy in my room, hey! Come to think of it, the two boys were somewhat similar, both with midnight-blue hair and matching eyes with ashen white skin. This was all getting too weird. Yup, I'm going crazy on my own birthday.

"This just got way easier than I expected, *aneki*[8]," a guy very close by spoke threateningly.

"I told you his friends would soon leave him all alone and helpless, ready to be taken to our King," a girl's voice also coming from behind me, replied.

I discretely looked behind me, and to my surprise, I saw, no more than a few feet away from me, a guy and a girl in their mid-twenties so identical that I wasn't sure which voice came from who. They were both dressed in black sweatpants, black t-shirts, and black running shoes. His hair was black, chin length, almost covering his also black eyes. Hers was also black and chin length, styled as her brother's. Apart from her barely present makeup and apparent female body, I wouldn't be able to differentiate the two Asian twins.

"Oh yeah, Marcus, we are coming for you," the guy spoke again with a grim smile on his face.

"Me?" I asked, "Who in the world are you?" I logically panicked again for the second time on my birthday. And it was barely noon.

---

[8] *Aneki:* Sis (Japanese)

"Oooh, he's feisty, *aniki*[9]," she mocked me, "I like it,"

"You'll have plenty of time to ask questions, Dogie. Right now, all we gotta do is take you to the King, whether you're willing or not," the grinning guy spoke again approaching faster. They both blinked at the same time, and the weirdest thing happened. Just like the Midnight-Blue Eyed Guy who visited me earlier in my room, their eyes became bright-white as if stars were trapped behind their eyes with no pupils.

"KING? You guys are crazy!" I turned away from them making my way around the aisles between books and comics and right there, in front of me, they appeared again. I turned back trying to find another way out into the next aisle, and impossibly enough they were right in front of me. Again. This time, even closer than before. I ran to the middle aisle where I could see all the rest of the store, every single row was a pair of twins. The same twins.

"Are you tired yet?" He asked grabbing my arm.

I looked around myself and thought that I had indeed gone crazy for there were two pairs of identical twins surrounding me.

"What? You guys can multiply?" I asked, trying to free myself from his grip.

"Something like that, silly Dogie." And just like that, the other pair of twins vanished in thin air, leaving only a trace of glittering dust floating around.

"What in the world?" I asked, terrified of them.

---

[9] *Aniki*: Bro (Japanese)

"As I said, you'll have plenty of time to ask questions once we take you to the King," the guy reminded me again. I hate his sarcasm.

"I'm not going anywhere!" I tried to free myself without any luck.

"You can't fight us boy, we are Wonderers," she said loud and proud, followed by a crazy laugh.

Both of them were holding me now. He had both of his hands gripping my right arm, and she was holding my left arm also with both hands. They dragged me a few feet away and then suddenly everything became bright in front of my eyes as if someone turned on a spotlight on my face. My whole body started tingling from inside out, head to toes.

"Guys, I'm not feeling well, please let me go," I pleaded, completely losing stability of my body. I guess it was a good thing they were both holding me.

"Nice try, Dogie," she told me.

"Dogie? Don't you mean 'doggie'?" I try to say out loud, but the words barely came out. My whole body was tingling, my arms and legs were getting heavier and heavier, and all I could see now was a blur of white light, with dark shadows replacing everything around me.

"Guys, I..." tried it again but also with no luck, no sound came out, my body was jerking in all directions

"Hey, what's happening?" The girl asked her brother.

"He is not a Porter yet, how is this even possible!?" He sounded freaked out about it.

I couldn't hear anything anymore. The pain and

the anger combined with the panic of trying to free myself had left me deaf. I decided to look at my arm but all I saw was this thin white fur. My hands were gone, covered in some sort of cow-shaped hooves and all I wanted to do was free myself. And I did.

I heard the girl let out a scream followed by the guy's plead to leave her alone. I thought to myself 'the cops are here,' but I couldn't see anything. My body was heavy as if my upper body had gotten one hundred pounds heavier and ***BANG*** - I fell face flat on the floor unconsciously.

"Marks? Are you okay? Marcus?" I heard a familiar voice asking me as she slapped my face, getting me back to consciousness.

"Yeah, I'm okay, Jena," I didn't have to look to recognize her voice followed by her hand. Her skin was well darker than mine, making me look paler than I actually am for a Brazilian-American like myself.

Jena Alvis used to go to the same school that I go to, and even though she's only fifteen years old and younger than all of us, she graduated last year before all of us. Yup, she is that smart. Her mother, Audrey Roosevelt, had passed away from cancer when she was only seven years old. Her father, Mr. Jamal Alvis, was a surgeon's assistant.

In one particular heart valve surgery, between operating on the aortic valve and pulmonary Valve, Jamal met Marisa, a thoracic doctor. She performs operations on hearts, lungs, esophagi, and other organs in the chest. Mr. Alvis asked her out, but she only said yes after he helped her save a patient's life. They have been married for over six years now, and even though Marisa is Jena's stepmom, they were pretty close as daughter and mother are.

"What happened?" I asked getting myself back up.

"Whoa, take your time there, buddy. You better stay seated for a minute or two, you just fainted." She told me as she handed me a glass of water that one of the employees had grabbed for me.

"I fainted? I've never fainted before," I finally got up to my feet.

"Did you eat at all today, Marks?" She asked concerned.

"Yeah, yeah. Hey, did you see what happened? Did you see where those two ran off to?" I looked around trying to spot the twins with no luck.

"Who? All I heard was a loud bang nearby and next thing I knew, you were passed out face flat on the floor. Oh, here they come."

I looked behind me afraid I was going to see the twins again. But it was Jacques and Mileena.

"Are you okay?" Mileena asked, squatting down quickly to feel my temperature.

"Yeah, yeah I'm fine," I said taking her hands off of my forehead.

"I'm glad you're here; he was just asking about you."

"Are you sure you're okay, Marks?" Jacques asked in a low, concerned voice.

"Yeah, Jax. Hey, you didn't see a couple of Asian twins, did you? A guy and a girl in their twenties all dressed in black?"

"You gotta be more specific than that Marks, there's a lot of people around us and I'm pretty sure you'll find a lot of Asian couples around us," Jacques spoke with concern.

"Never mind," I replied defeatedly trying to pretend that nothing happened and that indeed I wasn't going crazy on my sixteenth birthday.

"Let's go, Marks, your mom is waiting for us," concluded Mileena. "Oh, I love what you did with your hair today, Jena...," she continued as they both headed out of the store in front of Jacques and me.

On the way home I tried to keep it low key in the car, I opened the book Mileena got for me: Sun: The Star of our Solar System by Luz Silva. I pretended to read it, but the truth is astronomy was never my thing, so I wasn't too excited about it.

My mom gave me my new cell phone, which technically was a new phone but was the exact same phone I had. Jacques never really dropped it in the water, I did in hopes that I would get the new nPhone, the latest, freshest and dopiest phone out there right now. But that didn't work.

So far, I wasn't enjoying my birthday at all.

II

SURPRISE!

Once we got home, I went to my room to put my new book on the bookshelf, next to the other books to collect dust. Jacques came along, leaving Jena and Mileena with my mom downstairs as they were putting the house together for my party later on, which I was no longer looking forward to. This day has proven to be one of the weirdest days ever, in all of the History of Marcus Mathias. Great, now I'm talking in the third person.

"Marcus, now that it's just us here, what the heck is going on?" Jacques asked as he made himself comfortable on my chair by the desk. I sat across from him on my bed and grabbed one of the stones out of the shelves.

"Don't be silly Jacques, everything's fine."

"It's okay if you don't wanna tell me, but don't lie to me. I've known you since we were five years old, I can tell when you're lying."

"Jacques, I—"

"Hey Marks, today is your birthday, your sixteenth birthday! It can't be that bad, now can it? Well, in seven months it will be me turning sixteen so you can be there for me like I am here for you now. Whenever you're ready to talk about whatever it is that's bothering you, you know I'm here for you, *pote*[10]," Jacques smiled, assuring me of our friendship.

"Thanks, man, I'm just not sure what's going on with me right now. But, as soon as I know, you'll be the first to hear," I assured him.

"Whenever you're ready, man, whenever." Jacques faced the laptop screen now and turned it on. "Hey, give me your phone so I can sync it with your PackBook, and sorry your plan didn't work out."

"It's alright, man, I tried," I laughed. "Here," I handed him my phone.

"Who were the twins you were talking about it in the mall?" He asked as if to take my mind off of things, but little did he know that he achieved just the opposite.

"I saw a couple of Asian twins in the mall, and I think I saw them in school before, but I wasn't sure, so I was wondering if you've seen them before, that was it," I sort of lied. "I really don't know them," we

---

[10] *Pote:* Buddy (French)

both implicitly agreed to pretend I wasn't lying.

"Wait, were they Koreans?"

"I think they were Japanese. Why? Do you know them?" I said hopefully, maybe I wasn't going crazy after all.

"Well, there is this Korean girl in my English class, Nari I think is her name and she is pretty hot. Maybe it could have been her, but I don't know if she has any hot twin brother for you, bro," said Jacques teasing me.

"Hilarious Jax, hilarious," I said wrestling him out of the chair.

"Hey, while your phone syncs, do you wanna play some Mirabillis?" Jacques excitedly suggested.

"What about the girls?" I asked.

"They are too busy getting your party together. I'm sure we are better off staying up here out of their way," he convinced me.

"Yeah, you're right," I agreed, "but what about your bracelet?"

"Oh, don't you worry buddy, I have it right here." Jacques pulled up his jacket's right sleeve revealing the same bracelet-game that I have.

"Of course, you do," I said putting mine on my right wrist, turning Mirabillis on.

As we were about thirty minutes into the game, my mom shouted from downstairs: "Marcus, you have a phone call!"

"I love how your mom says phone call even though it's a video call," Jacques noted as we paused the game.

27

"Force of habit, I guess," I laughed as I turned on the video call by my desk.

"Hey son, *Feliz Aniversário!*[11]" A very familiar face that I've been missing for a while appeared on the screen; it was my dad.

"Thanks, Dad, how are you?"

"Marks, I'll go downstairs to see if they need help putting the rest of the decorations together, I'll see you in a few. Hi, Mr. Mathias." Jacques knew that this was a call that I had been waiting for all day. It was the first time that I was spending my birthday without my dad.

"Hey there, Jacques," replied my dad to Jacques, just before he left the room. "I'm fine, son," he continued, "I still have a lot of things to get done here before I can head back home to Boston, but hopefully I'll be there soon. Enough about me, today is all about you. Are you excited about your sixteenth birthday? I bet your mom is organizing a great party for you downstairs."

"No, not really, it's just gonna be a few close people from school, and that's it."

"I'm truly sorry, son, I wish I could be there with you. It's the first time we are apart on your birthday."

"It's okay, Dad. I understand. Grandpa and Grandma need you now, I know you'll be back here as soon as you can, or maybe Mom and I could visit you after my graduation if you're not back by then."

"Even though that's not a couple years from now,

---

[11] *Feliz Aniversário:* Happy Birthday (Portuguese)

that's a great idea. I'm not sure if we'll be able to af-
ford it, though. You know I got laid off from work because of this trip, and your mom is the only one working right now, so we'll see, son." Dad's voice was a bit
shaky. I knew this whole situation with my grandma
was taking a toll on him.

"Let me help, Dad! Maybe I could get a job after
school, just a part-time job to help out in the house,
you know?"

"No, I want you to focus on school first and—"

"But Dad, I don't see why not. You and Mom need
help, so let me. It would give me something to do, and
it would make me feel important."

"Are you sure, Marcus? I don't want you to feel
obligated."

"Yeah, I'm sure. Let me help out in the house," I
insisted.

"Alright. It would mean a lot to your mom and me.
As a matter of fact, I know just the place for you to
start. I know the owner; I'll send you the phone number. Ask for Ms. Margaret Hills," he said as he typed
in all of the info that I needed. "Tell her I sent you."

"Thanks, Dad. I'll call her first thing in the morning!" Words couldn't express my excitement.

"You mean after school, right, young man?" he
asked, making sure I didn't forget that tomorrow was
a school day.

"Yeah, after school, Dad," I said reluctantly.

"Son, have a great birthday and enjoy yourself
with your friends, okay? As soon as I get back home,
we will go out and celebrate, alright?"

"Ok, Dad, thanks."

"I love you, buddy, take care of your mom for me, alright? You're the man of the house now."

"I got this, Dad," I assured him.

"*Tchau*[12], son."

"Bye, Dad." I turned off the screen. My cell phone vibrated next to me. A phone number that I didn't recognize. "Hello?" I answered.

"Hello, is this Marcus?" A woman's voice spoke in such a sweet tone on the other side of the phone that it reminded of a candy cane that I was already craving from Christmas.

"Mhm, yeah...?" I said a bit skeptical.

"Oh yes, of course, it's you, Marcus, honey, it's your cell phone, how silly of me. Hahahaha, how are you? Good? Good. My name is Margaret Hills, your dad told me you'd stop by, tomorrow? Yes, tomorrow. I'm expecting you here tomorrow at the Lulu's Coffee Place, right after school, alright? Alright. Put on some comfortable clothes and shoes, 'kay? 'Kay. So, I'll see you then. By-ey." She spoke all of that in one breath, not giving me a chance to reply to any of it. "Oh, and Marcus, happy birthday!" She said just before hanging up.

"Thanks..." I said to the phone since there was no longer anyone on the other end.

That was totally weird, odd to say the least. How did she have my number? Maybe my dad must've texted her while we were on the call? Anyway, I guess

---

[12] *Tchau:* Bye (Portuguese)

I did get the job then. Nice! I can have my own money and buy whatever I want, maybe even the new nPhone. That would be so cool!

I am sure Jacques wouldn't understand the whole thing behind getting a job, but Mileena, on the other hand, would totally understand. She has had a job at a restaurant for a couple of years now. I went downstairs to tell everyone about it and see if they needed help finishing up the decorations.

"SURPRISE!" A choir of voices shouted just as I got to the bottom of the stairs, making me almost drop my new old phone.

"What? I thought the party was in a few hours from now?!" I exclaimed, surprised in seeing a bunch of people from school here and also a few friends from the neighborhood as well. Jacques' parents were there too, along with Jena's parents and Mileena's mom. I made my way through the crowd greeting and thanking everyone for coming over. I was utterly surprised.

"Happy birthday, Marcus!" Jena congratulated me as she handed my gift: the comics version of Mirabilis. "Jax got you hooked on this, didn't he?"

"I guess he did," I hugged her as Mileena, and Jacques joined in.

"Thanks, guys, and whose idea was it to decorate the house with Mirabilis' characters and zombies everywhere?" I asked, looking at all the mini-cupcakes topped with edible body parts.

"MINE!" shouted Jacques from behind of Mileena. "Oh, and they are Flesh—"

"Eaters, I know. A few more body parts and this birthday party would look more like an off-season Halloween party," I mocked him.

"HA! I told you," Mileena said elbowing Jacques.

"But it's cool nevertheless, buddy," I assured him.

"And once you start playing the game, you'll love it even more, Marks. Let me tell you about this guy right here..." Jacques went on and on about all the characters and decorations in the house, leaving Mileena and Jena behind by the snack table. Even though I didn't know any of the characters, I went with it. I know it meant a lot to Jacques, so it made me happy that he was happy. As a matter of fact, as Jacques and I walked around through the house, everyone seemed happy. I saw everyone with sodas in their hands, eating the Brazilian snacks that my mom learned to make because of how much I loved them. Everyone was having a good time. That made me happy.

"Oh Marcus, remember that girl I told you about that has English classes with me?"

"Nori, yes...?" I remembered Jacques telling me about this Korean girl when I asked him about the Japanese Twins after the incident in the mall.

"Turns out she does have a brother."

"Seriously?" My heart was beating fast, maybe I wasn't crazy. Maybe Jacques did know them.

"Yeah, I invited them both, and they are right there," Jacques gestured to this girl with her little brother on her arms. He couldn't have been older than five years old.

"They are clearly not twins, Jax," I said to him, kind of relieved noticing that she didn't look anything like one of the Japanese twins I met earlier in the mall. Somehow that reminded me that maybe I was still going crazy after all.

"Gather 'round everyone," Mom said loudly, as she made her way to the living room with a half–deceased–upper–body–of–a–now–turned–zombie–guy cake. Apparently, it was one of the badass zombies, Flash-Eaters actually. My mom lit up the finger-shaped candle, and everyone started singing "Happy Birthday" to me.

"Don't forget to make a wish, honey." Mom told me as I was about to blow off the finger-shaped candle. As I cut the first piece of the cake, fake blood splattered everywhere to my mom's delight.

"I hope you know how much I love you because there is no other way I would have allowed a zombie-themed party to happen with a cake that splatters blood everywhere…" As the words were coming out of her mouth, her volume was increasing just a tiny bit, obviously not knowing about the splattering blood coming out of the cake.

"I love you too, Mom," I said hugging her.

Mom took over and finished cutting the rest of the cake while I passed the pieces to everyone, with the help of Mileena and Jena since Jacques decided to go for one of the first pieces.

I noticed this guy near the doorway to the back porch that I didn't see before. I went to bring him a piece of cake, but when I turned to walk over to him, he was gone. I made my way to the back porch thinking that maybe he was over there. But no luck, no one was out there. I stared at my mom's mermaid statue and right there and then I thought of my dad.

The mermaid statue was somewhat of a wedding memory that my mom and dad had. I never knew the whole story, only that, while on their honeymoon, my mom saw this statue and said she had to have it. And clearly, she did. I got to think of my dad, and suddenly I felt a knot in my stomach.

"He is fine, Marcus."

I jumped, not expecting anyone behind me dropping the plate that I had in my hand. "What a waste, that cake looked delicious!" The same guy that was in my room earlier today was right there in front of me, with the same midnight-blue eyes staring at me with a half-smile on his face. "Sorry, I didn't mean to startle you."

"Who are you and how did you get in here?" I said it louder than I intended to.

"Marcus, I told you I'd see you later on, and this is later on..." he spoke casually.

"WHAT DO YOU WANT FROM ME?" I shouted; my anger took over me.

"Marcus, buddy, what are you doing out here by yourself?" Jacques asked as he looked around to see if anyone else was out there with me.

"I thought I saw someone out here," I didn't even have to look behind me to know that the Midnight-Blue Eyed Guy was gone.

"Come on inside *pote*[13], your mom is looking for you," he said closing the porch's door behind us as we went back inside.

"Oh, Marcus, there you are!" Aunty April had just walked in. "Sorry I'm late for your party, but I couldn't miss my favorite nephew's birthday!" She hugged me so tight that I thought I was going to die of asphyxiation in her huge bosom.

"I'm your only nephew, Aunty April," I said as I tried to free myself out of her enormous body. People on my mother's side of the family were not particularly small, but Aunty April was definitely bigger than big.

"Here, I got you something. I hope you like it," she handed me a massive package that I almost couldn't carry myself.

"Thanks, Aunty," I opened the package, and to my surprise, a stuffed character from the latest animation movie was standing right there as big as me.

"Isn't it adorable? I know how you and Mileena went to the movies as friends a few months ago, and your mom said how much you loved the movie, so I got this for you."

"Thanks!" I said glancing at my mom from behind her.

"Sorry," my mom muttered.

"I know you just turned sixteen, but we can never let the kid inside of us die. Did you like it? I can always return it if you didn't, I—"

---

[13] *Pote:* Buddy (French)

"I love it, Aunty April." I hugged her. "Let me put this upstairs in my room." Truth is, I actually did love it, but I couldn't let the other kids in school know that I'm still a kid. I know I had just turned sixteen, but I still like my animation movies, cartoons, and video-games; I'm not planning on leaving that behind any-time soon. I put my new gift on top of my bed. I went back downstairs, but not until I checked and closed all the windows in my room, I didn't want any more surprises later on. I wasn't sure if I was crazy or not, but I wanted to make sure either way. No more Mid-night-Blue Eyed Guy for today; that kid is getting under my skin.

"Hey Marcus, people are leaving already, go say goodbye," my mom met me at the bottom of the stairs.

"Yeah, sure..." I went around again thanking peo-ple for coming over and for all of the fantastic gifts I got. I must say that Aunty April's was my favo-rite. Mileena and Jacques stayed later, helping my mom and I put the stuff away. There were still a few mini-cupcakes left along with the Brazilian goodies, which Jacques already claimed for me to bring to school for him tomorrow.

"Hey guys, thanks so much for everything, I had a great time." I thanked Jacques and Mileena again once we finished wrapping the last tray of ~~corpses~~ mini cupcakes.

"Alright Marks, I'm off. Do you want a ride, Jax? Jax?" Mileena asked Jacques as she grabbed her jacket.

"Oh, *oui, ma petit chou-chou[14]*, thanks. Bye, Marks, see you at school," Jacques said as he waved goodbye. "She wants me," he mouthed to me.

"Bye guys, see you at school." I closed the door behind them as they left.

"Honey, did you have a good time?" My mom, who was putting the trash away, came back in through the back door.

"Yeah, I did. Thanks, Mom."

"For the record, I didn't know that the cake would splatter blood everywhere; otherwise I wouldn't have allowed it,"

"Oh, I know Mom. I'll clean it all up tomorrow after school, okay?" I said apologetically.

"It's alright, son, go get some rest. You gotta wake up early tomorrow for school."

"Can I skip school tomorrow, Mom, please?" I tried.

"Yeah right, you already skipped school today, you're not skipping it tomorrow."

"Alright, good night Mom." I made my way to the stairway.

"And son, I love you," she said before I went up.

"I love you too, Mom." I went back and hugged her goodnight.

"Don't forget, I want all the blood off the walls to-morrow after school, okay?"

"Goodnight, Mom," I said, and this time I did go upstairs to my room. I opened my bedroom door and

---

[14] *Oh, oui, ma petit chou-chou: Oh, yes, my little cabbage (French)*

took one step inside to see if a particular guy was in there. I even checked the bathroom, and no one was there. I turned on the fan, opened up the blinds, but left the windows shut. I had a long, crazy day and I didn't want any more surprises.

I laid on my bed, grabbed one of my rocks by the night-stand, and went to sleep.

III

COOKIE

Next day, I woke up late; twenty minutes late to be precise. I rushed out of bed, brushed my teeth, and didn't have a chance to jump in the shower. I ran downstairs and saw this note:

"Bom dia[15], Sleepy-head

I had to go to work early today

Don't forget to remove all of the blood from the walls

See you later after school, I should be home by 5

Love you, Mom."

---

[15] *Bom dia:* Good Morning (Portuguese)

I grabbed the snack Mom had left for me on the counter top and left to school.

"Hey, Marks hop in." Jacques and his mom were passing by the front of the house.

"Good morning Mrs. DüMicahellis, Jax. What are you doing here?" I asked as I made my way in the back of the S.U.V. Jacques' mom was driving.

"Your mom mentioned that she was going in early to work this morning to me last night, so I asked Jacques to call you. Since you didn't pick up the phone, I decided to stop by to make sure you get to school on time," she explained.

"My phone! I forgot my phone!" I noticed patting my pockets for it.

"Oh dear, I'm sorry but if we go back to your house we won't make to school on time." Mrs. DüMicahellis told me apologetically.

"It's alright, I guess one day without my phone won't kill me," I responded sadly.

"You okay, Marks?"

"Yeah, I'm fine," I assured him.

I usually don't stay without my phone for more than a few hours, but I guess I could do a school day without it. Soon enough the day would be over, and I'll be back home with my phone in my hand.

The first half of the morning went by uneventfully with a few teachers here and there wishing me a happy birthday. Once I made it to the cafeteria, I met up with Mileena and Jacques, as usual.

"Hey birthday boy, how's your day going so far?" Jacques asked as he bit off an apple.

"So far so good, except I have tons of homework already and science is not my favorite."

"I'll take science any day over math," inserted Mileena. "I just don't get it."

"Hey if you wanna come over after school, I could help you with that," Jacques offered.

I SAY DO THIS, NOT THAT, AND ASK HOW YOU GOT THAT. I SAID, MOVE THIS, LIKE THAT, AND SHOW ME HOW YOU GOT THAT

"Ugh sorry, guys that's my ringtone," Jacques explained a bit cocky and not apologetic at all.

"Who in the world is this?" I asked entirely taken by surprise.

I SAY DO THIS, NOT THAT, AND ASK HOW YOU GOT THAT. I SAID, MOVE THIS, LIKE THAT, AND SHOW ME HOW YOU GOT THAT

"It's Black Maze, I love his stuff—"

"JACQUES, answer the phone!" Mileena told him.

"Oh, yeah, uh... Hello? Oh okay, hold on. Marks it's for you," he handed me the phone, looking as puzzled as I was.

"Hello?"

"Hi, Marcus, sweetie, this is Ms. Hills. I'm just calling to remind you that I'll be waiting for you here at Lulu's Coffee Shop for your first day at work right after school, 'kay? 'Kay, I'll see later, alright? Right. By-ey." She hung up the phone before I could even say 'by-ey' back.

"Who was that?" Intrigued Mileena.

"Oh man, I totally forgot. Today is my first day at work," I said remembering out loud.

"You got a job?" Mileena and Jacques asked surprised at the same time.

"Yeah, I did. My father knows the owner of this coffee shop in Cambridge near Harvard Square..." Suddenly I was not happy for my first day at work.

"That's great!" They both said at the same time again but clearly with opposite feelings.

"That's exactly how I feel," I said back at them.

"Hey, how did she have my number?" Jacques asked.

"That's a good question," I said, mostly to myself than to them.

We went back to the class, and everything else went by almost like a blur. I didn't pay attention to the rest of the periods. I was still kind of bummed by that fact that I had to go to work. Sure, I wanted to go to work, but just not today. I wanted to go home and take a shower and grab my phone, play some Mirabilis. I also had to clean the fake blood off the wall. Not a great day so far, but I guess it could be worse, at least I was not having illusions of the Midnight-Blue Eyed Guy in desperate need to talk to me or those Japanese Twins coming to take me to their king, whoever these people might be.

After school, I head straight to work. It took me a few extra minutes than I expected to find the place. I've been to Harvard Square before, but Lulu's Coffee Shop was down one of those side streets. It had just one small sign at the top of the front door, making it somewhat tricky to find it.

I made my way in.

"Hello, how may I help you," asked a guy in his early twenties from behind the counter putting out a tray of cookies in the display case.

"Uh, I'm here to see—"

"ME! You're here to see me. You must be Marcus Mathias! Oh, honey, you look just like your dad when I first met him many, many years ago. Not that many, I'm not that old," she let out a laugh. Her laugh was so loud and spontaneous that made me laugh involuntarily with her.

"Come, Marcus, sit down and have a cookie, have two even..." She grabbed a tray full of cookies, the same tray that the guy had just put on display and put on the table right next to me, gesturing for me to sit down, and so I did.

Still somewhat laughing, the guy behind the counter was slightly annoyed that now he had to go grab another tray to replace the one she had just put on the table.

"I take it that white chocolate chips and macadamia nuts cookies are your favorites?" She guessed right. "Oh dear, where are my manners, I'm Margaret Hills, welcome to Lulu's Coffee Shop. He, right there, is Gingerbread. GINGERBREAD, honey, bring Marcus a glass of whole milk, could ya?" Her voice was so high and sweet - almost operatic - that it made me really want to have a glass of milk, whole milk like she said.

"It's Steve," he said as he put the glass in front of me and went right back to the kitchen to grab another tray of cookies.

"Steve, Steve... everyone here has a nickname related to our theme. Steve is Gingerbread. His beautiful red hair and freckles make me want to build a gingerbread house, oh but that would be off-season, it's only May, right? Right. Hahaha," she laughed out loud again, making me almost choke on my cookie.

"Oh Cookie, be careful, here have a glass of milk," she said handing me the glass of milk that was already in front of me. "COOKIE? Yes! Cookie, you are from now on Cookie. Alright, Cookie, have your cookies, and I'll be right back with the paperwork, 'kay? 'Kay. Hahahaha," she laughed again making her way to her office to grab the paperwork.

Margaret Hills was a very tall woman, around at least six-foot tall if not taller. Her body seemed like it was somewhat carved out of a wedding cake; her bottom bigger than her bosom and her face round with a high silvery-blonde hair bun on top. As for her skin, I couldn't tell if she was pale or had a makeup job from the 1820s. Or maybe it was flour. However, her icy blue eyes and red lipstick stood out in contrast, matching her equally red shoes, nails and polka dots in her white ruffled dress.

She was definitely something fun to look at.

The whole place was decorated with maroon seats and dark wood with copper details here and there. Tiny light strings were hanging from the ceiling to resemble stars shining in the night sky. They were so small and well-placed that it gave the feeling that they were detached from anything, floating there in mid-air. The whole place had a 1920s look, a century older than what Margaret was dressed like. I wonder if she got the centuries wrong.

"It's a beautiful place, isn't it?"

I looked behind me, and there was this huge man. He was about six-foot-five, his body was muscular build that made me feel like he could bend a car with his bare hands if he wanted.

"Mr. Hors, how are you? Black coffee with two sugars?" Steve asked the tall man confirming his coffee order.

"Yes, please, Steve. Thank you." Steve made his way from behind the counter, handing Mr. Hors his coffee. Now that I could clearly see him, I could tell that besides the fact that Steve did have red hair and freckles, he did not resemble the Gingerbread Man whatsoever. He was too skinny for that.

"You're okay there, buddy?" He was looking at me with those bright-green eyes, greener than lettuce.

"Yeah, I'm fine. Thanks," I responded.

"Oh, my Chocolate Cake has arrived," Ms. Hills' high pitched voice broke the icy air again. I was genuinely embarrassed for Mr. Hors, who did not seem embarrassed at all.

"Hi, Bread-Pudding," he smiled and kissed her on the lips, making her chuckle and wipe his red lipstick stained lips with a cloth she had hanging on her apron.

She turned to me to introduce him, "Marcus, this is Kent Hors. He is a very good friend of mine."

"Hello, Marcus," he stretched out a hand. Looking

at them now side by side I can understand why Ms. Hills calls him Chocolate Cake. His dark complexion was even darker in comparison to her pale skin. I could pass as their son; my olive skin complexion was right in the middle of theirs. Mr. Hors looked tough, but he definitely had a soft spot for Ms. Hills.

"Nice to meet you, Mr. Hors." I shook his hand.

"Very nice to meet you too, Marcus." He smiled at me then sat on one of those high stools by the counter, where Steve was organizing the cupcakes.

"Here, Cookie. Fill out this paperwork, and I'll be right back, 'kay? 'Kay," Ms. Hills said handing me the papers. She went to sit right next to Mr. Hors as Steve gave her a cup of coffee and made his way to the table.

"Marcus, right?" he asked with a welcoming smile on his face for the first time.

"Yes, it is."

"Well, Marcus, since you and I are gonna be working together, I might as well introduce myself. I'm Steve Reed," he extended out his right hand for me to shake it.

"Marcus Mathias." I met his hand, shaking it.

"Listen, Ms. Hills can be a little weird at first, but she's a good boss, almost like an aunt to me. I'm sure in time you'll come to like her too." Rightfully so, she did remind me of Aunty April, they could have been sisters.

"Gingerbread, honey, let Cookie finish up his paperwork, you guys will have plenty of time to chat, 'kay? 'Kay," Ms. Hills spoke from her seat without even glancing back at us.

"See ya, Marcus." Steve made his way back to the kitchen as I focused my attention back to the paperwork.

"So, this is him, huh? Marcus Mathias..." Mr. Hors spoke in a very low, whispering voice as if I couldn't hear him. "Are you sure Roberto is right? I mean, the kid just turned sixteen, he couldn't possibly be a Porter, at least not until he's eighteen, Marge."

"Shhh, I know you're right, but his father must have sensed something, right? Then again, it's not like he's enrolling to C.H.E.P. right now, he's only applying for a job here so we can keep a closer eye on him until the right time comes," Ms. Hills' voice was now normal as if her cartoonish operatic voice was part of a theatrical act.

"Actually, I'd be happier if he was going to Jupiter, at least he would have all of the Queen's Army there to protect him," Mr. Hors contested.

Ms. Hills glanced back at me. I pretended to not hear them, so I kept staring down at those words, not making sense out of them. What on Earth were they talking about?

"Everything alright, Cookie?" Ms. Hills asked, with her candied high pitch voice.

"Oh yeah, everything's fine," I replied, casually.

"Alright Marge, we'll keep an eye on him until his father returns, but as soon as he does, you, Roberto and I will sit down to talk to Marcus, he needs to know sooner than later, Pudding.

"I think this is something that we can both agree

on," she kissed him lightly on the lips. After I filled out the paperwork, Margaret gave me a tour. Lulu's Coffee Shop is a tiny place; it has three small booths on your left when you walk in, an "L" shaped countertop that goes from the center to the right of the shop, plastic cases everywhere displaying pastries of all different types of cookies, muffins, cupcakes, Danishes, cannoli, and other types of goodies I couldn't name. The kitchen was in the back of the coffee shop, divided by a folding door separating both the coffee shop and Ms. Hills' own kitchen. Lulu's was on the first level of a three-story building, occupying almost a third of the first floor. There was a beautiful view from both kitchens to the backyard with a tall, thick tree, right in the middle of the grass. White roses bushes contoured the other side of the backyard with a few sunflowers here and there.

"So, do you have any questions, Cookie?" She glanced at me with those big blue eyes and a broad smile on her face.

"Uh... why Lulu? Why not Marge's Coffee Shop?" I asked.

"Oh, this place is named after my Grandma Lucile, may she find peace among the stars, Lulu for short."

"Oh, I'm sorry, I—"

"Don't be silly, Cookie, she died centuries ago, I barely even remember her..." She laughed it off. "Now, if that's all, let's get you an apron, a hat, your name tag, and Steve to start training you."

Steve showed me how to take care of customers, how to ring in on the register, how to bake cookies, and how to brew coffee and iced tea. The hours went by quickly, and I was actually having fun on my first day at work.

"Alright sweeties let's close the shop up. Cookie bring the cookie trays to the back and wash them off for me while Gingerbread sweeps and mops the floor. Oh, and Marcus, all the pastries left, put them in a box so I can bring them to the veterans' homeless shelter," Ms. Hills directed us, as she went into her office by the kitchen to count the money out of the registers.

I brought a few trays back and put all the cookies in a box and started washing the trays. I looked outside the window and saw how beautiful Ms. Hills' backyard was. The weather suddenly changed; the sky got cloudy almost immediately as if a storm was coming. But this was May, and no storms were announced in the forecast.

I looked outside, and there was this young girl in her early twenties or so by the tree. Her dark-brown hair was covering her face so I couldn't see who she was. The clouds opened up, and rain started pouring very fast, but she didn't move at all. Instead, she let the rain pour down on her. I knocked on the window trying to get her attention to bring her inside, and with a blink of an eye, **BAM** she was right there in front of my face screaming on the other side of the window, making me jump and fall backward on the floor along with the dirty trays.

"Marcus, buddy, are you okay?" I woke up with Steve slapping my face.

"Oh, my goodness, what happened here?" Ms. Hills' high pitched and yet concerned voice brought me back to consciousness faster than Steve's slaps.

"I heard a noise of cookie trays hitting the floor, so I came in to check on him, that's when I found him there, lying unconscious on the floor with the water still running," Steve explained as he shut off the faucet, not before pouring me a glass of water.

"Oh dear, Marcus, are you okay, Cookie?" she helped me up.

"Yeah, I just saw this..." I looked outside, and nothing had happened, no rain, no storms and definitely no girl out there getting soaking wet in a terrifying, somber, gloomy kind of way, "...bird. This bird came crashing into the window and scared me. I wasn't expecting it," I try to sound convincing.

"Oh Cookie, get yourself cleaned up and you may go. Gingerbread and I will finish this up. See you tomorrow?"

I nodded.

I couldn't have left the store any quicker. I was so embarrassed, and I had no clue to what was happening to me. Yesterday was the dream about the lion or lioness - whatever, by the beach followed by the weird guy playing some sort of harp on a small boat. Then I was visited by the Midnight-Blue Eyed Guy. Twice. Oh, and let's not forget the Japanese Twins and now this girl in the rain in Ms. Hills' backyard. I've gone crazy, literally. I must have lost all my screws. Great! And all this on the second day after I've turned sixteen. I can only imagine what twenty-one is going to look like for me.

I took the subway back home, or the 'T' as we call it here in Boston, and in less than thirty minutes I was back home. I opened the door of my house, nothing changed, the house was the same way as I had left, my mom's note was still on the countertop where I left it earlier.

"Mom, I'm home," I said out loud, looking around for her.

"I'm in the kitchen, honey," she shouted.

"Oh hey, how was your day?" I dropped my jacket on the chair.

"Mine was okay, just got home like an hour ago. But how was your day? Your Dad told me you started a new job today over at Lulu's Coffee Shop, right?" She fixed me a plate of food.

"It was good, nothing eventful," I lied convincingly.

"Now, how is that I found out through your dad about your job and not through you?"

"Sorry, Mom, I meant to tell you yesterday when I came downstairs but the surprise party happened, so I didn't have a chance to tell you, and on the top of that, I forgot my cell phone at home this morning..." I explained.

"It's okay honey, now go eat before it gets cold. I'm gonna jump in the shower."

"Thanks, Mom."

"And don't forget, when you're done with the dishes, to remove that fake blood off the wall, I haven't forgotten about it," she reminded me before closing the bathroom door behind her.

"Got it," I assured her. Once I was done with the dishes, I went outside to the back porch to have a slice of my leftover birthday cake. It was a beautiful night. The sky was full of shining stars of all different sizes. The weather was nice too, warm but with a gentle breeze here and there.

I sat down on the stairs by the porch facing the mermaid water fountain again; at this hour yesterday, I was certain I was going crazy talking to the Midnight-Blue Eyed Guy. But this time, it was just me.

"Olá, querido, como está você?[16]*"*

I guess I wasn't by myself anymore. I looked behind me, and there was Grandma Maria, my dad's mom, standing there with a beautiful floral dress and long silver locks down to her shoulders. My Portuguese wasn't great, but it was good enough to understand what Grandma was saying.

"Hi, Grandma. I'm okay," I put my plate down and was about to get up to hug her, but she motioned me to stop.

"Please sweetie, finish your cake, I can come to you."

I glanced down at my plate and grabbed another bite. "So, Grandma, when d—?" I looked at Grandma, and she was gone. Just that, in a blink of an eye.

Yup, I've lost it. I have gone completely bonkers.

I looked at the sky as I had another bite. The sky looked so much brighter now, fuller with stars. As if

---

[16] *"Olá, querido, como está você?:* Hi, honey, how are you?" (Portuguese)

they had somehow multiplied. Then I saw a falling star. I made a wish. I wished that my grandmother could get better. I know wishing on a star is superstitious, but it didn't hurt to try. Another falling star went by, that was rare. Another one, then another one; there were falling stars everywhere. I called my mom, but she didn't respond. I got up and walked out to the backyard to look at all those falling stars, it was beautiful yet scary at the same time.

"It's beautiful, isn't?" I jumped, not noticing my grandma next to me again.

"You! You were the lion, the lioness," I remembered her voice from my dream. I asked her, but the noise of all the falling stars was getting louder and louder. I looked up to the sky as one seemed to pass very close and looked back to Grandma, but this time she wasn't there. The enormous, beautiful white lioness of my dream was right there, where Grandma had been just a moment ago.

"Don't be afraid Marcus, it's only me..." I was so in shocked in my dream that I couldn't recognize my own grandma's voice and now she's right here in front of me, as a lioness.

"How is this possible?"

"Marcus, tell your parents that I'll be okay. I shall find peace among the stars."

"No!" I went to touch the lioness, but she exploded in a cloud of what seemed like glitter. "Honey, what are you doing out here?" My mom asked by the door to the back porch.

Of course, everything was gone now, and I looked

like a crazy person again. "Mom, is Grandma? Is she...?" But before I could finish the sentence, a knot took over my throat, and the tears fell down my eyes involuntarily.

"Oh, honey come here, I know, I just got off the phone with your dad, and he just told me. But how did you know?" She seemed surprised as she embraced me on a hug. I hugged her back hiding my tears, avoiding the answer.

IV

BUMPER-CAR RIDE

"Good morning." Mom was fixing breakfast as I greeted her in the kitchen. She was on the phone with my dad, so she just nodded in affirmation. By the way the conversation was going, I could tell my dad was not okay, and neither was Mom. I decided to leave early to school so she wouldn't have to drive me there. The school was only a few blocks away from the house anyway, and my mom still had to get ready to go to work.

Mom, Dad, and I are very close, it wasn't always like this. After a lot of tribulations in the past when we had no one but ourselves to lean on, we learned how to trust and always support each other no matter what. When Grandma Maria got sick, my dad did everything he could in his power to help her get the proper medical treatment she needed. Six months ago, he moved back to Brazil to be with his mom after the doctors diagnosed her with only a few months left to live.

With Dad gone indefinitely, Mom took on more hours at work. She worked as a cashier on a local market close by just to help in the household income, but now she really needed more than just twenty-something hours a week; she could use all of the hours she could get.

Dad was a salesman at a car dealership who had laid him off from work after he took indefinite time off to go to Brazil; none of us knew if he would have his job back once he was back in Boston.

"Hey Marks, how was your first day at work?" Mileena asked as soon as I arrived at the school.

"It was fine," I replied, almost as if programmed.

"Are you alright?"

"My Grandma passed away last night..."

"Oh, Marcus, I'm sorry." She comforted me.

"What's up, guys?" Jacques was just passing by. "Gee, what's with the funeral faces, who died?" he asked playfully.

"His grandmother, you fool," Mileena said giving him a not so happy look.

"Oh man, I'm sorry, I didn't kn—" the bell inter-rupted him.

"It's okay, Jax, it's not like we weren't expecting it," I managed to say, making my way to class.

"Way to go Jax," I heard Miles' disapproval comment as she elbowed him.

"Marcus, can I talk to you?" Our math teacher approached me before we could make our way to class.

"Sure, Mr. Stuart."

"Your dad just called Principal Dewars; I'm sorry for your loss, you can be excused for the day, okay? Go home, be with your mom."

I waved good-bye to both of them and left.

I'LL STOP BY YOUR PLACE AFTER SCHOOL, BUDDY. FEEL BETTER Jacques texted me before I even made my way out of school.

I didn't go home.

Mom must have already left for work, and I did not want to be home by myself. I made my way into a comic store nearby and picked up a copy of Mirabilis to read. Jacques' favorite game was everywhere in every format. First as a book, then it became a comic book and lastly a video game; according to Jacques, a T.V. show was supposed to start by the end of summer in the fall T.V. lineup.

My phone vibrated. It was Ms. Hills calling.

"Hello, Marcus, I'm sorry to hear about your grandma, she was a great person and a strong warrior, but rest assured she is now in a much better place. Yes, she is. No need to come to work today, Steve and I have this covered, 'kay? 'Kay. By-ey."

Ms. Hills' high-pitched voice always brought a smile to my face. The fact that I didn't need to say anything to her on the phone was a big plus, she never leaves any room for me to reply. I wonder if she thinks she called my voicemail.

I paid for the comics and made my way home.

My mom, as expected, was at work. I cleaned the fake blood off the kitchen walls and some that ended up in the living room as well. I grabbed a leftover corpse cupcake from my birthday party and sat on the couch facing the T.V. without turning it on. I was getting used to the weird silence in my house. There was a time when there were four of us: Dad, Mom, me and my big sister Daniella.

One day, my mom took my sister, who was seven years old at the time, and I to play in the park near our house; as we sometimes did on the week-ends. She was playing by the swings, and I was going up and down the slides at the playhouse with the other kids. My mom was sitting nearby on a bench watching all of us. And then, as I was climbing up the playhouse, I fell backward to my mom's despair, she came running to check on me. Luckily, I just had a scratch and was back up and running again in no time.

'Daniella, DANIELLA!' I remembered my mom screaming my sister's name. She was running around like crazy, screaming my sister's name asking anyone if they had seen her, but no one had. She fell down on her knees and started sobbing. The last thing I remember was my dad coming over and taking me out of the top of the playhouse with the police sirens approaching us. I was only five years old.

My sister's room was next to the living room, and since that day it hasn't been touched. We all made a vow to never speak of it again, and to always be there for each other, no matter what. Mom and Dad had never truly recovered from losing their precious little princess. And I, my big sister.

My phone vibrated in my pocket, snapping me out of that terrible memory.

"Hey, Marks, where on Earth are you? I've been ringing your doorbell, and nobody answered it," Jacques seemed a bit frustrated on the phone.

"What? I... hold on, let me get the door for you." I jumped off of the couch and let him in.

"Were you playing Mirabilis without me?" He looked at me questionably.

"No, no, I just sat at the couch to read some comics and next thing I knew, you were calling my phone,"

"Wow, you must have dozed off, look what time it is." To my surprise, it was already mid-afternoon. I don't remember falling asleep. I wondered if my mom came in and didn't see me or decided not to wake me up.

"Are you okay, *pote17*? You have that look again..."

"Yeah, no, I'm fine. I was just wondering if my mom was home or not, but anyways have a seat. Let me go upstairs to my room to grab Mirabilis so we can play," I made my way up the stairs.

"Cool, I—" Jacques' voice broke as if he suddenly had vanished.

WHOOSH

And he did vanish.

"Jax?" I stopped halfway upstairs. "Jacques? Where did you go? JACQUES?" I looked around the living room, then the kitchen and then the bathroom. My sister's room was locked as always. I checked the backyard, nothing. I went to my mom's bedroom, and to my surprise, the whole place was torn as if a mini tornado had passed through it.

"MARKS, help—" Jacques' voice echoed throughout the house. I saw just a glimpse of him being dragged out of the kitchen door just as I made my way back to the living room.

"JACQUES!" I ran halfway to the living room, and then the doorbell rang. I ran to open it.

"Mom, I was ju—"

"Aww, that's so sweet, now if you'll excuse me..." Ms. Hills was there in my house with her whole 1820's look gone, wearing jeans and a flowery red shirt. Hair was still up in a bun, but more like this century. Her voice was not the high pitch sweet voice that I was used to, but normal just like when she was talking to Mr. Hors back at the coffee shop yesterday.

"This is not a good time, Ms. Hills. Jacques is mis—" I said after her, as she made herself comfortable on the couch before she could interrupt me.

"I know, I just saw it, and your mom is also—" the house phone rang, interrupting her.

"Hi, Marge, what's going on? Is the boy safe?" Mr. Hors said as he appeared on the other side of the screen that Ms. Hills had turned on.

"Yeah, I just got here, and Roberto was right, Kathy is gone," she told him.

"Kathy? As in Katherine, my mom?" I asked but no

one answered.

"Well, you know what to do. I'm on my way."

"Oh, and Kent," she said before he could hang up. "they took Jacques too."

"I'll be right there." He hung up.

"What was that all about?" I was perplexed about all that was going on. "Marcus, get ready, I'll explain everything on the way."

The doorbell rang again.

"Mom is here, there's no need for—" I opened the door.

"Hi Marcus, I thought Margaret told you to get ready so we could leave." Mr. Hors was standing at my door; he was just as tall as my door.

"How did you—?" I was stunned by his sudden appearance. I saw the background of the screen, and he was nowhere near the house.

"I'll explain it on the way, now go get ready so we can get going." He made his way inside the house and sat on the couch across Ms. Hills.

"They got Jacques too, Kent," I heard Ms. Hills saying before I made my way upstairs.

I didn't hang around to hear what Mr. Hors said, I was already upstairs. I grabbed one of my lucky rocks and sat down on my bed. I called my mom, but no answer. I called my dad. The phone went straight to voicemail. I honestly had no idea what was going on. It wasn't long enough before we were all inside Ms. Hills' car.

"Is anyone gonna tell me what's going on or not?" I asked a bit louder than I'm comfortable with as I buckled my seatbelt.

"Marcus, Cookie, I think Kat and your friend are in trouble," Ms. Hills said, not taking her eyes off the road.

"What are you talking about? My mom is at work!" I stated clearly annoyed by it.

"She never went to work today. She was supposed to go pick up your dad at the airport in a few minutes, but hasn't contacted Roberto at all today," Mr. Hors said as he turned on a small device that looked like a G.P.S., except it wasn't giving directions, it was just showing the map of everywhere we went.

"My dad? He is not coming back from Brazil today; Mom would've told me."

"They wanted to make it a surprise for you, Cookie. Anything, Kent?" Ms. Hills asked as if she was expecting a call from someone.

I took my cell phone out to call my mom.

No answer.

I called again.

Straight to voicemail.

"Mom, it's me. Call me when you get this, I really need to talk to you. Bye," I left a message. "So, how do you two know my parents and how have I never heard of either one of you before?"

They both exchanged a look to which Ms. Hills just nodded at Mr. Hors and then he began: "Marcus, your father and I—"

BAM

A car came out of nowhere and smashed against

the passenger seat where Mr. Hors was sitting, making our car spin out of control hitting a mailbox next to my window, crashing it.

"Is everyone okay?" Ms. Hills asked, wiping some blood off her forehead.

"I'm fine, I just—"

"They are running away Marge, go after them," Mr. Hors told Ms. Hills as he was pointing to a red sports car that was apparently fleeing the scene.

"I'm on it." She switched gears and went after the red car.

"Wait, what? A car-chase? Really? What in the world are—"

"Hold on tight there, buddy, there's a reason she's on the wheel and not me." Mr. Hors' serious and yet excited face glanced back at me through the mirror. Ms. Hills' car was a yellow hybrid car, not an S.U.V. or a sports car. I was sure those guys were going to be able to get away from us before we could even move. But I was wrong.

The little yellow hybrid car did not hold back whatsoever. Ms. Hills switched gears and, soon enough, caught up to them. They tried to get rid of us by turning on a corner, but that was not a problem for her. She was right behind them right now. They took a right turn, and they were gone.

I mean, gone as in vanished, disappeared in the thin air. I couldn't believe what I saw or didn't actually. One moment they were right in front of us and the second after they were gone.

"I think they've given up," Ms. Hills said as she

pulled over.

"I doubt that. If they were who I think they were, they will be back," Mr. Hors said looking at his little device again.

"Who were they?" I demanded out of them.

"Well, if this is true, Kent, then we should keep going before they catch up to us," Ms. Hills stated, completely ignoring my question.

"Can somebody tell me what the hell is going on?" I lost a bit of my temper.

"Watch the language, young man and buckle up," Ms. Hills said as she raced out again.

"I didn't even unbuckle...," I mumbled.

I really had no idea what was going on. If the car wasn't moving at seventy-five miles per hour, I would ultimately have jumped out of it. But I wanted to stay, by now I had no idea where I was anyways.

Where were the cops? I wondered why they haven't caught up with us yet. I was pretty sure we were way over the speed limit.

We took a few more turns before Mr. Hors glanced at Ms. Hills.

"What? What now?" I said it to the air because no one bothered to answer me.

"I got this, Kent. They came after the wrong Porter," she smiled at him in assurance, and that made me a bit worried.

"Porter? What in hell? I mean, what is a Porter?" The only sound I heard was of the tires screeching right behind us. "Oh man, not again." I looked behind us, and there they were. The red sports car right behind us. Besides the shining eyes on both the passenger and the driver, I couldn't see anything else.

"Marcus, honey—"

"I know, I know, Ms. Hills, 'hold on tight'." And I did. I knew we weren't joking around and this time, they were after us, so we had to do our best to get rid of them.

"How far are we?" Mr. Hors asked.

"Five," was all she said.

"Make it three, they will catch up to us before we hit the bridge," he warned her.

"No, they won't." It was scary to see Ms. Hills, my obsessed with sweets boss, completely turned into a mad car racer. I wasn't sure if it enticed me or scared me. She truly never ceases to amaze me.

POW

"What's that?" I asked.

"They are hitting us, Marge." Mr. Hors cool face was now wearing a somewhat concerned look.

"Hold on!" Before she could even finish her sentence, Ms. Hills turned to the right and then to the left and sped so fast that I was surprised the other car was still behind us. She turned left and right again and by now I was bouncing side to side on the backseat. She then accelerated so fast that my whole body was being pushed against the seat.

"Marge?" Mr. Hors inquired. "MARGARET?" A swift right turn made all of us lean to our left sides.

And she stopped.

"Why did you stop?" I asked. "Aren't they still behind us?" I saw the car approaching us. And then they stopped. "Why did they stop? Why did everyone stop?" I was surprised more than curious.

"They won't cross the bridge," Mr. Hors said. "Good thinking, Marge." He kissed her.

Just then I noticed we were on the top of the bridge and they stopped right before they could get on the bridge. Now that was weird.

"So, is anyone gonna tell me what that was all about?" I asked to the air again.

A few minutes later we were at the airport.

"Margaret, stay here while Marcus and I go look for his Roberto," Mr. Hors said as he got out of the car and opened the undamaged back door for me.

"According to your dad, he should have been here about thirty minutes ago," Mr. Hors said looking around. "Stay here while I ask if his flight is late."

I sat in one of those benches watching the big screen hanging from the ceiling announcing flight deals to Hawai'i, Bali, and Iceland. 'Who goes to Iceland on vacation?' I thought to myself.

"Don't knock it until you've tried it," this guy on the screen appeared with a profound voice staring at me with his dark eyes and sunless complexion partnered with a creepy smile.

"What in the world," I said to myself.

I looked around, but no one else seemed to have noticed him.

"I'm serious. In Reykjavík there's this place called Blue Lagoon which has naturally heated water, great place for relaxation," he continued. His voice was deep, melodic, yet mature just like of those reality T.V. show hosts.

"What's the matter, Marcus? Rather go to Hawai'i instead?" I jumped to my feet by the sound of my name. "What? Don't you recognize me?"

His skin got paler, losing its melanin. His hair from the top of his head fell to one side, turning blue, just like his eyes from black to blue, midnight-blue.

"YOU!" I'd recognize those eyes anywhere. "WHAT DO YOU WANT FROM ME?" I shouted not worrying about anyone around me.

"You? What makes you think I want something to do with you?" His voice was that of a twenty-some-thing-year-old again, calm and eerie. "I'm merely stalling you," he grimed.

"Dad..." I said under my breath.

"Attaboy," he congratulated me jumping from inside of the screen to the right in front of me. "WHERE'S MY DAD?" I demanded.

"Calm down now, Dogie, you do not wanna lose your temper. I'm here to help you," he spoke every word with every step he took.

"Dogie?" My body was getting a numb and tingling sensation all over again. "What in the world is 'Dogie' and why does everyone keep calling me tha-argh!" I shouted in pain.

My head was bursting with pain from inside out as if my brain suddenly had a hold of a baseball bat and was trying to break itself free.

"Marcus, are you okay?" The midnight-blue-eyed

guy asked clearly concerned, but I couldn't see him anymore. All around me started to shine as if there were a spotlight coming from inside my own body. I looked at my legs and arms, and all I saw was hooves and cow-like skin all around where my skin was. My legs bent backward, I let out a scream of pain, but all I heard was a loud ***MOO***. It was as if a bull got hit by a truck or something. I couldn't hold my body upward anymore. My chest got bigger and bigger. I put my arms out to catch myself from falling but the weight was too great, so I fell, followed by a loud ***BOOM***

All I could hear was Mr. Hors' voice from afar asking me if I was okay before passing out.

V

NATURAL

I woke up in a very different environment than I last remembered being in it. I was laying down on a maroon colored couch. Everything around me was a bit dark. I could tell I was in a basement. I sat down and tried to get a glimpse of the location, but my head was still hurting and throbbing.

"I think he's up." I heard Mr. Hors voice coming from somewhere behind me in the room.

"Whoa, Marcus, take it easy. Everything is okay now, you're okay." Ms. Hills sat next to me on my right, offering me a glass of water.

"Thanks, what happened?" I asked drinking the water.

"Don't you remember?" Mr. Hors was standing in front of me a bit concerned.

"No," I lied, "I remember being in the airport and—"

A RARE ACCIDENT HAPPENED THIS AFTER-NOON IN BOSTON The T.V. interrupted me from behind Mr. Hors, ***A SMALL EARTHQUAKE SHOOK LOGAN INTERNATIONAL AIRPORT IN THE MID-DLE OF THE AFTERNOON. NO ONE KNOWS THE CAUSE OF IT OR HOW IT CAME TO HAPPEN. THE LAST TIME WE HAVE SEEN AN EARTHQUAKE IN THE BEANTOWN WAS BACK IN—***

Mr. Hors turned off the T.V.

"Marcus, you don't remember anything?" Mr. Hors still looked puzzled with my answer.

"An earthquake at the airport? How come I don't remember? We were there!" I got up asking both one of them. Of course, I remembered what happened. I had a hallucination and fainted again, just like with the Japanese Twins at the mall. "How long was I out?"

"A couple of hours." Mr. Hors answered casually sitting on the sofa across from me.

"What? What happened?" I didn't want to tell them what I remembered; I'm sure I was going crazy for good. I have to see a doctor once I find my mom.

"Cookie, we were hoping to have your father here to have this conversation with you, but I think we are gonna have to do this without him." Ms. Hills got up and walked to the far back of the room. With a swift move of her right hand, she turned all the lights off.

"What's going on?" I asked not moving an inch

since I couldn't see anything around me.

"Marcus, I need to show you something." A large computer screen showed up in mid-air, floating just like a hologram in front of Mr. Hors. "We believe what's happening to you is, you are a Natural Porter, however rare that is."

"A Natural Porter? What the—"

"Language Mr. Mathias." Ms. Hills interceded from across the room.

"Sorry. What's a Porter?" I asked.

Mr. Hors touched the screen, and a definition balloon popped up on the screen. "Porter: A person employed to carry luggage and other loads, particularly in a railroad station, airport or hotel." He read it out loud. "That's the definition of the word porter. However," he continued, "in our terms we use it as a guardian, a holder, a carrier," He stopped to see if I had understood him so far.

"Yeah, I'm following. What am I naturally holding, guarding or carrying, or whatever is the term you use?"

"We think you are a Natural Porter of the Taurus Constellation." Ms. Hills spoke loudly and excited that her high pitch voice almost came out again.

"What?" I asked.

"A Natural—"

"I heard what you said Ms. Hills, but what does it mean?" I interrupted her ruder than I had intended to.

"Let's show it to him, Marge." Mr. Hors said to Ms. Hills, not happy with the way I had addressed her.

With another move of her hand, the whole place became illuminated like the night sky. There were stars shining everywhere and all around us, even on the floor under my feet. I had the surreal feeling that I was floating out in the middle of the Universe.

Mr. Hors touched the 'air' and I could see our Galaxy right in front of us. "This is the Milky Way Galaxy," he began, "And in the Milky Way Galaxy is where our Solar System is located." With another touch, Mr. Hors made our Solar System appear closer to us with everything floating all around. The Sun was right in the center of the room with all the other planets rotating around it, including our own planet, Earth, and its moon.

"Whoa, this is so cool. Are all of the planets here?" I asked analyzing the rings of Saturn.

"All of which we know the existence so far." Mr. Hors explained. "You see, our Universe is always expanding; is always creating new planets, new moons, new stars, new suns. All that is allowed for the human race on Earth to know we know. If whenever a new planet is discovered by N.A.S.A., we get a notification right here in this room."

"This is all cool and all, but what does this have anything to do with me and with what happened in the airport earlier?"

"Here is where the fun begins." Mr. Hors stepped in closer to the Sun and pressed a button again, and all the planets now had a small screen in front of them, each with its own symbol that I've seen before when reading about my horoscope. "Do you know anything about astrology?"

"All I know is that I'm a Taurean—"

"A Taurus." He corrected me. "You are a Taurus just like me." He pulled up his right left arm's sleeve revealing a tattoo. "Marge, over there, is an Aries." She waved proudly at us, also showing her tattoo under her left arm.

"Cool tat, and...?" I'm not a very patient person; clearly, I was having a hard time connecting the dots.

"Every planet in our Solar System plus the Moon and the Sun has a symbol, an Astrological Sign; the same one you see in the newspaper, Internet when you're reading about your Horoscope. For instance, touch the symbol of Taurus in front of our Planet." He asked.

I did touch the screen, and a smaller screen popped open with an image of a huge black bull in front of it.

"Touch it again."

All the other stars went dark beside a few ones that were shining much brighter than before, matching the same tattoo that Mr. Hors had under his left bicep. Next to the bull appeared a bunch of information, such as birth year, height, location, appearance and his name: Kent Hors.

"So, is this an astrology book you are writing?" I was trying hard to follow, but none of this was making any sense.

"Marcus, this is who I am. I'm the Porter of the Taurus Constellation, just like you, same as Ms. Hills being the Porter of the Aries Constellation and just like—"

"Wait, what are you trying to tell me exactly?"

"That as a Porter, we have the ability to transform ourselves into our very own Astrological Sign, as I mentioned I'm a Taurus so I can transform myself into a bull, Ms. Hills into a ram—"

"A ram? What's a ram? Never mind, this is all nonsense! No one can transform themselves into anything, not without the special effects of Hollywood or James Cameron."

"Marcus, Cookie, let me show you what—" Ms. Hills approached me.

"Show me what? All I want to know is where my Mom is and what happened to Jacques. Did you actually forget that he's missing?" I was getting really impatient.

"No, we didn't, and that's why we are here trying to help you." She insisted.

"Do you wanna help? Then get out of my way!" I passed right through Ms. Hills only to realize something: "How do I get out of here?" I shouted without looking back at either one of them.

"The door to your left, behind Pluto, takes you back upstairs to Lulu's Coffee Shop; where I'm sure you'll be able to find your way out." I didn't have to look at Ms. Hills to see her disapproval face. It was stamped in every word coming out of her mouth.

"Marcus, you may be in danger; we have to protect you before they strike again." Mr. Hors pleaded one last time.

"Who, Kent? Who strikes again?" I yelled out.

"We are not sure." He said with a very defeated voice.

"Let me know when you find out who! And by the way, Pluto is no longer considered a planet." I stormed out of the room, slamming the door behind me. Sure enough, once I made my way up two sets of stairs, I was back at Lulu's Coffee Shop.

I left the coffee shop on a haze. I made turns unthinkingly on random streets over and over again, replaying in my head everything that's been happening to me since the morning of my birthday, up until now and how all this just didn't add up.

I wondered how my new boss somehow became this woman, still lovely and sweet, but affected somehow; and worse, her friend was also playing this trick on me, and let's not mention the fact that I have no idea what happened to Jacques and my mom.

And then I lost my sense of direction; I walked far too long without realizing that I was going in the opposite direction from the nearest subway station. I turned abruptly to my right and slammed into this girl.

"Hey, watch it!" She said as her books flew out of her hands by the impact. "Marcus, what are you doing here?"

"Jena, hi! What are you doing here?" I kneeled over to help her pick up the books.

"I asked you first, Marks," she said, smiling at me. "I borrowed these books from the library and am heading home now, what about you?"

"I, well, just left work..." Which technically wasn't

a lie, but I didn't know if I should tell her everything that had just happened. "What's up with the books?"

"Just some books I'm reading." She looked at me clearly knowing I was hiding something. "Are you okay?"

"Yeah, I'm fine." I lied.

"Hey, are you on your way home? Since I'm heading home, I was wondering if you wanna catch the T together?" She asked casually.

I wasn't sure if I wanted to take the subway back home with her because I knew she would ask a lot of questions and I didn't want to lie to her any more than I already had. At the same time, I didn't want to be alone and, right now, I could really use a friend's company to take my mind off of things.

"Yeah, sure," I replied.

On the way home, we talked about the most random stuff, and it was kind of fun to talk about usual things, like school, and reality T.V. shows for a change. Finally, we arrived in front of my house.

"Okay, Mr. Secrecy, so I know you didn't want to talk in public but now that we are here, would you like to tell me what's going on?" The thing about Jena is that she's too smart, she could tell I wasn't being myself. Or maybe it was clear that I was really annoyed.

"Why don't you come inside for a few minutes?" I asked as I opened the door. "Well, in a few words, I am the newest Porter of the Taurus Constellation."

"WHAT?" She asked even though she had heard me. We both burst out laughing. We sat down in the living room, and in very few words, I explained everything that's been happening to me, bit by bit, not forgetting one detail; if I was going crazy, I needed someone, a friend to look after me.

"Wow, you must have hit your head pretty hard when you fell on the airport." She stated, making fun of me, as we both laughed.

"Well, I beg to differ." A voice came from behind us, startling us both.

"DAD!" I said in disbelief.

"*Olá*[17], Marcus, aren't you gonna give your dad a hug?"

"Dad, you're home! When did you get here?" I went and hugged him.

"Well, I thought I had told your mom that I would be arriving today from Brazil, she was supposed to pick me up at the airport, but never showed up. After a small and yet unexplainable earthquake, I decided to grab a cab and leave. It took me way longer than expected. Talking about that, where's your mom? I was expecting a welcoming party and all..."

"Dad, I..., Mom is..., something's happened, and to be honest, I don't know where Mom is, and Jacques is missing too." I sat back on the couch feeling completely inutile.

"Marcus, I think is best to tell your dad what's going on," Jena suggested.

"No need, son, I heard everything you told Jena from the bedroom..." He sat next to me on the couch.

---

[17] *Olá:* Hello (Portuguese)

"It's absurd, right Dad? I mean, Mr. Hors and Ms. Hills have to be playing a trick on me, it's all just crazy, to say the least, I—"

"Marcus, how about you go to your room and take a shower, freshen up? I gotta make a few phone calls and see if I can find Katherine..."

"But Dad, I—"

"Marcus, go to your room. Please, son, we will find where your mom is, and then we can figure out what happened to Jacques." Suddenly, my dad's voice went from 'chill dad' to 'concerned dad' in two seconds. I learned many times before to not argue with him when he had that tone.

I went upstairs to my room with Jena, leaving my dad in the living room, sitting down on the couch as he reached for the phone.

"Marks, this is all too weird. I mean, why would anyone lie to you like this?" Jena intrigued.

"I don't know, but I don't get why Dad got all paranoid. It's almost as if he believes them." I sat on my bed, getting one of my rocks out of the shelf.

"True, but maybe he's just concerned about your mom. By the way, cool tattoo your dad has." She said trying to get my head off of things.

"Tattoo? What are you talking about? My dad doesn't have any tattoo..." I said, getting up to my feet.

"He does now, I mean I never saw your dad with a tank top shirt before so it's not like I could have seen your dad's biceps before," she blushed a little. "I'm not sure how long he had it for but clearly has been for a while."

"Jena, I'm gonna go downstairs. I think I left my cell phone in the living room."

I hadn't mentioned to Jena or to my dad about the tattoo I saw on Mr. Hors' arm, I didn't think it matters. But if Jena was right, Dad was one of them. I had to check it out.

I sat on the top of the stairs to make sure my dad didn't see me. He was too focused on the phone that he didn't hear me at all. I looked at him hard, trying to see his tattoo, but nothing was there.

"We had agreed to talk about this once the time was near, and not when I was away on my mother's funeral, for crying out loud." My dad argued over the phone, not wanting anyone to hear who he was talking to. I had never heard my dad talking to someone like that, and it was a bit scary.

I decided to step down a few more steps, to get a better glimpse on my dad's right arm.

"I know, Margaret, but you and Kent had promised me to just look after him while I was in Brazil. Now, what am I gonna tell my kid? He is upstairs, scared of all this madness." He turned halfway toward me and almost saw me, but I hid off his view.

I wasn't scared. I just thought it was some sort of joke, a prank someone was playing on me. Hey, he was talking to Ms. Hills on the phone, was he confronting her about the joke? I wondered if I still had a job.

"All right, I'll bring him tomorrow when he's feeling better, okay? Talk to you later."

As he hung up the phone, I turned around, making my way back upstairs to my room quickly before he could have noticed me, but I missed a step, two actually, and I fell all the way down the stairs to the living room.

"MARCUS!" Both my dad and Jena shouted at the same time.

"I'm okay..., ouch!" My dad came to help me up, and that's when I saw the tattoo under his left arm. It was exactly the same tattoo Mr. Hors had, same location and all. It gave me the chills. I knew something wasn't right.

"Marcus, son, what were you doing? Are you alright?" He helped me up.

"Yeah, Dad, I was just looking for my phone. I think I left it over there by the coffee table." I reached out for my phone. "C'mon, Jena," I gestured to her as I head to the kitchen leaving my dad behind.

"Marcus, what's going on? If I didn't know you better, I think you actually believe in all of this..." She asked as soon as we got in the kitchen.

"No, no. I just tripped down the stairs on my way down, that was it." I lied.

"You sure you're okay? My mom is expecting me home soon, but if you want, I could call her and say that I'm staying over."

"No, it's okay, Jena. You can go. I'm gonna head back upstairs, take a shower and then eat something. I had a long day. I'll text you later, okay?" She knew I was lying, but I had no choice. For now, I decided to keep it to myself. Something wasn't right, and I had to find out what. Even if I had to do it all by myself.

"All right, if you're okay, then I'm gonna head home. Call me later, okay?" She opened the back door.

"Yeah, sure, definitely. I'll call you later; yeah, go, I'm okay, thanks for listening to me, and not thinking that I've gone crazy."

"I'm not so sure about that, buddy." She mocked me. "See you later."

She waved and walked out, leaving me alone in the kitchen feeling as lost as ever. I pulled up a chair and got to thinking about my dad and his connections with Kent and Margaret and their matching tattoos. Was Dad one of them? And if so, could I really trust him? There's only one way to find out. I gotta go talk to him. I need to know what was going on.

But before I could head back to the living room, my phone vibrated.

"Marcus, Marcus, can you hear me?" A very disturbed Jacques was on the other side of the phone.

"Jacques? What's going on? Where are you?" I could see him, but I could not make out where he was.

"Marcus, I don't know where I am. Listen, I am in some kind of park; some cars are passing by, and there's a river in front of me, and a big old metal bridge..."

"Hey, Jax, I need you to focus; look around you and find a building or something that can help me find you, show me through the camera..." I told him.

"I don't know. I don't think I've been here before, how did I get here?"

"Jacques, I cannot make out where you are, you're

shaking too much..." I told him.

"Oh wait, there—" and just like that, the phone call was dropped.

"What? Wait, Jacques? Where are you? Jacques? JACQUES?" But it was too late no one was on the other side. I tried to call him again, but his phone went straight to voicemail. Now I was more worried than before, but also relieved that Jacques was somewhat okay, but where was Mom? Was she with him? I had to go talk to Dad.

"Son, is everything okay? I heard you talking on the phone." He walked in the kitchen.

"Dad, it was Jacques, he's okay, but he's lost; we gotta go find him."

"Yes, sure, but first I need to talk to you, son."

"Right now? We gotta go find him, Dad!"

"I know, Marcus, but we don't even know where to begin. But I know someone who might be able to help us. You're gonna have to trust me.

VI

YOU TOO?

We left the house in my dad's car toward Boston. He said we should go over to the house of one of his friends and maybe he would be able to help us find where Jacques might be. On the way, Dad was anxious about people following us. He told me to keep an eye on the road for any suspicious cars. I did not know what he was talking about, except maybe he meant the same people who followed me in the car chase earlier with Ms. Hills and Mr. Hors. But how did he know that? Either way, I decided to keep a lookout just in case they, or anyone else, show up.

I wanted to ask how he knew my boss, Ms. Hills, but I decided not to. Dad was not his usual self, and I didn't want to make him upset any more than he was.

We passed the Financial District, then down to the New England Aquarium. We continued on, passing the Rowes Wharf. I always loved the arched structure of that building. Dad parked the car, and we started walking between restaurants, people staring out at the ocean and then, Dad stopped right on the top of a metal bridge across from Boston's Seaport.

"So, are we supposed to wait for your friend here?" I asked my dad, wondering why he had stopped in the middle of the bridge.

"Hold on, son. I'm looking for something. There it is,"

I saw what my dad was talking about. There was a little boat under the bridge, unattached to anything. It was just there, floating in the middle of the river. Dad walked over to the exact location where the boat was, and then he called me over.

"Marcus, come here."

"Dad, I can see the boat perfectly from here." This was not a good time to go boat-sighting, especially that little boat that had nothing special about it.

"Son come here. We gotta get moving, it's already late." He insisted, calling me over one more time.

You see, I am a very impatient person, especially when I have something on my mind that needs to get done soon. But I went anyway, and in a glimpse, my dad was gone. Vanished right there in front of my eyes.

"Dad, where did you go? DAD?" I said looking around.

"Shhhh, Marcus, over here."

Then I saw the creepiest thing ever: His arm, bodiless, coming from nowhere in mid-air, grabbing my arms to where his body should be. I closed my eyes by impulse. I opened them and noticed that we were inside a crystal-clear box, and my dad was there, body and all, smirking at me curiously.

"What in the world? How did you do that?" I asked, surprised, looking around the glass box. It was shaped like an elevator, except it had no resemblance to one at all, except for its shape. There were no cables, no visible numbers pad anywhere, nothing at all.

"This is an elevator that no one outside can see in." My father told me, as if it was too obvious of an answer. He then pressed a button that wasn't there before, and it lit up with the down arrow on it. It occurred to me that we were in fact right in the middle of a bridge, nothing above us, nothing under us. Just the river. The RIVER! We then descended. The elevator went all the way down to the top of the boat that was under the bridge. Before the elevator could hit the boat, it stopped and its floor opened, letting us fall inside the boat with no damages whatsoever.

My dad obviously had done that a few times before since he went and turned on the boat, leading us to this small, abandoned house in the middle of the water, just across from the Rowes Wharf Hotel. The house was on the top of a few tall, large trunks of trees that were cut down and put in the middle of the water just so it could hold the small house. The place had to have been abandoned for at least a few decades.

Once under the house, before I could ask my dad anything, the boat stopped. Dad stepped out of the boat, and just as I thought he was going to fall, he didn't. He was standing still and smiling at me; I could swear my dad was enjoying doing this to me. I realized then that it was another elevator, so I followed him inside the clear glass box again. This time, we went upward. The elevator stopped in front of the only door in the tiny house.

My dad stepped out of it and opened the door. I followed him in.

Inside, it was equally weird and strange as the outside; yet fresh and new, full of high-tech equipment, computers, and large-screen monitors. A telescope out in a window pointed to the Rowes Wharf building right in front of us.

"Hello again, Marcus!" A voice that, I wasn't sure if I wanted to hear again anytime soon, greeted me. Ms. Hills and Mr. Hors were sitting comfortably on a red couch, quite similar to the one I woke up in earlier over Ms. Hills' basement after the airport incident this afternoon.

"Dad, what are we doing here?" I asked, with a mixture of surprised and annoyed expression at the same time. "Weren't we supposed to be looking for Mom and Jacques?"

"Son, I think we need to have a very serious conversation about some things that are happening to you right now." He sat on a lounge chair across from Mr. Hors.

"But Dad, not here, not now, not in front of them

either!" I said, a little bit embarrassed by it. I mean, I didn't like it when my father spoke to me as if I was only twelve. I had just turned sixteen!

"I think this is the perfect time and place. Kent and Margaret might actually be able to help us. They are also very close friends of mine," he assured me. "Maybe we should give them a chance and see what they have to say."

"No, Dad. I'm sorry, but I'm not gonna be sitting here and listening to that story about Porters, and Constellations, and Astrological Signs, and pretend that is all true!"

"But it is true, Cookie." Ms. Hills spoke with her sweet and calm voice, completely the opposite of mine.

"No, Ms. Hills, it isn't. I'm sorry, but I refuse to believe in this madness. Have all of you lost your mind? Am I supposed to believe in all this craziness? I stopped believing in Santa Claus when I was six. I have never believed in fairy tales, and it's not about to change now." Was I really having this conversation with them? Shouldn't it be the other way around? Shouldn't I be the one telling them that the fantasy world was real, and they tell me to wake up from my dreams?

"Marcus, please just give us a chance to explain it to you." My dad asked, unflustered.

"What, Dad? What is so important that you have to say that is gonna change my mind? That somehow is gonna make me believe in all of this?"

"Because I am also one of them." My father exposed his tattoo lit up just like how Ms. Hills and Mr. Hors did.

"How did you...?" I stepped closer in disbelief. It was as if their tattoos were made out of light, electricity. I'm not talking as in glow-in-the-dark light; I'm talking as in a small-tiny-teeny-mini-light-bulbs-were-inside-of-their-skin light.

"Marcus, son, Kent is a Porter of the Taurus Constellation, Margaret is a Porter of the Aries Constellation, and I am also a Porter of the Taurus Constellation," my dad began explaining calmly to me. "You see, long ago before you were born, Kent and Margaret came to me, asking me to take over the Taurus Constellation becoming a Porter and then a Wonderer, I'll get to that in a minute..."

"Your dad's mother, Grandma Maria, was also a Porter of the Leo Constellation. She served as the Wonderer of Sun for a couple of centuries before meeting Rafael, whom she decided to marry and therefore resigning her post as a Wonderer and then later, a Porter altogether, allowing Leonard Lark to take over." Ms. Hills explained.

"Did you know Grandma Maria?" I sat down, giving them a chance to explain everything.

"Did I know your grandma? I trained your grandma when she had just turned eighteen years old." She smiled at me, sitting by my side.

"How old are you?" I was completely puzzled.

"Oh dear, what kind of question is that?" She was said embarrassedly.

"Kent and Margaret have been protecting the Earth for a very long time, son.

"And then your father was born, Marcus." Mr. Hors joined in for the first time. "I thought, after protecting Earth for over five-hundred years, it was time to stop being a Wonderer and enjoy the rest of my life."

Mr. Hors reached out for Ms. Hills' hands, and she blushed. I knew exactly what he meant. He fell in love with her just like my Grandma and Grandpa did way back then.

"What's a Wonderer?" I asked, still puzzled and confused.

"There are plenty of Porters out there. Every Wonderer is a Porter, but not every Porter is a Wonderer," Mr. Hors explained. "Hit the lights, Marge."

The whole place went dark, and then everything got bright again. All the stars, the Moon, the Sun, and all the planets of our Solar System was right there in front of me, floating in 3D holograms just as if I indeed was out in the Universe.

"We call this place G.O.L., Galaxy's Observatory and Laboratory, just like the one you saw over Ms. Hills' place under Lulu's Coffee Shop earlier with us." Mr. Hors continued.

"Every Wonderer has one. Margaret used to be a Wonderer a while ago, but she resigned, allowing Jennifer Lowell to become the Wonderer of Mars, Porter of the Aries Constellation."

"Every planet in our Solar System, including our

Moon and Sun, has a Wonderer, someone who's responsible for protecting their assigned location." My dad explained.

"Protect it from what?" Everything was so hard to believe, but I had never seen anything like this before, so I was just going with it.

"Not from what but from who, Marcus, the Wanderers," Mr. Hors got up to his feet as he approached me. "Wanderers are Porters of Constellations without an assigned location. Look at the planets in front of you. In all those planets you see a Wonderer's name and their Astrological Sign, but then you have this."

With a swift hand movement, he sent our Solar System away, leaving only the stars. "Pay attention," Mr. Hors connected a few stars in front of him as if he was playing Connect-The-Dots. "This is the Pegasus Constellation, the late Wanderer Louis Neil died about fifty years ago of solitude. He was a great warrior but after 467 years leaving alone, he took his own life."

"Indeed, his funeral was very touching, he truly was a beautiful black winged horse." Ms. Hills' comments made me a bit uncomfortable, resulting on Mr. Hors giving her a not so happy look.

"What? He truly was. Poor thing was found dead in one of the moons of Jupiter, Themisto, I think. Did you know Jupiter has over sixty—"

"As I was saying," Mr. Hors continued, "his Constellation had no planet, so he literally wandered from planet to planet, moon to moon. And he is not the only one. In total, there are eighty-eight Constellations, twelve of which are Wonderers and the remaining sixty-six are Wanderers..."

"There are many more Wanderers than Wonderers..." I analyzed.

"Five and half of them to one of us." My dad said.

"Yes, but we also have the elements - Earth, Air, Fire, and Water - that they do not possess." Ms. Hills included.

"Okay, so why don't we go after them and just lock them all up?" I asked impatiently.

"Is not that simple son, not all Wanderers are bad and not all Wonderers are trustworthy either. That's why we are here."

"You think they have something to do with Mom and Jacques?" Now things were finally going somewhere.

"We don't know for sure Marcus, but we think something bad is coming and it has to do with your mom and your friend's disappearance." Ms. Hills stated.

"Wait, why are they after my mom? Or Jacques? Unless if they are not at all after us, they are trying to get to you, Dad. I mean you're a Porter but not a Wonderer, Mr. Hors is. Why is that?" I got closer to my dad. "You never succeeded in becoming a Wonderer, did you? Did you fail or did you resign it so you can be with Mom? That's why Kent and Margaret were looking after me so I could be the next Wonderer of Earth, Porter of the Taurus Constellation, right? But guess what, Dad? I don't wanna be a Porter, even less a

Wonderer! I don't want to follow on the steps that you, yourself, never succeeded. I've never asked for any of this madness! All I want is to find Mom and Jacques. I gotta get out of here! How do I get out of here? Where's the invisible elevator?" I looked around with no luck.

"Marcus, wait, you can't leave like that on your own, it's late." Ms. Hills warned me.

"I AM LEAVING RIGHT NOW!" I shouted at the three of them. All three of them blinked and their eyes were gone. Instead, shining eyeballs just like the Japanese Twins and the Midnight-Blue Eyed Guy took their place.

"Those eyes..., I've seen those before, you are all in this together, you're all the same." I pushed the telescope out of the way and jumped through the only open window; all the way down to the water with a 'no' echoing from all three of them inside of the not-so-abandoned small house.

I apparently didn't think this through. The water was icy cold even though the weather was nice out. I didn't realize how high I was, about three stories high, making me sink quite fast to the bottom. I thought I was going to find the little boat, but it was nowhere to be seen. I tried to swim back up to the surface, only to feel quite heavy, and realized that I wasn't the excellent swimmer I thought I was. The salty, icy water made it harder to see under it; the water was not as clear as I thought it was either, as a matter of fact, it was quite dark once I was immersed in it.

The water carried me further away. I was up on the surface, but I couldn't find the energy to swim to the shore. My body gave up quicker than I expected, and then, just like that, I sank. My mind went blank. I could hear nothing but my own heart slowly giving up. Maybe I did overreact about everything that my father was trying to tell me. After all, he is my father. Perhaps all of that would make more sense if I actually put some thought into it, but now it was too late to think about that. I had lost him. I had lost my mom. I had lost it all.

And just when I had given in completely, a hand grab- bed my arm, pulling me back to the surface. I realized that the water hadn't taken me too far from the small house; I wasn't immersed under water for too long. I was still close to the Rowes Wharf hotel. Amid coughing and water expelling out of my lungs, I rolled to my side and thanked whoever the person who rescued me was, barely looking up to see his face.

VII

MIDNIGHT-BLUE EYED GUY

Are you okay there, buddy?" This guy said with a concerned yet laughing kind of voice. "You must be really hot to go swimming at this hour."

"I'm okay," I said, shivering with cold.

"Whoa, we should get you dried up. Are you staying at the Rowes Wharf as well?" He took off his jacket and laid it on me.

"Where? Oh no, I'm from here. Everett actually. I'm okay. I'll just walk home or take a bus or something, I will dry up along the way." I tried to get up to my feet, only to shiver again and fall down to my knees.

"Hold on there, buddy." He said, holding me up

before I could collapse on the floor. "Listen, I am staying at the Rowes Wharf Hotel. I'll take you there, get you some towels, and make a phone call to your parents to pick you up, okay?"

I didn't have much of a choice. I could barely walk, and even though it was nice for me outside, apparently, it wasn't the same after being immersed in thirty-degree water.

"Let's go. The hotel is just a few feet away from us. You can lean on my shoulders."

And I did. Once in the hotel lobby, I dried up and comfortably sat at a lounge chair. I finally had a chance to take a look at him and thank him for helping me get out of the water.

"Feeling better now?" He gave me a cup of hot cocoa.

"Yeah, thank you again..." I stopped mid-sentence, staring at him.

"You sure you okay, there? Cause the way you're looking at me it's super weird."

"I'm sorry, you look like someone I met a few days ago." And he did.

"Is his name William Chase?" He asked smiling at me, and for a second, I could swear I saw his eyes change color.

"I should get going, thanks for the towels and saving me from that freezing water."

"You sure, you're good? You could use the phone here in the lobby to call someone or a cab." He assured me.

"No, it's all right. They're not home, and I can take

the bus back home myself." I looked for my wallet, but no luck. Great! I didn't know how to go back home from here, nor did I have any money for the bus. How was I gonna go back home? I searched for my phone, but it was not working obviously. I wonder if Mom would believe that I fell again in the water, damaging my phone. Maybe if I head back to that weird house in the middle of the water, I could still find my dad there. Then again, that was not an option. I ran away from them for a reason. My father and his so-called friends were all acting weird with all this astrological nonsense that supposedly, now out of the blue, existed. So no, I needed time for myself. Walking home it is.

"Is everything alright?" William asked me, realizing that I really haven't moved much.

"Yeah, I guess. I think I lost my wallet when I fell in the water." I said still patting my pockets. "And of course, my phone is damaged."

"Hey, no worries. I can give you a lift to where you need to go if you're okay with that. I mean, I'm technically not a stranger anymore, and I just saved you, it's not like I'm gonna try to kill you or anything." He laughed.

I just looked at him.

"Okay, that did not help my case. I got a car, and Everett is not that far from here if you want a ride..." he offered again.

"No, it's okay. My dad is out there. I just gotta go find him." I lied.

"Okay then, but be careful out there and don't go

swimming again, okay?" He said, mocking me.

"Yeah, I'll try." I laughed back. "Thank you again for helping me get out of the water."

"Hey, sure. See you around, Marcus."

"Yeah, see ya." I walked out of the hotel lobby toward the water again and saw the small house right there, in the middle of nowhere, as if it was a house-island; only instead of land under it, there were trunks of trees. I wondered if my father and his 'crew' were still inside. The house seemed all closed up. I couldn't tell if they were able to see me or not.

I got to think on how I would be able to find Jacques. I was alone with no money, and my cell phone was filled with water. And even if I wanted to go to my dad, I didn't know how. How was I to find the invisible glass elevator that took us to the boat? Maybe I should have had accepted William's offer to give me a ride home. I knew it wasn't right to lie to him, but then again, I didn't know him, so I was not going to go jumping in some stranger's car for a ride to my place. Who knows what he could do? I mean, it's not like he saved my life or anything – oh wait, he did actually. I just realized something; he knew my name! I never said my name to him, but he did say 'see you around, Marcus'. How did he know my name?

Before I could finish my train of thought, something glistening caught my eye. It was a glare made out from a mirror's reflection, which annoyed me. And just to my surprise, when I looked down to see where it was coming from, it was coming from the water that I was just in a few minutes ago. I looked closely, and I saw Jacques under the water, panicking, mouthing something that I couldn't hear or make out. He seemed locked inside of what looked like a clear box and seemed to be running out of air. Following my guts, I jumped into the water. Again!

The second time around, the water wasn't so cold or so dirty. Or maybe I was just getting used to it by now. I tried to reach out for Jacques, but something caught up on me. I looked back to see if my shirt was stuck on something, but the only thing I could make sense out of it was that someone else's hand was pulling me back to the surface again. I tried to free myself without any luck. And before I realized, I was on the surface, again by the Rowes Wharf.

"What the heck are you doing?" I yelled, repelling myself out of whoever had grabbed me. "My friend is under water I need to help him."

"I leave you alone for a minute, and you jump right back in the water!"

I looked back not believing and yet frustrated to see who was. "William, what were you thinking? My friend is underwater, trapped or something. I gotta go help him."

"What's up with you guys from Boston and this dirty water? Stay here!" He demanded, jumping into the icy cold, dirty water.

"He's not here Marcus," He assured me with his head out of the water."

"He has to be, I just saw him. There!" I pointed where Jacques was; about fifty-feet away from us, unconscious.

"I'm sorry, Marcus." William apologized.

"Wait, no, you gotta do something, you gotta help him,"

And then I saw what I didn't wanna see.

William's eyes turned bright-white like stars, his skin was covered in blue feathers as he flew out of the water going over to get Jacques. William Chase was the Midnight-Blue Eyed Guy, the blue feathered bird guy.

"Get away from him, leave him alone, you freak! Let him be. I'll kill you myself if you hurt him, WIL-LIAM!"

He ignored all my comments and insults. He grabbed Jacques out of the water with his bird claws and brought him to where I was standing, dropping him gently on the ground; transforming himself back into the white, pale complexion guy with his midnight-blue eyes again. His smile was gone entirely.

"Get away from him," I shouted pushing William out of the way.

"Marcus, let me help him before he dies. He's been underwater for too long."

"No! NO! You will not touch him, you're just like the rest of them." I sat down on the ground crying uncontrollably by Jacques' body.

William ignored me and started doing C.P.R. on Jacques. I knew Jacques was dead; I couldn't believe it. I just couldn't.

Jacques then opened his eyes, coughing out all of the water he'd swallowed.

"Jacques, are you okay?" I rushed to him as William stepped back.

"Hey, slow down *pote*[18], I'm alright," he replied as he lost consciousness again.

"Jacques! JACQUES!"

"Marcus, he may be suffering from hypothermia, let's take him inside to the hotel room, we can put him under a hot bath," William suggested.

"Please, don't hurt him." I was feeling lost, cold, and too tired to argue with him.

"Give me your hand." He stretched out his hand to me while grabbing Jacques with his other hand. I did. "Hold on." His eyes went from midnight-blue to bright-white shining like stars again, his body shifted in the blink of an eye to that of an angel, a blue feathered angel that is.

He moved us from the ground up to twenty-three stories high in a matter of seconds, throwing me inside through the window first and then handing me Jacques, as he swiftly made his way into his room; transforming himself back into the twenty-something-year-old guy that I was getting used to by now, before his feet had even touched the floor. We took Jacques into the bathtub, removed his clothes, and ran the warm water.

"I'm gonna put his clothes in the dryer and grab something to warm you both. Here, give me your clothes." He handed me one of the bathrobes to change into.

---

[18] *Pote:* Buddy (French)

I did.

I left Jacques in the bathtub and went back in the room. I sat there facing the water outside of the window, wondering what I was doing. William seemed like a good guy, but he is somewhat of a stranger, and yet, he saved Jacques and me from drowning.

I woke up in one of the lounge chairs in William's hotel room. I must've fallen asleep for about twenty minutes or so. Jacques was sleeping on the bed, and William was nowhere to be found. I decided to go find him. He probably went downstairs to the restaurant or something.

The hotel was quiet, even in the lobby. I wondered how late it was, but I couldn't find any clocks around either. How could a hotel of this magnitude have no clocks?

Once outside, I realized how dark it was. Maybe somewhere around three in the morning, maybe my twenty minutes nap was way longer than I thought. There was also no one outside of the hotel, and the restaurant facing the water that Jacques and I had just fallen in was undoubtedly closed. The only thing I could hear was low instrumental music playing through the speakers of the patio. I walked near the water, remembering the struggle that I had been through. The thought of it made me shiver. Thankfully, we were all saved now, thanks very much to William, who, besides my early suspicions, seemed like a decent guy after all.

Just as fast as my thoughts came, they vanished in a flash. I saw something bubbling under the water. At first, I thought it was just a fish or something, but then the bubbles became more and more intense. I approached closer to the edge to see what was under there, and then I fell in the water again! I tried to swim back up, but I was locked inside of what seemed like an air box, just like the one Jacques was in a few hours ago, there was no air in it. I tried to scream, but no sound came out. I could not break through the air box.

I wanted to kick it, punch it, but nothing happened. Then everything started going white around me. Sparkles were coming out of my eyes. My body was getting tired and heavier by the second, and then it happened again: my legs were gone; they were replaced by two white legs with hooves like that of a bull. When I touched them, my hands were also the front hooves of a cow, and then I let a very loud and frightening **MOO** come out. I wrestled trying to free myself out of the box, only to find myself back on the floor of William's hotel room.

"Marcus, are you okay?" William was standing nearby the window we had flown through a few moments ago, staring at me.

"Yeah, I'm fine. It was just a bad dream." I said embarrassedly. After all, he and Jacques were both looking at me weirdly. I wondered if I had said something or screamed in my sleep.

"Jacques, you're awake! How are you feeling? Are you alright? What happened?" I clustered him with questions as I sat next to him on the bed.

"Hey, slow down there, *mon ami*[19]. One question at a time. I can barely remember what happened." He said getting up to a setting position.

"What do you mean? You were gone for hours." It's impossible that he could have forgotten what happened to him.

"I don't know. I was over your place waiting for you downstairs, then the doorbell rang—"

"The doorbell rang? I didn't hear the bell ringing." I was getting a little frustrated and confused at the same time.

"Easy, Marcus, let him finish the story, then you ask questions," William told me. "Thanks, uh, who are you?" Jacques asked, noticing William for the first time. "I'm William Chase, Porter of—"

"He saved you when you fell in the water," I interrupted him.

"And you too, Mr. Mathias." William reminded me, making me feel somewhat embarrassed and uncomfortable.

"What does he mean by 'you too', Marcus?"

"I'll tell you my story once you finish yours," I tried to avoid the subject. I did not want to talk about what had happened to me. It was somewhat ludicrous. "Now tell me, what happened after you got to the door?"

"Well," Jacques continued, "when I opened the door, no one was there. I went outside for not more than a few feet away from the door, wondering that

---

[19] *Mon ami:* My friend (French)

maybe someone rang it and ran away; but nothing, so I went back inside. Once I closed the door, I realized that it was rather windy inside the house, in a very unusual way. I called out your name, but no one answered. I went outside to the back porch, and it felt like a tornado was staggering still on your backyard. I went back inside, and then I fell."

"What do you mean you fell?" None of this makes any sense.

"I don't know. I saw a glimpse of someone in the living room, and then before I could define who it was, something or someone kayoed me." He concluded.

"Kayoed you?" William looked puzzled.

"Knocked him out," I said, kind of aggravated at William for not knowing what kayoed meant. "Someone knocked him out. Go on, Jacques."

"I didn't see anyone there. I just felt this blow of air so strong on my face that I was knocked off my feet, falling unconscious on the floor, and that was it."

"Did you hear or see anything or anyone?" William looked intrigued.

"I heard two people speaking in a foreign language that seemed to be Japanese or something like that," Jacques remembered.

"Japanese? Are you sure of that, Jax?" The Japanese Twins, I thought to myself.

"Maybe Chinese? Korean? Something like that, Marcus. How am I to know? I'm only fluent in English and barely in French." he sounded a bit aggravated by my question.

"Marcus, hold on. Let me ask him something," William sat next to us in the bed facing Jacques. "How did you get here to Rowes Wharf and got left underwater?"

"I..., I don't know... I don't remember. When I gained my consciousness back again, I was there locked inside of what seemed like a box made out of air, and I couldn't free myself out of it. I tried to call you, Marcus, but my phone was not working. I could see people out, but no one seemed to notice me, so I started kicking and punching the box, trying to break free. I was running out of air, and that's when I saw you, Marks. And you know the rest. That's all I remember." Jacques finished his story, or at least what he remembered of it.

"Wait a minute, you said you tried to call me, right? But you did call me earlier, remember? We talked for a minute and then?" I asked.

"Yes, yes, I remember that I was walking on the park when I called you, I had no idea where I was till I saw the Rowes Wharf Hotel and then I saw a woman, not sure, but I guess it was your mom, Marcus," His words barely came out once he remembered it. I'm sure he didn't want to tell me that part of the story.

"My MOM? What happened?"

"Something hit me in the head, and I fell unconscious. Again! A sense of failure came out of Jacques' voice.

"That does not make any sense at all, Jacques, and I know you're telling the truth, but I just can't wrap my head around all of this. My Mom? I mean, does this make any sense to either one of you?" I asked out loud almost as if to myself; confused, as if some explanation would come to me out of thin air.

"Sense or nonsense, Marcus, one thing is for sure: it's getting very late, and I gotta get you guys home. Your parents must be worried sick about you two. Let's go, I'll drive." William grabbed our clothes all dried up and folded.

Only then I realized how late it was and how hungry I was. It had been such a crazy long day that I couldn't even argue with William. And even though I knew I shouldn't trust him, I decided to accept his ride home; besides neither Jacques nor I had any money or cell phone right now.

On the way home, I told Jacques everything that had happened since my vision on the back porch till when I found him. Not putting any detail aside, including the incident in the airport, the disappearance of my mom, and how my dad was allied to Ms. Margaret Hills, my new boss and her boyfriend, Kent Hors. I told him about this whole 'Porter' thing that I was supposed to be. How I, freaked out by everyone's eyes bright-white like stars, jumped in the same water that he was in just a few hours ago and was also saved from it by William. I left out the part that William appeared in my house many times before and how he solely was responsible for me freaking out in the airport and how he transformed himself into a big blue bird and saved Jacques out the water and flew us into his hotel room. I thought my story was already crazy as it is. I didn't want him to freak out. found him.

"Wow, what do you think about all that? I mean, do you think that any of this could be possible?" Jacques finally asked after a long pause.

VIII

DESTROYED

I didn't reply. I looked at William who was driving the car. I was sure he was clinging on every word I said. I wanted to know his thoughts, almost hoping that he would laugh at any point and that somehow, it would all go back to normal and him, being a little older than us, would have an explanation for all of this. But instead, he just looked at me, smiled, and then looked back to the road as if I had told Jacques about my day at school yesterday.

I kept my thoughts to myself. Deep inside, as crazy as it all sounded, I knew my father wasn't one to lie, and after seeing William transform himself into a bluebird over and over again, I knew I was not going crazy. But what was I to do? Protect the world from the

Wanderers? Become a Porter? How cliché! It was just not for me. I'm not that guy.

"What's your sign, William?" I tried to break the ice.

"You can call me Will, and I'm a Libra," he answered, kind of confused about my question, leaving me more confused than ever. After all, Libra was represented by a scale and not a big blue bird.

"Uh, Marcus, are you sure you put the right address in the G.P.S.?" William interrupted my train of thought.

"Will, you think I don't know my own address?" I looked around, not recognizing the place where we had just parked. "Where are we?"

"Marks, I think this is your house, or at least what's left of it," Jacques spoke with a tone of concern.

"It can't be. There are only ruins there." I got out of the car followed by Jacques and Will. "Hey, look at this!"

I got closer to Jacques to see what he was found. It was one of my lucky rocks. I didn't know how he found it in the middle of that wreckage, but he found it. Only then I looked around and recognized my place, destroyed, in front of my own eyes. There were only ruins everywhere I looked. It seemed like an earthquake had happened here. My clothes were all over the floor, at least whatever was left of it, my parent's stuff too. It was all destroyed, all gone. I did, though, find some more of my rocks, about five of them. I found one old brown hoodie and a family portrait with all of us in it, including my big sister, Daniella, before she went missing. I sat on the back porch, which was somewhat still there, and cried. A sense of loss was upon me, an empty hole inside my chest, a sense of no direction, not knowing what to do next. I didn't cry of sadness. I cried of frustration, of defeat. I was defeated.

I wasn't sure on what to do next. I could go to Jacques' house and all, but what about Mom and Dad? Where were they? Did they know about our home, how it was all destroyed? What was I supposed to say to Mr. and Mrs. DüMicahellis once we got to their place? I was never the lying type. Well, at least not the big kind of lies.

"Hey, Marcus, let's go over to my place. I'm sure Mom and Dad are gonna let you stay the night." Jacques comforted me.

"Thanks, Jax, but I don't know if that's a good idea. I think I'm gonna try to find my dad. I mean, Will, would you mind taking me back to the Wharf?"

"Hey, not at all, Marks. I have to go back there anyway. Did you forget I'm staying there?" William pointed out.

"Okay, but do you know where even to find him?" Jacques asked.

"Yeah, sure. I think I know where he is." I lied. Well, sort of. I did know where I saw my dad last at the small abandoned house in the middle of the water, across from the Rowes Wharf Hotel. But is he still there? Is anyone still in there? I guess the only way to find out is to go there.

"Marcus, I think it's best if we go to my place and stay there for the night. I mean, it's already late, and there's not much we can do now anyway." Jacques suggested.

"I have to say, I don't mind driving you back at all, but Jacques is right. It is kind of late."

Of course, they are both right. It is late, and there is nothing that I can do at this hour. But at the same time, I knew I had to find my dad. I need to tell him about the house. I am sure he doesn't know, but where can I find him?

"All right," I agreed, "we'll go to Jacques' place, rest for the remainder of the night, and we can start fresh tomorrow."

"Okay, awesome, let's go to my place. We need new clothes too." Jacques emphasized.

"All right, guys, jump in. I'll drive you there." William said excitedly, turning the car's engine on.

We got in Will's car and headed off to Jacques' house, which was very close to mine. I was relieved to see that his place was still standing with no sign of destruction. The lights were on, which probably meant that his family was still awake. William pulled the car over in the drive-way.

"Here we are, guys, safe and sound," William said, parking the car.

"Thank you very much, Will, for driving us to my place, I really appreciate that, and for rescuing us from out of the water and all." Jacques made fun of our recent situation, which made me somewhat embarrassed.

"Hey, no problem at all, guys. Anyone else would have done the same," he smiled.

I know it sounds weird, but somehow William seemed like a good guy, and after spending a few hours with him, I feel like he is becoming a friend. I still need answers though, like why he's been hovering around me lately. We need to have a conversation soon.

"By the way, how are you guys planning your 'little adventure' tomorrow morning? Riding the town on a bus?" William asked jokingly.

"Hum, I don't know yet. We'll figure something out in the morning once we're up." I said, not laughing, not because it wasn't funny the way he said 'our little adventure' but only because he was right. I had no idea how we were going to do all that without a car.

"How about if I come back here tomorrow morning and drive you guys back to the Rowes Wharf?" William offered.

"Thank you, Will, but I can't ask any more of your help."

"Marcus, c'mon, Will is right. We are better off with him. We need someone with a car to drive us around." Jacques insisted.

"I know, Jacques, but I'm sure William has other plans for his vacation."

"Yes, it is true, Marks, but you need my help, and I feel like helping you. And what better way to spend the rest of my vacation than helping you with your missing dad and destroyed house? I would definitely have a great vacation story to tell when I get back home."

Somehow, I knew that Will was lying about all this. Not sure if it was by his tone of voice or his smirk stamped all over his face.

"All right, you're right," I finally agreed, "tomorrow morning, meet us here at Jacques' place around ten, okay?" At least this will give me a chance to get to know him better, and maybe ask all the questions that have been bothering me since the day I met him on my birthday.

"Awesome! See you guys in the morning." William was weirdly excited about all this, which made me wonder if I had made the right choice or not.

"Later, Will," Jacques said, as William pulled out of the driveway in his blue S.U.V.

"Okay, so what are we supposed to say to your mom and dad?" I asked.

"What do you mean? They know me, Marcus, I live here, remember?" Jacques said, smiling at me, clearly not understanding my question.

"What are we gonna tell them about me?"

"Nothing Marcus, you're my friend. You're staying over just like many times before, *toqué*[20]."

He clearly doesn't see a big deal in any of this. Maybe he is right. Maybe, I'm worrying too much about nothing. Truth is, I have no idea what's going

---

[20] *Toqué:* Goofy (French)

on. I don't know what to do or who to trust anymore. I don't know who this William guy indeed is and why he is helping us out after he crept upon me many times before. But come to think about it, even my dad has now shown his bright shining star-like eyes, so clearly, for all I could tell, they may very well be on the same team. Or worse, I have officially gone crazy. Yep, that totally makes more sense.

Jacques opened the door with a key he found hidden inside the mailbox allowing ourselves in. His dad was in the living room watching a soccer match on T.V. with his back to us.

"Ça va bien, Papa?[21]" Jacques spoke to his dad.

"Bien, bien, fils[22], ah not again, he missed it. Seriously he was right in front of it..." he replied without even glancing back at us.

"My dad gets very intense watching soccer," Jacques said, gesturing to his room.

We got to his room, and Jacques opened up his sofa bed just like many times before whenever I slept there. His bedroom is the size of my living room.

"Hey, do you need anything?" he asked, as he handed me a pair of shorts for me to change into.

"No, I'm good Jax, thanks," I said getting off my clothes and putting on the shorts.

"Try to get some sleep, buddy, I know you had a long day today, but hopefully tomorrow everything

---

[21] *Ça va bien, Papa?:* How are you, Papa? (French)

[22] *Bien, bien, fils:* Good, good, son (French)

should make more sense. Or should I say later on?" He pointed to a clock on the wall displaying the time way past three.

"Haha, thanks, Jax. See you later, then."

"G'night man." he fell in his bed.

"'Night." I laid down on my bed too.

I couldn't go to sleep, and not because Jacques was snoring or his dad's constant curses in French at the T.V., but only because I couldn't get my mind off of things that happened today. I'm genuinely lost and confused; all I want is my dad and mom back in my house like everything was a couple of days ago. My home is destroyed, my mom's gone, kidnapped or something. My cellphone is water damaged after falling in the water more than once. I wouldn't have this problem if my mom had got me the nPhone since it's waterproof. I have no idea if my dad is still at the small house in the middle of the water with Ms. Hills and Mr. Hors. Luckily enough, I haven't had one of my episodes yet. Not that it matters since everything else around me seems like an episode of hallucination.

I got up and made my way to the kitchen to grab a cup of water. The whole house was dark. Jacques' father was passed out asleep on the couch with the T.V. still on. I got to the kitchen and opened up the cabinet to grab a glass then headed to the fridge for some water.

"Can't sleep either?" A voice that was becoming more familiar than ever spoke from behind the refrigerator's door. I dropped the glass, but it got picked up in midair by him. "Sorry, didn't mean to startle you," He said handing me back the glass.

"William, you gotta stop sneaking up on me like that." I grabbed the glass out of his hand filling it up with water. "Want some?"

"No, I'm good." Will made himself comfortable in one of the chairs by the dining table.

"What are you doing here at this hour?" I asked sitting across from him. To ask about how he got in the house would be a waste of time. I know Will has a way of getting inside of any place by now.

"I came here to check on you, to see if you're okay." He sounded very truthful.

"You know I'm not okay. Truth is I have no idea what's going on. My dad, Kent and Margaret, the Japanese Twins and now you. What in the world are you?"

"I'm William Chase!" He sneered at me.

"That I know! What I mean is what sign are you?" I asked angrily.

"Libra, I told you that already. You gotta be more specific than that."

"How can a Libra become a bluebird? I thought you were represented by scales or something,"

"A Lyrebird," he interrupted me, "I'm William Chase, Porter of the Lyra Constellation, a Wanderer." Something about the way he spoke, sounded as if he is royalty just like the way my dad spoke of himself about being Porter of the Taurus Constellation, a Wonderer.

"Wait, I thought you were a Libra. How can you be a Libra and also a Lyrebird?" I was more confused than ever.

Just when I thought I was getting the hang of things.

"I was born on the 14th day of the month of October under the regent sign of Libra, and I also am a Lyrebird. Lyrebirds get their name after their tail shaped like a lyre. The Lyra Constellation is based on the lyre instrument as well. That's why when I first saw you, I was in a tiny boat playing the lyre,"

"That was you? My Grandma warned me about you. She told me not to trust you, that you were coming after me." I indignantly got up to my feet.

"No, Marcus, she wasn't talking about me. I'm your friend, not your enemy."

"Yeah, right! How did you know of my dream? Was that even a dream? ANSWER ME!" I demanded.

"Marcus, who are you talking to?" Jacques walked in the kitchen looking at me with a puzzled face.

"Myself." I didn't need to look around me to know William was gone. I knew he was gone just like always. "I needed some water..."

"Alright let's go back to bed, we gotta be up in less than four hours." He turned back to his room half asleep.

I followed.

IX

THAT'S MY BOY!

"**M**arcus! Marks, get up! William is gonna be here soon. MARCUS!" I heard Jacques shouting around the room waking me up. I opened my eyes.

"William, William, William. All I hear lately is William this, William that..."

"Geesh, did you sleep okay?" Jacques asked, once he realized how annoyed I was.

"I'm sorry. Bad dream. That's all." I lied, I was tired and confused, and now I was not even sure if I could trust Will anymore. Not after knowing that he was the one my grandmother was talking about in the morning of my birthday in my dream, vision, or whatever that was.

"It's okay, buddy, go get ready, Will should be here soon."

Jacques stepped out of the room, leaving me by myself to get dressed. Once I was ready, I made my way to Jacques' kitchen where he and his mom was getting the table ready.

"Good morning, Marcus. Jacques told me you guys have a big day ahead." Mrs. DüMicahellis greeted me as she put down a plate of scrambled eggs with crispy bacon strips on the table.

"Uh?" I looked at Jacques wondering how much he'd told her.

"Aren't you guys off to play soccer?" She asked, confused, looking at Jacques as if she had misunderstood him.

"Yes, yes of course. I thought we were going for football, but I guess soccer it is." I lied, as I drank a glass of orange juice.

"Soccer, football, it's all the same. After marrying Jean, I get those messed up all the time. You see, Americans are the only people in the world who call football, soccer. Go on now, eat up. You don't want to be hungry before the game." She went to the countertop to grab the toasts out of the toaster.

Just when I was done brushing off my teeth after breakfast, I heard Will's S.U.V. pulling over.

"Let's go, Marks. Will's outside." Jacques said, heading out through the kitchen door waving at Will.

"Who's Will?" Jacques' mom asked curiously.

"New kid that just moved in next door, I lied before quickly leaving the house.

"What's up, Will?" I heard Jacques saying as he got into the blue S.U.V. parked in the driveway sitting on the backseat wearing his favorite blue baseball cap with the New England Patriots logo in it, his favorite football team.

"Good morning, buddy. Ready for our 'little adventure'?" William greeted me with the same sneer he uses all the time.

"G'Mornin', Will. Glad to see you woke up in a good mood." I mumbled.

"Gee, Marcus, bad dream?"

"Yeah, something like that," I said as I was getting myself in the passenger seat.

You see, the problem was, I didn't know what was happening to me. My life was completely upside down. I couldn't tell what a dream or reality was anymore. I didn't know where my parents were, and my house was destroyed. I didn't know who to trust, what to do, or where to go from here. Nevertheless, I decided to keep calm and retrace my moves from yesterday, and then maybe I would be able to find my dad. If only my cell was working.

"Hey, where are you guys going?" A very much familiar voice said outside the car next to my window as we stopped by the traffic lights.

"Oh hey, Mileena, good morning! How are you?" I let the words roll out of my mouth instantaneously.

"Hum, I'm good..." She said as she looked inside the car, a little bit taken by Will, who I just realized she hadn't met yet.

"Miles, this my friend William. He is giving me a ride to work." I introduced him.

"Hi, Mileena, nice to meet you," Will greeted her.

"Nice meeting you, William," she greeted him back, turning her attention back to me, "I thought you had weekends off?"

"Inventory," Jacques shouted from the backseat once he realized I didn't know what to say. To be fair, I had no idea today was Sunday, the days seemed to all be blending into one lately. *"Bon jour, mademoiselle![23]"*

"Hey Jax, are you working there too?" She mocked him, knowing that Jacques would never work a day in his life if he didn't have to.

"Moral support." he smiled, followed by my own awkward laugh.

"Okay," She looked suspiciously at me. "What are you guys up to later on? Wanna hang out or something? Maybe movies?"

"Sure, yeah. I mean, I'm not sure how long we're gonna take, but yeah, I'll text you." I replied nervously.

"All right. I'm on my way to Bianca's house. Tell your mom I'll stop by later on to have some of her cookies. They are so good."

"Yeah, sure, I mean, okay. Haha." I laughed way harder than I intended to. "Well, it was nice seeing you. I gotta go. I'll talk to you later, okay?"

---

[23] *Bon jour, mademoiselle:* Good morning, my lady. (French)

"See ya," Mileena said as she walked away, look-ing back at us, somewhat not buying the whole story. I'm such a bad liar.

"Au revoir, ma belle[24]," Jacques shouted from the back-seat. "That right there, Willie, that's my future wife, okay? Don't get any ideas alright, buddy?"

"William or Will, never Willie or Billy, alright buddy?" William's tone of voice made it very clear that he didn't like nicknames.

Lying to Miles was something I didn't like to do, but I had no other choice. What was I supposed to tell her? I would have eventually to tell her the whole story about Porters, but not now. Not when I don't have a clue about what's going on.

We headed just a couple of blocks down the street from Jacques' house, near Everett High School, and only then I noticed how cloudy it was. I mean, we were in Spring right now, but for some reason, the weather was always coming and going. After all, this is New England weather, and you never know what the day has in store for you. One time we had all the four seasons in one day, hail and all. Will stopped the car abruptly, taking my head off the clouds quite li-terally.

"What happened?" I turned to Will to find out why he had stopped.

"They happened!" William said pointing out to the front of the car.

"Not them again!" I couldn't believe who was

---

[24] *Au revoir, ma belle:* Goodbye, my beauty (French)

standing in front of the car, blocking our way.

"Who are they?" Jacques asked confused from the back-seat.

"The Japanese Twins." I was definitely annoyed, but glad to see that they were not part of one of my 'delusional dreams'.

"We call them the Gemini Porters or Wonderers of Mercury if you wanna be more specific," William informed me. "Do you know them?"

"Yeah, I met them briefly before." I remembered vividly the day I met them in the bookstore trying to kidnap me to their king.

"Excuse me, but we are trying to get through!" I yelled out of the window, but they didn't move.

"We need to talk to you, Marcus. Please step out of the car. You and you only." The girl spoke; truthfully, I did not miss her tone of voice.

"What is she talking about, Marcus?" Jacques said with a weak voice from the backseat.

"So, you did meet them before." William's sense of humor was very well timed as always.

"Listen, I don't want any trouble. Can we please, get through?" I pleaded from the window.

"We need to talk to you, Marcus. Please step out of the car. You and you only. We are not going to repeat ourselves." This time, the boy spoke.

"Okay, I'm gonna see what they want. If anything happens, just run over us. I'm sure I'll be fine." I wasn't sure if I was gonna be fine or not but, I didn't care if he ran over me and those annoying twins. "Alright, I'm stepping out,"

"Marcus, don't." William tried to stop me.

"Marcus Mathias, you need to come with us. We need to talk about your future." They said in unison.

"Wait, wait a moment. What do you want from me? Who are you, people?"

"Sorry about our manners," the girl spoke, "my name is Lynne Yang, and this is my twin brother, Lee."

"We are the Porters of the Gemini Constellation, Wonderers of Mercury," Lee continued, "more will be explained once we bring you to our king." His voice was harsh, just like that of a law enforcement officer.

"I am not going anywhere. I'm not the person you think I am," I told them, a bit aggravated.

"Aren't you Marcus Mathias?" They asked.

"Yes, but—"

"You're coming with us, Dogie." Lynne imposed before I could finish my sentence.

"Listen, I'm gonna return to the car, and you are gonna let us pass through, okay? I don't have time for this nonsense right now." I made my way back to the car.

"No, you are not," they told me as their eyes went from black to white, shinning bright like stars, frighteningly just how I remembered.

I turned around and found one more pair of twins behind me. I turned to the 'original' pair of twins in front of me, and I tried one more time. "Listen, guys, I don't want any trouble."

"Marcus, I don't think they are going to reason with you anymore." William stepped out of the car.

"You stay out of this, Birdie!" Lee's copy of himself moved from behind me to in front of William in less than a second; it was definitely inhumanely impossible to run that fast.

"William!" I tried to warn him, but the guy already had William in a chokehold. "LET HIM GO!" I warned them.

"Come with us, and no one gets hurt, Dogie," Lynne warned me.

"Hey, what's going on? Let them go!" Jacques demanded, stepping out of the car.

"Jacques, get back in the car," I told him.

"Nuh-uh-uh." This time was Lynne's copy which was in front of the door, trapping Jacques inside the car, waving her finger in front of Jacques.

"How did you get here?" Jacques tried to move her out of his way, but in a flash, she moved, and Jacques fell on the floor. Her foot was on his head holding him down.

"Pathetic!" Lynne's copy told him with an air of superiority.

"So, where were we, *Aneki*[25]?" Lee grimed at Lynne clearly waiting for her move.

"Let's just get this over with, *Aniki*.[26]" she snapped.

They moved from fifty-feet away from me to holding me with both arms in the air; in less than a second.

---

[25] *Aneki:* Sis (Japanese)

[26] *Aniki:* Bro (Japanese)

126

"So, you guys have super speed and can multiply yourselves. Not bad!" Jacques spoke with his mouth half stuck to the floor.

"SHUT UP!" The twins and their copies shouted at him at the same time.

"LET THEM GO!" A voice that I recognized with a very demanding tone spoke from behind us.

"Can it be?" Lynne asked mockingly.

What I saw was pretty hard to describe. A huge black, muscular bull with shining eyes just like those of the Gemini Porters, was standing right there less than a few feet away from us. To his left was a brown bull, a bit smaller but much more significant than any other bull I had ever seen. On its right was a very large, bigger-than-ordinary, tan-colored ram not more prominent than the bulls, but twice as big as any other sheep. Mr. Hors' voice came out of the black bull again with a thunderous, almost deafening tone:

"LET THEM GO. HE IS NOT GOING ANYWHERE!" he threatened them.

"HA HA HA HA HA HA! Look at this, the rest of the cattle decided to join the party." Lee's voice was deafening too but not as loud as the bull's voice.

"And you're gonna try to stop us? You? Irrational animals?" Lynne's mockery was far from over.

I heard something that apparently could only mean that I was dreaming again: My father's voice coming out of the brown bull with a calm but solemn tone; clearly, a facade to hold his fury. "We do not wish to fight you, Gemini, so please, LET THEM GO!"

The nostrils of the brown bull expelled air so vigorously that I was somewhat grateful they were on my side.

"Oh, but we do wish to fight you, stupid four-legged. Hold the boy, *Aniki*[27]." Lynne let me free only for a second as Lee wrapped his two arms around my own arms holding me against his chest. He was definitely taller and stronger than I remembered.

"I'll take care of them myself," he said.

The large animals charged toward us. The bulls and the ram ran toward the twins as they all dispersed. Lynne's copy let Jacques loose and went after the ram, while Lee's copy went after the brown bull, as Lynne herself went for the big black bull.

They were fast, jumping and running around the animals, which made it hard to look. They were putting up a fight, but clearly, they were not even half as fast to keep up with the Gemini Porters.

The ram finally grabbed hold of one the twins, holding her with its horns against the car, damaging Will's car.

The black bull was charging after Lynne, but she was enjoying herself with mad laughter echoing all over the streets.

"Aaaahh!" I looked, and the brown bull was kicked to the floor by Lee's copy falling backward. Hearing my dad's voice coming out of the brown bull was definitely painful, making me feel even more useless and confused. Was this all real?

"Roberto, are you okay?" Ms. Hills' voice came out

---

[27] *Aniki:* Bro (Japanese)

of the ram confirming who the ram was.

"Marge, be careful!" The black bull, Mr. Hors, tried to warn her but it was too late; Lynne's copy had already kicked the ram's face, freeing herself out of her grip.

They were not losing the battle, but they were far from winning it. I had to do something to help my dad. I tried to free myself, but Lee was much stronger than I was.

"You can't free yourself from my grip, Dogie." Lee's hold was getting tighter and tighter, making it impossible for me to breathe.

I started losing air and my body was getting that tingling feeling again. The same as it had happened before in the bookstore and in the airport. But this time I went for it. I could feel my legs folding backward, my hands turning into hooves, my head pounding like a drummer in a drumline competition; my vision was getting brighter and brighter, but I somehow could still make out what was happening around me. I saw Jacques getting knocked out by Lee's copy to the other side of the fully damaged S.U.V. William is gonna be so pissed.

My chest pounded from inside, becoming heavier and heavier. I let out a loud, deafening bellow, taking everyone by surprise. I shook Lee's out of my neck as if he was just a bug. And then, I couldn't be on my legs anymore. I fell forward allowing my two front hooves to hit the floor. A massive wave of asphalt and earth came from under me, striking everything and everyone around me in a matter of seconds.

I lost consciousness but not before hearing the brown bull proudly say, "That's my boy!"

X

G.O.L.
(GALAXY'S OBSERVATORY & LABORATORY)

I woke up and jumped out of Ms. Hills' lap, to which she told me: "Shhh, everything's okay now, Marcus."

We were sitting in the backseat of Mr. Hors' car. He was driving, my dad was on the passenger seat, and Jacques was on my right. My dad looked back with a proud smile and asked me if everything was okay. I nodded. My head was still hurting a lot, but I didn't mention it. I didn't know what was going on.

If everything I saw was right, then I was truly delusional, crazy, or something of that nature. But even though everything seemed so real, I knew deep inside that none of that could possibly be real. All the images kept replaying back in my head, like a movie on re-peat. I couldn't shake off the grin of the Twins and their eyes shining like stars. And every time I relived the scene of me falling, I shook back to reality, only to have Ms. Hills' arms wrapped around me, trying to comfort me, which didn't help at all. It made me feel even worse, as a matter of fact. I couldn't stay quiet anymore; I had to ask Jacques.

"Hey, are you okay?" He asked me first, just be-fore any words could have gotten out of my mouth.

"Yeah, I guess," I said somewhat confused, "can I ask you something? Please be honest with me."

"Of course, Marcus. What's up, man?"

I looked down, took a deep breath and asked: "Was it all real?"

"C'était magnifique, pote[28]! Mr. Mathias said he was gonna explain everything to us once we get there." Jacques' smile couldn't be any bigger. He was definitely proud and excited about everything that happened which didn't help me at all. If Jacques thought this was all real just like everyone else around me, I had to be in a dream, logically.

"We're here." Mr. Hors spoke as he parked the car. I looked outside the window and recognized the place: Lulu's Coffee Shop, owned and operated by Ms. Margaret Hills, the place where I got my first job and probably the last.

Lulu's Coffee Shop occupied most of the first floor of Ms. Hills' house. I remember the large industrial

---

[28] *C'était magnifique, pote:* It was magnificent, buddy (French)

kitchen where she cooks her famous white chocolate chips and macadamia nut cookies that I love very much. The kitchen was big, and very modern, with a dining room table for at least twelve people. It also had a beautiful view of the backyard. A yard that had a lot of different types of flowers everywhere, including this five-foot-tall white rose bush, which made a statement in the yard. In the middle of it all was a very tall, thick tree, a tree where once I saw a woman calling out my name just before I passed out in one of my crazy dreams on my first day at work.

The next floor up was the rest of Ms. Hills' house. Upstairs was the living room and three bedrooms and a full bathroom. On the top of the house was the master suite where she sleeps.

Ms. Hills took me upstairs to one of the guest rooms where I took a shower, and at the same time, I had time to think as well. She had left me some clothes on the bed. I didn't know who's those were, but they were definitely not hers. And luckily, they fit just fine.

"Marcus, your dad wants to talk to you downstairs in the kitchen." Jacques came in the bedroom to let me know.

"I'll be right down, Jax." The truth was, I was dying to ask him a lot of questions, but I didn't know how. Any of this just didn't make any sense. I was also scared. If all this was a reality, then what now? What was I supposed to do? Become a Porter? A Wonderer? I just wanted to be a football player.

I made my way downstairs and into the coffee

shop. My father was sitting on a table with Mr. Hors across from him. Ms. Hills was getting some cookies for Jacques, who was sitting on one of the stools by the counter.

The room got quiet once they noticed me there.

"You look good in my old clothes." My father looked at me and gave me a half smile, sort of happy and sorry at the same time.

I pulled up a chair next to my dad and sat down. Mr. Hors got up and left into the kitchen almost at the same time as I sat down. I didn't say anything. I knew something was up, and we needed to be left alone. Everybody else went too, one by one, even Jacques, who was vividly talking and happy with his chocolate chunk cookies.

"Dad, am I going crazy?" I broke the ice, afraid of what he might say.

"Son, I think you know the answer. Even though you don't know how or why, you do know that this is all truly happening. And as you noticed, you can't run away from it," he explained, almost regretting the words that were coming out of his mouth.

"What am I?" I asked.

"Remember when you manifested your ability for the first time in public at the Logan International Airport?" He began.

"Yes. No, I mean, wasn't that just a crazy dream, one of my delusional dreams?" I interrupted him, annoyed with that statement.

"Marcus, son, just listen to me. For once, would you?"

"Sorry, Dad." My dad and I always had good communication, but he was right. Ever since all of this started, I wasn't really listening to him like I used to.

"Margaret and Kent brought you here and showed you our hologram lab downstairs in the basement, right?"

"Yes, G.O.L. they call it," I remembered.

"They also explained to you about the Porters, Wonderers, Wanderers and how you are most likely the next Porter of the Taurus Constellation, the Wonderer of our planet—"

"No! I mean, yes, they implied that I was a Natural Porter, whatever that is. But that's crazy, right? It's just that—"

"Son, I'm not finished," this time he interrupted me, "I think Kent might be right. We have had some strong reasons to believe that you truly are a Natural Porter, and your life might depend on it; worse, maybe even your mother's, for that matter. Those people back then weren't kidding around. They knew what they wanted and who they were going after. Who knows if any of us are gonna be there to help you next time that happens? We need to train you, to get you ready in case they do come back for you, Marcus."

I just listened like I promised, even though I didn't necessarily believe in any of this, but it was the only plausible explanation for now. "Okay, if I were to say I believe in all of this, how is this even possible? How can any of this make sense, Dad? I'm lost. I don't know what part of me is dreaming or what part of me is awake. I see lions, bulls, rams, birds; much larger than their normal size that I've ever seen before. I don't know where to go from here."

"Did something else happen that you're not telling me?"

I forgot to tell him about William before, the big blue lyrebird. So, I decided to tell him everything. It couldn't get any worse than this.

"Dad, on the night before my birthday, I had my first, what I call them now, 'delusional dreams'. I saw this massive white lion on the beach who came warning me about people coming after me, then, in the same dream, this boy came in on a tiny boat playing this harp, lyre actually, looking for me. Before I could ask the lion, who was now a lioness, she jumped on me and disappeared. I woke up in my bedroom with Mom knocking on the door. Afterward, before we left the house to the mall, this guy appeared in my room to tell me something, but we got interrupted by Jacques, and then he left through the window. He flew out of the window.

Then at the mall," I continued, "we went to return the gift that Mileena gave to me since she and Jacques had a miscommunication and ended up buying me the same gift. I then ran, for the first time, into the Japanese Twins, the Gemini Porters. They tried to grab me and take me to their King or whatever, but I freed myself having my first episode ever. I thought it was just a dream so when Jena woke me up with a slap on my face, I completely avoided the incident. I realized that I was probably the only one who saw them. That's when I realized that my 'delusional dreams' were becoming a constant.

Later on, we had my birthday party, and the same guy of my dream decided to show up again in the backyard, disappearing just before Jacques came to check on me. Who now started wondering if I was going crazy, and to be fair, so did I.

The following day I came here for my first day of work at Lulu's Coffee Shop, only to have another episode after meeting Steve, Ms. Hills, and Mr. Hors for the first time. I saw this woman in her 20's in the backyard who made everything dark, raining and scary. She screamed at me, and I fell backward, embarrassed as hell—"

"Language, young man." My dad interrupted me.

"Sorry," I apologized before continuing, "oh yeah, and what in the world is C.H.E.P.? Never mind I'm sure I'm gonna find out soon. Then my mom and Jacques got kidnapped. Ms. Hills and Mr. Hors appeared in the front of my house to take me to the airport to pick you up, who I had no idea was coming back home, to only then maybe find Mom, but no one was there. Instead, the same guy from my dream was there, again, making me have another episode in public. Two on the same day now, and that's not even counting my 'delusional dreams'. Oh, and on the way to the airport, we had to get rid of this car chasing us. Yes. We had a real car chase, Dad, just like in the movies,"

"Son, I—"

"No, let me finish, I don't wanna forget anything," I interrupted him and continued, "when I woke up, I was here. Actually, in the basement at G.O.L, where both Ms. Hills and Mr. Hors were trying to convince me that everything that was going on, was real and made sense. Needless to say, I didn't buy any of that and ran out of here. By the way, is Pluto still considered a planet? Who cares, I never really liked Pluto anyways. I ran into Jena, and we went to the house to find you, who was surprisingly back from Brazil; then you took me to Mr. Hors' place, his G.O.L, and tried to explain things to me. I was somewhat doing okay, but your eyes, you know, the ones that shine like there's a star coming from inside of them? Right, all of you have them, Ms. Hills, Mr. Hors and you, Dad; reminding me of the Japanese Twins, so I panicked and jumped in the water. I thought I was gonna drown, but I got saved by this guy who I realized was the same guy from the boat in my dream, the same one who appeared in my room and flew through the window on my birthday. By the way, what happened to our home?" I had just remembered about our home being completely destroyed.

"We destroyed our home, son."

"YOU WHAT?" I heard what he said, but I couldn't believe.

"Knowing that everyone was after you, and with your mom nowhere to be found, Marge, Kent and I decided that it would be best if we stick together here at her place, this way we could keep an eye on each other and protect you too. I'm not planning on losing you too." He explained.

"What about our stuff?"

"We packed a few of our clothes and stuff and took them with us before destroying the house. I would have given you some of your clothes, but they are still in storage."

"So, then we went to Jacques' place to stay for the night; since we both had no cell phones, we couldn't call you. In the morning, we made our way to go find you at Mr. Hors' place, but the Twins found us first. And so did you. You know the rest." I finished exhaustedly.

"Listen son, I know the last couple of days were crazy and it's too much for you to understand, but trust me, I truly know how all of this sounds," my dad tried to comfort me, "I've been there before; when I was eighteen, Kent also came to me asking to be the next Porter, a Wonderer. It didn't work out for me but, that doesn't mean it won't work out for you. We need to clarify everything that's happening to you. Well, at least the part that I know."

My dad and I went upstairs to Ms. Hill's living room. It was rather cozy. It felt big and small at the same time. I guess the place was average size, but the furniture was so bulky and significant for the room, that it made us feel cramped. Overall, it was very well put together, oddly, it actually felt like home. She had a lot of weird picture frames and paintings hanging on the wall of places she'd been, but I didn't recognize any of those places; as a matter of fact, it seems like it was even from another, well, planet! But of course, that was just my imagination going crazy. Things that looked abnormal were becoming quite normal lately.

"Marcus, everything that's been happening to you is happening for a reason." My dad sat at one of the beige couches, under Ms. Hills' picture of herself holding a surgical instrument when she was maybe about sixteen with such a happy face.

"And what reason could that be?" I pretty much shouted at him, "sorry," I said, right after I realized my tone of voice.

"Son, try to listen to me first, okay? Let me explain all you need to know, and then you can ask all the questions you have," he suggested.

"Okay." I followed his idea and sat on the other smaller couch across from him.

"I know this seems rather strange, and there's so much to tell you, but we also have to hurry. I might have an idea of where your mom might be, so I'm gonna make this quick, okay?"

I nodded.

"At first," he began, "I didn't think that any of this was gonna happen to you, at least not this soon, so I'm sorry for have not prepared you for this sooner. Kent and Margaret are right about everything they told you. You are a Natural Porter, and possibly the next Wonderer of the planet Earth. I know it's crazy but bear with me for a minute. Every planet is represented by a Wonderer, and every Wonderer is allowed to travel from planet to planet, however, most of the time they would have a Wanderer travel for them, so their planet wouldn't be without its protector, its Wonderer. All the other Porters and beings are forbidden to leave their planet."

"Beings?" I asked puzzled.

"Yes, you know, other non-human creatures?" He told me with such a tone of obviousness to it.

"You mean aliens?"

"Technically, everyone is an alien. You see, humans were brought to our Solar System many years ago. Humans like you and I exist in pretty much every planet of the Universe. You didn't think we were the only ones, did you?" The obviousness tone of my dad was somewhat annoying. Was I the only one who didn't know any of this?

"Sometimes Porters do leave their planets, and it's the responsibility of the Wonderer to make sure that doesn't happen."

"But isn't that forbidden?"

"Yes, Marcus. It's not a perfect system."

"How do they travel?" I asked.

"Every Wonderer and Wanderer have a way to travel between planets, sort of teleportation system,"

"You mean, disappear here and reappear anywhere they want?" I interjected him.

"Yes. It's a Wormhole, an Exotic Matter System. You'll learn more about that once you'll enroll at C.H.E.P."

"C.H.E.P.?"

"Center of Higher Education for Porters. But again, missing the point here,"

"Okay, let's say I get this, right? Where does Mom fall in all of this?"

"That's what we are having a hard time figuring out. You see, you're a Natural—"

"Porter, I know, but how so?"

"You don't need the ink to transform yourself into your astrological sign, Taurus, the Bull," he explained, "you know, that ink that we have in our tattoo." He rolled up his sleeve, revealing his tattoo to me once he saw my confused face. "This ink gives Porters the ability to transform themselves into their astrological sign."

"How's that possible?"

"The ink in every Porter's tattoo is made out of the stars that make out their own Constellation, combined with Halley Comet's dust. Victor Tool, Porter of the Pictor Constellation, applies the tattoo under their left upper-arm. That allows Porters to transform themselves at will with ease, no pain, no headaches, into their astrological sign.

However," he continued, "every one-hundred years they have to redo their tattoo; if they choose not to, they will grow old and eventually lose their ability to shift. They will slowly become humans again. That's why a lot of them don't grow old, they can pretty much choose how they're gonna look for eternity, just like Kent."

"How old are you, dad?" I knew how old my dad was, but I was just making sure.

"Forty-four." He replied looking at me confused.

"But how can I transform myself without the ink?"

"We don't know exactly how you can do it without the ink. Usually, Naturals are only able to do so if both of their parents are Porters, but they would still have to do their tattoo to avoid them from fainting just like you do every time you have one of your so-called delusional dreams."

"So, Mom is a Porter, too?"

"No, your mom never wanted anything to do with this. She refuses to talk about it. To her, this life of mine doesn't exist. That's why this is very confusing to all of us. You're an exception of the exceptions."

"All right, so let's see if I got this." I began. "I'm supposed to be the new Porter of the Taurus Constellation, Wonderer of Earth, right?"

"Most likely, yeah"

"What about Mr. Hors?"

"Kent has been looking for someone to replace him way before I was born," my dad replied, quite normally as if saying that the sky is blue, logically.

"How old is he?" I asked.

"I don't know. I lost count after his 276th birthday."

I laughed only for a second after realizing that my dad wasn't joking about Mr. Hors' age. "So, am I supposed to protect the planet from other Porters...?"

"Porters, Wonderers, Wanderers and other beings, Marcus," he reminded me.

"Porters," I continued, "can they travel from planet to planet?"

"Only a Wonderer or a Wanderer can travel between planets; Porters, humans and other species aren't allowed, myself included. We can't open Wormholes on our own; we don't possess the Exotic Matter Sphere."

"Let me see if I got this right, if a Wonderer or a Wanderer decides to appear here right now with any other 'beings' they can, right?" I asked.

"They're not allowed to—"

"But they can?" I asked impatiently.

"Yes, Marcus, they can. What's your point?"

"Hmm, and they can take whoever and whatever they want, right?"

"I'm not following you." My dad looked puzzled.

"They could very well have taken my mom, right?" I questioned in a much serious and concerned voice now.

"I doubt that this would be the case, son—"

"But they can, right?" I insisted.

"Yes, son, yes. What's your point?"

"Dad, if Mom is gone and these people, these 'beings', are out there, they could have very well taken Mom to some other planet," I concluded.

"No, that would be impossible. She would die out there without Stardust in her blood system."

"But they could've taken here to any place on this planet, right?"

"Yes, but what would be the reason behind it?" My dad asked, getting up to his feet.

"Well, if they are after me, they could have very well kidnapped Mom trying to get to me. By the way, what do they want to do with me?"

"That is the question I don't have the answer to, Marcus."

"What do you suppose the Gemini Porters want with me?"

"Don't know the answer to that one either, son."

"Okay, so where do we go from here? How do we find who took my mom and why? And what can I do to have more control over my abilities?"

"All of this and more will be more understandable to you once you get your tattoo." Ms. Hills' high pitch voice interrupted the dialogue between my dad and I as she entered the room, "I'm sorry to interrupt, but lunch's ready."

We went downstairs to the kitchen where the table was set.

"Feeling better, buddy?" Jacques asked as I sat on the chair across from him.

"Yeah. I'm still a bit overwhelmed, but I'm fine. You?"

"Oh, I'm awesome, Ms. Hills and Mr. Hors explained everything to me while you were upstairs talking to your dad; this whole situation happening to you is freaking awesome," he said very excitedly.

"You think so?" I asked, mostly to myself than to him.

"Alright, everyone let's eat. I know we don't have our moms here right now, but Happy Mother's Day," Ms. Hills said as she laid a plate of roasted turkey on the table.

"Marge, aren't you vegan?" My dad asked her.

"I am, but no one else is, plus Marcus must be starving." She said cutting a piece of drumstick and placing it on my plate.

"I don't know about Marcus, but I know I am." Jacques snatched the drumstick out of my plate and took a big bite out of it, followed by everyone's laughter, except Ms. Hills who had a disapproving look.

I had completely forgotten that today was Mother's Day. With everything that was going on, every day kind of blended into one. And now I felt even worse knowing that it was Mother's Day and I was not spending it with my mom. I wondered what she was doing; if she was aware that it was her day today. Was she even still alive?

XI

LYREBIRD

Once we were done eating, I helped remove the dishes off the table while Jacques helped Ms. Hills wash them. I looked around and saw my dad on the chair talking to Mr. Hors, clearly covering his face to not let me see him crying. His mom, my Grandma, just passed away two days ago and his wife, my mom, was nowhere to be found. I could not imagine the pain he was going through right now.

I went upstairs to the bedroom where I was staying over to think about all this and try to make sense of it all. After all, they were all adults and had no reason to lie or to just to play a prank on me. It was clear that all of this was getting truer by the hour.

If Mileena was here, maybe she could help me make some sense out of it or even William; he seems so clever. I wondered whatever happened to him. I forgot to ask my dad what happened to him after our encounter with the Gemini Porters.

'Marcus Mathias, Porter of the Taurus Constellation, the new Wonderer of Earth.' A different and yet somehow familiar voice spoke outside of my window. I opened the French doors and stepped outside to the balcony but couldn't see anyone there. I looked everywhere, but no one was there, not even at the backyard of Ms. Hills' house. Maybe it was one of my delusional dreams kicking in again, but this somehow felt much more real than ever before.

'You really can't see me, can you?' The same melodic voice spoke again.

"No, I can't, and honestly, I think you're inside my head," I spoke just loud enough for whoever was around me to hear. I didn't want anyone downstairs listening to me and thinking that I was going crazy again. Then again, crazy would make a whole lot of sense to me right now.

'Look again, hard enough to where my voice is coming from. Listen to it inside your mind and find me,' he told me.

Even though the voice seemed inside of my head, somehow it felt like it was echoing from outside, as if expelling it out of my body without me speaking it. I looked hard for a few seconds at this huge, tall tree, a few feet away from the porch and saw the same beautiful blue bird that I saw before at my place when I

148

first turned Mirabilis on. It seemed to smile at me.

"Is that...?" I asked mostly to myself.

'Good job, Marcus. I knew you could do it if you put your heart into it.' When the bird was done speaking, I almost felt it inside of me, loud and clear. He flew toward me and just before he landed, the bird stopped midair and started transforming himself into the guy I was growing used to. Where the bird's short legs were, a pair of human legs and feet sprung. His chest smoothly started to open up, forming into a man's chest and lower body. His face was now that of a guy with a very light skinned complexion as if it was only touched by the Moon. His eyes were bright-white, as if stars took their places. In a blink of an eye, from white they changed to the midnight shade of blue just like the sky at night with a bit of light streaming out of it, as if a star was trapped inside his eye sockets, covered by a navy-blue veil, now revealed its pupils. His wings, slowly flapping as he landed on the porch, now had two slim but toned arms, finally allowing himself to fully look like a guy in his early twenties who I very well recognized: William Chase.

"Surprised, Marcus?" William had a proud smile.

"William, huh, how did you do that? And how did you find me? Am I hallucinating again?" I mumbled my words out.

"You are never hallucinating Marks, everything is real. You should be getting used to it by now. I can change my voice at will, it's one of my many talents," he proudly explained. "I have often watched over you whenever no one seemed to pay attention or notice all this craziness happening to you. I wanted to make sure that you were being, well, portered." He sat down on the balcony's parapet, oblivious to the laws of gravity.

"Interesting choice of words, Will," I said, walking back to the room, leaving the window open so Will could follow me inside as I knew he would. I was somewhat surprised and in shock with all this. But at the same time, Will seemed to be the right guy to talk to right now. I barely even knew him, but he always had a way of calming me down just by talking to me.

"I know Marcus, how you're feeling right now about this whole 'Porter' thing. It's too crazy to believe in it, but also too real to ignore it, right?" He sat on the lounge chair across from the bed.

"Exactly!" I agreed. "I don't even know if I want to become a Porter. It doesn't make sense to me. My father is a Porter and expects me to follow in his footsteps as Mr. Hors and Ms. Hills do too. But what if I don't want to? I just want to be a regular kid, you know?" I sat on the bed.

"I understand, but if your father's right you don't have much of choice. After all, you're a Natural," he reminded.

"What do you mean?"

"Marcus, they kidnapped your best friend, who we rescued from the waters of the Rowes Wharf Hotel, your mom is missing, and no one seems to know where she is; also, your father destroyed his own house. So, why don't you just go along with it for now?" He suggested.

"I'm listening, and I think I get what you're saying. I'll do as I'm told just so I can get to my mom again, and then once everything is back to normal, I'll walk away from it all. There's no way they can keep me as Earth's Wonderer. I just want to be a football player."

"You got it, Marcus. See, you gotta give yourself more credit. You're young and have a lot to learn, but if you ever need anything, just say my name, and I'll be there," he assured me.

"William, you're not that much older than me,"

"Give or take a couple hundred years," he laughed followed by my own laugh wondering if he was joking or serious about his last comment.

"As much as it pains me, you're a cool guy, Will, besides all the frightening moments you gave me before,"

"Marcus, can I come in?" Jacques' voice echoed from the hallway outside of the room.

"Yeah, sure." I opened the door, allowing Jacques in.

"Who were you talking to?" He looked around the room.

I didn't have to look behind me to know William was gone. "Myself, Jacques, I was just talking to myself."

Jacques walked in clearly not believing me, but he kept it to himself. I didn't know if he thought I was really going crazy or, just like me, he didn't know what to believe in either. So, we did what best friends do, we ignore the issues and move on.

"Hey, Marks, how are you, buddy?" He asked sitting in the exact chair where William was not less than a few seconds ago.

"I'm okay, I guess. A little confused. But I guess this is the only thing that makes any sense, right? I mean, everything that they've told us,"

"I guess so," he agreed with me, "dude, all this 'Porter', 'Wonderer-of-the-Earth' thing is pretty awesome!"

"Yeah, you're right. I guess there's only one way to find out, right?"

"And what do you propose?" He asked curiously.

"To go with it. Just to see how far all this will go," I quoted Will.

"I agree. Maybe everything will make sense in the end," Jacques agreed.

"Hey, can I come in?" My dad sneaked up in the room.

"Dad, sure," It was more like 'I-don't-have-much-of-a-choice-but-say-yes' thing than actually allowing him in.

"Son, I think we should let you get some rest. You have a lot of things in your mind and too much to process right now, right Jacques?"

But before Jacques could say anything, my dad's cell phone rang. Ever since the whole incident with Jacques over the Rowes Wharf, we no longer had working cell phones, and we didn't quite have had the chance to go get new ones yet.

"Mileena, hey! What's up?" Dad answered the phone. I wondered what she wanted with my dad.

"It's for you." He gave me the phone.

"Hey, Miles!"

"Marks, I was wondering if you and Jacques wanted to hang out later on. I went over to your place, and no one answered. I called you and Jax but it went straight to voicemail. After talking to Jena, she told me that your dad was back in town, so I tried his phone, I figure if you weren't with him, he at least would know where you are," she seemed worried about me on the other side of the phone.

"Yeah, I'm home. Jacques and I are playing Mirabilis upstairs in my room," I lied casually. "We could meet you somewhere later."

"Uh, yeah. You see, I am already over your place, and besides debris, there's nothing left here, so..."

"Oh yeah, I forgot to mention we, uh, we, sort of moved. Yeah, we moved to Cambridge." I read the words out of my father's mouth.

"So sudden? Anyways, do you want to meet up?"

"How about we meet up at our hangout spot?" I said enthusiastically.

"Sure, sounds good. I'll see you in an hour."

As soon as I hang up, my father advised me not to tell her anything. The less people knew about it, the better it was for them. I had to agree with him. I already had told Jena about all this craziness happening in my life, I didn't need to bring Mileena into this either; in a way, it was a relief going out with somebody outside of this mad circle around me.

I wanted to hang out and have a typical afternoon

with a friend, and maybe forget about all this non-sense for at least a couple of hours. Even though I couldn't stop thinking about Mom; I figured if my dad was on the case, then there was not much else I could do that he hadn't tried yet.

Dad dropped off Jacques at his place so that he could celebrate the rest of Mother's Day with his parents, but not before dropping me off at our hangout spot, this place called Coffee & Books by Bella. The place was a mixture of a bookstore and library that sold plenty of old books and all types of fancy coffee and pastries; small but tasty pastries.

"Hello, Marcus. How are you this afternoon?" A friendly voice greeted me.

"Zara!" I greeted her back. "How are you? I didn't know you were working today."

Besides Jacques and I, Mileena would only spend time with three other people: Bianca, Jena, and Zara. I didn't know much of Bianca Drugov; for all I knew they were good friends, but Bianca always seemed too full of herself and, knowing Miles, I knew that there was only so much time she could spend with Bianca.

"She's just misunderstood, Marks. People look at her differently because of her Russian roots." Miles would try to convince me every time Bianca did something mean or bullied the other girls at school.

"Nationality is not an excuse for someone to be mean or not. She is a bully, regardless if she is Russian, Canadian or even American," I would tell her but somehow, Miles always saw the good in people, and

Bianca was not an exception.

Zara Gupta, on another hand, is a lovely girl. She is from an impoverished family from India; her parents moved here less than three years ago. Zara grew very closely to Mileena, especially now that Jena was no longer in high school with the rest of us.

"I work every Sunday, silly!" She joked. "The usual?"

"Yup," I agreed. I got a frozen chocolate milk with a dash of cinnamon.

"Here it is, Marcus. Hey, are you doing anything later? I know it's Mother's Day and all, but if you want to hang out? I'll be done in an hour," she asked while I paid for my chocolate milk.

"Actually, I'm meeting up with Mileena and—"

"Mileena, right. Of course," she interrupted me, "okay then, have fun you two. Next!" Somehow, I think she did not like my response.

I made my way to the tables in the back of the shop, by a large window so I could see the people coming and going while I waited for Mileena, and just as I sat down, she walked in and picked up a cup of frozen mocha cappuccino. I didn't know how, but Miles always enjoyed her coffee, something that Jacques and I never really got into.

"What's the deal with Zara? She seems upset, barely even made any eye contact with me," Mileena sat on the chair across from me.

"I have no idea…" I replied.

"Anyway, how are you?"

"Oh, nothing much. I was just over my new place,

chilling," I said, trying to avoid Mileena's eyes. For some reason she always knew when I was hiding something.

"Marcus, you and I both know you're bad at lying. Something is going on that you're not telling me."

Yeah, she knew I was lying. She and Jacques always knew. I guess I did suck at lying.

"You've been acting kinda weird since when last I saw you the other day."

"Too many things have been happening lately, and I can't seem to keep track of what is real and what is a dream. It all seems to blur into one." So much for wanting to have a 'normal' day out with a friend.

"Marks, I've told you before, you can trust me with anything, regardless of how crazy it sounds. You know I'll never judge you, right? So, tell me, what's bothering that little brain of yours?" Mileena was right. Ever since I met her, I knew I could trust her. I knew she would always be there for me, and she has.

I remember once in elementary school; she was the only one who knew about my obsession with rocks. When people found out and started making fun of me, she stood up for me, saying to everyone that at least I had a hobby and that I wasn't a loser like the rest of them. I thought that was kind of harsh on everybody else, but secretly, I liked it.

"Do you know anything about astrology at all?" If I was going to tell her about it, I had to start from the start, for starters, of course.

"If there's one place that has all sorts of books, it's here at Coffee & Books by Bella," she said, getting up.

Mileena walked over to some bookshelves located just a few feet away from where we were sitting. She went to a section that read "Astrology". I followed her. I didn't even know where to look, but she seemed to know exactly where to find those types of books. She grabbed book after book and put them on a different table, stacking them neatly by astrology, astronomy, and constellations. Apparently, they were all different things but somewhat connected.

The time passed by quite quickly as she and I looked over some pages. And even though everything was very well explained, none of the books mentioned anything about Porters, Wonderers or Wanderers at all. As a matter of fact, everything seemed a bit too foolish for me. I mean, I respect everyone who believes in Astrological maps and everything, but to me, it just didn't seem possible. How could a bunch of aligned stars be able to tell your personality, your love life, or your lifeline anyways?

But at this point, I didn't have much to back me up. And everything that always seemed unreal, impossible, and unbelievable was becoming very much real, possible, and believable, so I just went with it. It was a good thing that Mileena was into all of this because if I had to do all by myself, I wouldn't even be able to find the astrology section.

'Marcus, Marcus, it's getting late. Danger approaches as the Sun sets. Get your friend and run away before your enemies find their way... TO YOU!'

A voice inside of my head sang this song, emphasizing very loudly on the 'to you' part as it stopped singing. I looked outside a nearby window and saw the blue bird that I recognized very well, William Chase. It was so weird to look at the bird and hear it singing to me, and yet no one else did. As a matter of fact, no one even seemed to notice the beautiful bird just tweeting its song on a tall tree's branch outside the bookstore. I turned to Mileena and asked her a question that just came to me.

"Miles, is there a sign whose symbol is a lyre-bird?"

"Not that I know of. I mean, the symbol for Gemini can be a swan, but not a lyrebird. But that was over-ruled once they discovered the Constellation of Cygnus. Why?"

"The Constellation of Cygnus?" I wondered.

"Yup, there are about eighty-eight constellations, of which, twelve make up our astrological signs that I'm sure you've heard of like, for instance, I'm Virgoan,"

"Virgo," I remembered William correcting me once when I said I was a Taurean, "you're a Virgo. Proceed."

"Okay, so then we have Capricornus, Aquarius, Pisces, Aries, Taurus, Gemini, Cancer, Leo, Virgo, Libra, Scorpius, and Sagittarius. They're all assigned to a month from January to December. They're also ruled by a planet in our Solar System, including the Moon and the Sun."

'Marcus, Marcus, it's getting late. Danger approaches as the Sun sets. Get your friend and run away before your enemies find their way... TO YOU!' William

once again sang in my head.

"Okay, that I know. What about the remaining sixty-six constellations?" I shook off Will's voice in my head.

"That's when everything starts to get interesting. The other sixty-six Constellations are not assigned to any month or any planet for that matter. A lot of people don't even know of their existence. I just found out a few minutes ago myself. Give me a minute, and I'll let you know more about this. I need to find this other book about constellations..."

I hadn't told Mileena yet about William, the car incident, and everything else that happened afterward, especially the fact that my dad had also transformed himself into a bull and got in a battle with the Gemini Porters. Once again, the more I found out, the more I got confused. Then something hit me. The lyrics of the song that William Chase was singing so beautifully inside of my head: 'Marcus, Marcus, it's getting late. Danger approaches as the Sun sets. Get your friend and run away before the enemies find their way... TO YOU!' Was it just a song, or was there really any danger approaching me as the evening approaches?

I decided not to take any risks. I turned to Mileena, who apparently hadn't moved an inch in the last couple of minutes or so, to let her know we should be leaving soon. But something caught my eyes, something I remembered very well. A grin in the far corner to my right, in the library, a Japanese boy with his eyes looking down at a newspaper as if he was expecting something to happen. Lee Yang. On the other corner, I saw the same boy whose grin was slightly faded, but it was menacing as his Lee's.

I grabbed Mileena's arm, but before we could even turn, I saw Lee's sister Lynne Yang with her copy right behind us. They had just walked into the library.

"Marcus, what's going on?" Mileena freaked out, freeing herself out of my grip.

"Well, well, Mr. Mathias, how rude. Aren't you going to introduce us to your girlfriend?" Lee spoke on my right as he and his copy coordinately walked toward me.

"This time you are not getting away, Dogie." Lynne and her copy got close to her brother and were standing no more than a few feet away from us.

"Who are these people, Marcus?" Mileena kind of demanded, a bit scared.

"We, my dear Miss Watson, are the Porters of the Gemini Constellation, Wonderers of Mercury." All of them, Lee, Lynne, and their copies, spoke simultaneously.

"Are they all twins?" Mileena asked me, curiously.

"Something like that." I walked in front of Miles, trying to protect her as I also walked backward, trying to get more space between the twins and us.

"WHAT DO YOU WANT WITH US?" Mileena shouted at them, to my surprise.

"'Us'? What makes you think we want anything to do with you, dear? We want him!" Lynne pointed to me, followed by their laughter echoing throughout the bookstore. To my surprise, no one seemed to notice what was going on, at least not the three people in here. The books must be fascinating since they did not look up at all. Neither did the girl behind the counter listening to her music, reading some sort of teenager magazine. I wonder if Zara had already left.

"We gotta get out of here, Miles," I told her.

"Not so fast, girlie." Lynne moved from across from us to behind Mileena in a blink of an eye.

"You've seen too much; we can't just let you walk out of here like that." She threw Mileena across the room moving faster than lightning.

"MILES!" I yelled out, but with their swift moves, both Lee and his copy, were right in front of me.

"You, on another hand, are coming with us!" Lee's copy moved from in front of me, to behind me holding my arms, not allowing me to move.

"Let me go!" I struggled to try to free myself.

"Not this time." Lynne and her copy now moved close to me, and they both grabbed me too, entirely leaving me with no room for movements.

"MARCUS!" Miles shouted from across the bookstore.

"MILES, RUN! GET OUT OF HERE. GO FIND ME DAD. GO!" I shouted.

Mileena got up to her feet and ran for about two seconds. That's how long it took for Lynne's copy to leave me and grab her. It felt idiotic trying to move when you can barely even see your opponents.

"LET HER GO!" I warned her.

"No, no, no, Dogie. The plan was to take you, but

I'm pretty sure our King will be very pleased if I bring him an extra gift." Lynne spoke behind me.

"NO! Let her go, you want me. Not her," I pleaded, "Let her—"

'Marcus, cover your ears.' Will's voice spoke inside my head. But even before I could react, the window behind me exploded, shattering pieces of glass everywhere, followed by this high-pitched screech. The bigger than me midnight-blue bird flew in. It was William Chase. The impact of the glass shattering made the twins and their copies fall down to their back on the floor, me and Miles included.

'You okay?' His voice spoke again inside of my head, still flying above us, staring at me with those eyes shining as bright as stars.

"MARCUS, are you okay?" He repeated the question, this time really using his voice since I didn't have any reaction the first time. Will looked now like a blue feathered angel. His body was that of a boy except for his skin color, still midnight-blue, matching his wings.

"I'm fine." I finally said, standing up.

"William Chase, the great Porter of the Lyra Constellation." Lynne mocked him.

'Marcus, quick! Grab Miles and go.' I ran toward Mileena who was too scared to move.

"Marcus is our jurisdiction, fly away." Lee shooed him.

"Not anymore!" William flew fast passed the Twins toward Mileena.

'Cover your ears.' He alerted me speaking inside my head again.

Will opened his lyre-shaped tail, and just before I could cover my ears, I heard a very light stringed melody played by the strings of his tail; it was so melodic, almost surreal. Then, everything went in slow motion. I managed to reach to the window, the same one William had shattered a few moments ago, but I could no longer move. As I looked around me, everyone had fallen down, even the people reading their books nearby, the girl listening to her music and reading the magazine behind the counter, and both twins. Their eyes stopped shining, revealing their natural black color. Mileena fell asleep also, but as she was about to hit the floor, Will grabbed her and flew toward me. And that was the last thing I saw before closing my eyes, giving in to the urge of falling asleep.

XII

SCORPION RIDE

I woke up.

We were outside, around Downtown Boston. I was sitting on a bench, and William and Mileena were standing in front of me deep in conversation. I got up as if I had just woken up from a nap, feeling somewhat rested. Was it all a dream?

"Marks, you're up!" Miles exclaimed rushing to hug me.

"Hey, are you okay?" I asked her.

"Yeah, I'm fine. Your friend William is super cool. He explained everything that's happening to you," she smiled at Will.

"He did?" I wondered how much he'd explained to her.

"Hey buddy, are you feeling alright?" Will asked me.

"I'm fine," I stared at him, "how did you do that?"

"What do you mean, Marcus?"

"The screech, the music, the voice inside my head," I named a few things that needed explanation.

"Those are some of my abilities. I'll explain everything on the way; first, we gotta keep moving, just like you two woke up right now, the Gemini Porters should be waking up too. We should head back to Margaret's place."

Mileena and I agreed on it. We walked a few blocks toward the Downtown Crossing T station. In the subway, there were a couple of people here and there, but no one suspicious. Well, no one Porter, Wonderer, or whatever-you-wanna-call-'em suspicious. I waited for the red line train to go to the Harvard Square stop. Miles couldn't stop staring at William. Her curiosity and fascination were written all over her face. Will, on the other hand, was looking around for anyone suspicious, pretty much the same way Ms. Hills and Mr. Hors looked in the car before our car chase happened on the way to the airport.

"Here comes our train," William's voice broke the silence. The train's doors opened, allowing us in. There were about fifteen people in the car. Will looked around the train as if scanning people's mind. "Let's sit," he finally said with a much-relaxed voice. Mileena sat down between William and me.

"YOU! How did you do that? I mean, I saw my dad transforming into a bull and all, but you, what are you? How did you do that?" I asked.

"Marcus, calm down. The whole train can hear you." Mileena whispered.

"It's okay, Miles. I'll explain to you both, but not now. There are too many ears around, and we don't want them to think we are crazy." He said, almost as in the same tone as Mileena.

"Okay, alright, I'm sorry. But that was kinda crazy, and it's not like I'm not grateful and all, I'm just a bit confused. That's all," I apologized. "What kind of bird are you again?"

"I'm the Porter of the Lyra Constellation, a Wanderer," William spoke with the same air of superiority as the Gemini Porters did. There was something about the way they spoke about themselves that it sounded like they were all some sort of royalty. "Lyrebirds have lyre-shaped tails. When I open up my tail, I can play it, making people fall asleep and even create dream dialogues with them; think of hypnotic effects. Everyone in the coffee shop that was put to sleep, are all waking up now, going back to their business as if nothing had ever happened," Will explained to me, calmly yet with a certain tone of authority in his voice.

"Alright, I might not know anything about astrology, but I don't recall anything about a lyrebird being a sign, or am I missing something here?" Mileena asked confused.

"Listen to me carefully, you two. I am a Wanderer, not Wonderer. Wonderers are what you know to be the astrological signs. Wanderers are all the rest of the constellations, sixty-six to be more specific," he explained it.

"How come I never heard of this before?" I asked.

"Actually, your father tried to explain this to you before, but you were too deaf with anger to hear it." I looked down, completely regretting taking my father's story for granted.

"Marcus, I'm sorry I didn't know you weren't prepared. Assuming your father's past, I thought he would have told you about us, them, you," William spoke in an apologetic way that made me feel sort of bad about my burst of emotions, but I didn't say anything. "I know it's weird and all, but you have to bear with me, alright? The twelve Wonderers are chosen by the Queen of our Solar System, Mariah—"

"CAREY?" Mileena shouted completely surprised.

"Who's Mariah Carey?" Great, now even Mileena knew about Porters, not only knew them but clearly, she knew the Queen of our Solar System.

"Who's Mariah Carey? WHO'S MARIAH CAREY? The greatest female singer of all time?" Mileena looked at me with a face of 'where have I been in the last century?' Or something.

"STARS! Mariah Stars!" William looked at both of us in disbelief, "wait, hush you two," William got up murmuring the words 'not here, not now' as his eyes went from midnight-blue to entirely white, shining like stars, a look that by now I knew it meant one thing: trouble.

"What's going on?" Mileena said before I could. Then I just realized the train had stopped moving. We were only one stop away from our stop at Harvard Square.

"Marcus, we gotta get out of here. Now!" William said with a frightening voice that I had never heard before.

"What am I supposed to do, break a hole in the train?"

"YES!" He and Mileena said together.

"What? I don't know how! In case you've forgotten, I still don't know how to control my abilities." I folded my arms sitting back down.

"Marcus, I know I'm asking too much out of you right now, but you have to try it. Think of all the people on the train." William almost begged me. His skin was now turning blue with shining dots all over it, as if it was made of blue crystal in a shape of little blue feathers about to spring up open any time.

Before I could reply to his plea, the whole train got quiet and dark, screeches of metal echoed throughout the tunnels, followed by screams. Screams that made my skin crawl. I looked outside of the windows and saw people running through the tunnels, completely terrified of whatever was after them than of tumbling down and falling in one of those third rails that could kill you instantly electrocuted.

I still couldn't tell what people were freaking out about. Something must have happened, but was it enough reason for me to transform into a bull and break a hole through the train? Seriously?

Before I could make up my mind, something sort

of helped me make that decision: the same metal screech, now-louder-than-before, burst through the tunnels again. This time, closer than before, making all of us jump. The screech came from the opposite side of the train where we were sitting. And just as I turned to see what was making the noise, I saw something that if I hadn't seen it for myself with my own eyes, I would not have believed it. A scorpion almost as tall as the train, ripping the car open as if it was made out of aluminum foil.

The scorpion was not your average scorpion. It was much bigger, bigger than all of us. Its claws were just as big and thick as my whole body was. I realized that two things were similar between the guy in front of me and the scorpion approaching us; its skin was made out of the same material as William's feathers, but instead of blue, it was a dark cherry color. It shone like it was made out of glass or crystal and had little shining dots all over it, just like glitter. But something inside told me that there was no glitter at all on that creature.

And another thing was its eyes. The scorpion had lots of eyes from what I could see: two eyes on the top of the head, followed by three eyes on each side of the head, equaling to four pairs of eyes. And forgive the pun, but something caught my eye about this scorpion's eyes: all of its eight eyes were shining like stars. Just like Will's.

I was mesmerized by all this. After all, it's not every day you see a twenty-something-foot-long scorpion right in front of you.

All of that changed in a flash. All eight eyes of the scorpion looked our way, and I could swear the scorpion smiled at me. The scorpion finished throwing the last person out of the train with its pincers, making the poor guy fall down on the floor, missing the third rail just by a few inches. And it walked nice and smooth over to us with a glance that made us all stand still and wonder where that pointy bright-red tail was going to land. Then, if none of this wasn't already weird enough, the scorpion spoke.

"Well, well, well, isn't this the so-called Earth's new Wonderer, Marcus Mathias?" The voice that came out of it was a velvet-smooth woman's voice, speaking every word as if she was describing a delicious dessert in front of her but wasn't quite so sure of its taste.

"And you must be Mileena Watson," she continued, staring at Miles as if studying her, "and of course, how are you, Mr. Chase?" She stretched a hand in place of where her right pincer was, transforming herself back into a woman.

The transformation, just like Will's, didn't take more than a few seconds. She was just a little bit taller than William, about a head taller than me. Her beautiful dark-red hair dangled down to her waistline, reminding me of the same shade of color of her now-vanished scorpion body. She had a very well-sculpted body and wore tight clothes. Her blood-red tank top revealed her olive skin tone, tight black jeans, and knee-high black boots. Her eyes were now a shade of ripe cherry. A not-so-friendly smile made her appearance less frightening but still dangerous.

"Allison Prior, what a surprise to see you here on Earth all the way from your home planet Pluto," William said with an icy voice. He was not happy to see her.

"Wait! Wasn't Pluto disqualified as a planet?" Mileena asked out loud, almost involuntarily.

"Shush, girl," Allison told her, "oh, William, you know very well I have some business to attend, and I got to make sure that the job gets done this time. Those stupid twins never get anything done, like always," Allison said as she looked from Mileena back to William, not very happy to see me standing right behind him.

"Well, if you'll excuse me, Allison, I don't think you have any matter in this case. Marcus is under my protection, and you're not taking him anywhere," William imposed.

"But I beg to differ. I believe Marcus is capable of making his own choices, my dear friend. Isn't that right, Marcus?" Allison looked from Will to me again, this time trying to forge a smile as if suddenly we had become the best of friends.

"And what makes you think I would choose to go anywhere with you, Allison?" I demanded her to answer.

"Ms. Prior to you, little boy. You're not a Wonderer yet. You're still an insignificant boy whom I can crush at any second before you could even say 'mommy,'" she said with the fake smile completely vanished from her face.

"Don't you bring my mom into this, you—" I exploded.

"You what, little boy? What are you gonna do? Do you even know where your mom is?" She smiled and walked all the way back to where she came from.

"Do you know where my mom is?" I pleaded, stepping a few feet closer to her.

"Marcus, no!" Mileena shouted from behind me. For a moment, I had almost forgotten that she was there.

"Now, there's only one way to find out, isn't there, dear?" She said, stepping out of the train.

"ALLISON, WAIT! I mean, Ms. Prior, could you please wait?" I ran after her with Will and Miles right behind me.

"Marcus, wait!" William said, fully transformed in his bluebird shape.

"OH, YOU TEST MY PATIENCE, STUPID BOY!" She yelled, getting back in the train. This time, she had transformed herself partially into a scorpion. Her upper body was still that of a woman, but from her waist down, it was a scorpion's body with the eight legs and a piercing tail hanging atop of her head, ready to strike at any moment. Her arms were now the two pincers well known in scorpions, and her eyes were shining bright-white like stars again.

Everything happened so fast that I didn't have time to stop. I had crashed onto her body, falling backward on the floor. When I was finally able to look up, I saw her right claw coming to snatch me; I knew I wouldn't have time to escape it. But just like that, I felt claws piercing both my shoulders, throwing me all the way back to the train as if I was just an old used toy.

"Leave the boy alone, Allison. He's with me!" William said in his full lyrebird form, with a voice that seemed more like that of a singer but yet dark, deep, and creepy that gave Mileena and me goosebumps.

"Is that so, William?" She smiled and snatched Will as if he was a simple insect, one pincer holding his neck and another one holding his legs. William let out a screech so loud and high that it broke all the windows of the train. His body was flickering back and forth, from human to bird in a matter of seconds, trying to free himself with only his wings flapping in the air with no success.

"Now, you know that you were never able to defeat me, right, Mr. Chase? I am a Wonderer after all. Need I remind you?" She smiled at him as she dangled her pointy red tail near his face, aiming on where to strike.

I couldn't let her do that. I couldn't just sit there and watch her kill him. I ran. Everything was getting shinier and shinier, but this time, I was not going to stop. I didn't have to see to know where I was going. My arms got heavy again, and I knew it was coming. I was now running on fours, fully transformed into a white bull that I was getting used to. And the only reason why I knew it was because of my own shadow; I didn't care. I was running, and I wouldn't stop until I hit the target. And I did. I heard a noise of something crash against the train followed by Allison's scream,

William's cry of pain, and Mileena screaming my name from the back of the train.

And just like that, everything was over.

I opened my eyes to find myself outside of the train, lying down on the floor between the tracks. William was inside of the train unconscious, back in his human form. On the other side, all the way into the tunnel, about ten feet away from me was Allison; also passed out in her human form. It was unbelievable to think that just a few moments ago, that beautiful woman wanted to kill William. Far away, I heard Mileena's voice and steps approaching, suddenly getting louder and louder; my head was pounding.

"Marcus! Are you okay?" Her voice was shaken, so uneven that it was very hard to believe that this was Mileena.

"Miles, what happened?" I somewhat remembered what happened till the moment I hit Allison, but not so much afterward.

"You... you're AWESOME!" Mileena hugged me with such excitement that I was not expecting it, "I mean, it was somewhat scary at first, but as soon as you hit her like a bowling ball, she flew out of the car hitting the third rail losing her conscious with the electric charge. William passed out just as he hit the floor. The sound of the crash, oh my gosh! I thought it had broken everyone's bones! Such a loud bang that I thought you'd be hurt."

"Really?" I didn't recall the so-loud bang, but whatever. I guess I couldn't have heard it anyway. "How long was I passed out for?"

"About five minutes or so..."

"Miles, we gotta get Will and get out of here. We can go to my place. If we go through the tunnels, we'll be there in seconds. Harvard Square is the next stop."

"Cool, let's get Will and get off on the other side. That should get us to Harvard Square in a few minutes, hopefully," she said, hopeful.

"Miles, how come none of us got electrocuted on those third rails?" I asked as we were climbing back into the train.

"Oh, but she did," she said, smiling, "she hit the rail before you did, and everything went black. I saw the electrical waves run through her body.

"Holy cannoli, is she dead?" Allison looked very still, lying right there. Don't get me wrong. I didn't want her to kill Will, but I didn't want to kill her either.

"I don't know, Marcus, but we better get going soon before the police arrive, and it would be almost impossible to explain how the train got ripped wide open like a can of tuna."

"You're right. Let's get William and go."

"Marcus, wait. Marcus...?" A faint, familiar voice called my name from outside the train, exactly coming from where I was afraid it could be coming from.

Allison.

I looked back outside the train and saw her still lying down on the floor between the tracks, trying to get herself back up.

"I know who has your mother. Marcus... help me,

and I'll take you to her." Her voice was now sweet and calm, almost as human as it could possibly be. All the traces of evil totally vanished from her face, almost looking like a friend I hadn't seen in a long time. Mileena saw me standing there and called my name.

"Marcus, you don't believe her now, do you?" But I did for a moment.

Mileena and I grabbed William by his arms, putting him between us, and pretty much dragged him out of the tunnel with Allison in the background, screaming my name and begging me to turn back and get her out of there too. Mileena seemed not to notice her, but I couldn't ignore the fact that, of all people and everything else in between I had met lately, she was the only one who might know where my mom is. But the question is, should I trust her? Should I believe her?

We finally reached the platform. Luckily enough, there weren't many people there, and just like Mileena said, we were there in less than three minutes walking, which was a good thing since Miles and I couldn't carry Will much longer, and I couldn't possibly carry him all by myself. We put him on a nearby bench as we both sat on either side of him. I was tired, yeah, but I was fine, and then the unexpected occurred to me.

"Miles, stay here with Will. I'll be right back." I jumped back inside the tunnel toward the train we were in a few moments ago.

"Marks! Marcus, where are you going? MARCUS!

Are you CRAZY?" I could hear Miles speaking and increasing her voice as I was getting farther and farther from her.

She might be right. It might be the wrong thing to do, but I had to do it. Allison was all alone, and even though I was no match for her, I had to know if what she said about my mom was true. I walked for a few minutes into the tunnel, my heart racing, not knowing what our encounter might turn out like.

I saw the train we were in. I climbed back through the front door and ran two cars down, then it was there: the car where it all had happened. At that time, I did transform at will, quite not sure how, but I did. I approached the end of the car, still ripped open by the deadly pincers of the Scorpius Constellation's Porter, Allison Prior, Wonderer of Pluto. She was now standing still with her back to me, outside of the train, on the same spot we had left her.

"I knew you would be back, Marcus. There's something different about you, and you just don't know it yet, do you?" Her words were calm and well enunciated as if she was talking to a five-year-old child.

"Where is my mom, Allison? That's all I care about right now." I asked firmly, nice but as firm as I could.

"Easy, boy. Be patient. Everything in its own time."

"I think time's one thing that we don't have right now, the police will be here soon."

"Your mom's been taken by some people who are willing to kill her in the very near future, Marcus, and

I hate to say that to you, but I agree with their decision. You see, your mom is not a very nice person, you know?"

"What are you talking about? Who took my mom? Where is she?" My patience was running out.

"Marcus, I think it's time for us to get going." I didn't have to look behind me to recognize Will's voice, and I knew Mileena was right next to him.

"Oh, isn't that nice? The blue birdie is back for the rescue." Allison's voice was back in its sarcastic way.

"William, I have to know. Allison, talk to me! Forget about him and tell me, where is my mom?" This time, I said it calmly as if it was just the two of us again, trying to get Allison's trust back on me.

"All right, Marcus, I think you deserve to know. After all, if I had an evil mother, I would like people to warn me if she was trying to kill me."

"KILL ME?" I interrupted her. "My mom would never try to kill me. Are you out of your mind?"

"Allison, that's enough. Marcus, let's go!" Will told her.

"Oh, so sweet of you, William, always trying to look after the fragile ones. But it's not me you should protect Marcus from. It's his own mother, and you know it." Allison this time was sweet and also very sure of what she was saying, which was even scarier.

"Marcus, this is nonsense. She is just playing with your mind. Let's go before the police get here," William pleaded.

"I'm not leaving until she tells me what I wanna know. WHERE IS MY MOM?" I was getting freaking tired of this game. Could anyone just help me find my mom?

"Oh, but dear, dear boy, this is a conversation we shall have soon, just not now," Allison's stomach, where her belly button supposed to be, had a half-sphere, a bit smaller than a baseball. The sphere looked as if it had a mini-Universe trapped inside.

"Bye for now, Dogie." She pressed the small sphere and disappeared, as if sucked inside of a vacuum cleaner, leaving nothing but a trace of glittery dust in the air.

"What was that?" I asked.

"Stardust. The same material that our exoskeleton is made out of," Will explained.

"You mean, the stuff the covers your full body when you're a, you know, a bird?"

"Lyrebird. And yes, the stuff that allows our bodies to transform itself into our sign is Stardust."

"How was she able to disappear just like that?" Mileena asked.

"Through the Exotic Matter Sphere in every Porter's belly button, they are able to disappear inside of it and out anywhere in the Solar Sys—"

"Over here!" Just before William could finish his sentence, we heard noises of people approaching us from both sides.

"What are we gonna do? We have no way out!" Mileena was right. I could hear the footsteps from the police approaching from the train and the flashlights coming in front of us.

"Hey, I think I see something," another policeman

spoke, coming from the same place where Allison was standing just moments ago. I turned and could already see his shape in the darkness, turning his flashlight toward us. Then just before I could turn back, something grabbed my right arm, lifting me up in midair. It was Will.

"Don't speak, don't breathe. Stay still," he whispered so only Mileena and I could hear.

I looked up and saw the beautiful bluebird flapping its wings with an apprehensive look as we stood there in midair. Mileena was also hanging by her right hand, her face more frightened than ever. I don't know if it was because of the heights, Will's grip, or the policemen now staring, walking, looking everywhere for victims trapped somewhere.

William flew into the tunnels above the police. We took a few turns, and in less than a minute, we were at the Harvard Square T station. He landed us on the floor as he transformed himself back into his human shape. Weirdly enough, I was getting used to this whole nonsense of William transforming back and forth at will into a lyrebird.

We joined the busy crowd of people going in every direction. All of them seemed entirely oblivious to us, only just blending in the crowd. That's the good thing about living in Boston. No one cares what you look like or where you come from. They just keep minding their own business.

XIII

THE MOON QUEENDOM

We went up two sets of escalators that led us straight into Harvard Square. Even though it was late in the evening, there were still a lot of people out, which somewhat was a good thing. I don't think any of the Porters would go after us in the middle of the crowd. It was just too risky for them to expose themselves. But then again, what do I know?

We took a few turns out in the streets in silence. Words were not needed to be spoken. We all knew we needed to get to someplace safe as soon as possible. Will had taken the lead, and Miles was right behind me. His idea was to take us to Lulu's Coffee Shop; Ms. Hills' house is where we have all been staying lately. My dad was there, and I needed to get some rest. It has been a week of madness, and I was still losing my sense of reality.

Sort of.

We just crossed a bridge halfway when Will stopped abruptly. His eyes suddenly widened up with happiness, and a smile now dominated his once concerned face.

"Angela!" He murmured.

I looked around us and saw no one.

William looked down into the river and Mileena and I looked right after him. We saw this beautiful woman in her mid-twenties. Her eyes were dark-brown like chocolate. Her hair was a faded shade of brown mixed with what was once blonde. Her skin was ashen, just like Will's. Her smile was very subtle, almost as if she didn't need to show her teeth for us to realize that she was genuinely smiling. She was standing on the top of the water as if the water was made out of concrete, or maybe she was just too light to sink in. She was floating above the water, but of course, it must have been just one of those boats made out of glass just like the one over Mr. Hors' place. After all, it is impossible to walk on water, right?

"Marcus, I'd like you to meet a very good old friend of mine, come with me." William's wings sprang open out of under his blue t-shirt. He flew up and down again, facing me from the other side of the parapet, with nothing but water and his friend under there.

"Are you ready?" He stretched out his hands with a big smile on his face. His eyes bright-white like stars.

"What about Miles?" I asked concerned, before leaving her all by herself.

"I'll come back for her," he insisted again, with his hands stretched out still waiting for me to grab.

"Will, I don't think it's a—"

"You think too much," he said, grabbing my hand with a swift movement, upward and down again; passing in front of Miles, landing right where his mysterious friend was. I looked around and under me afraid I was going sink in, but nothing.

This was somewhat different than how it felt before on Mr. Hors' boat with my dad. I felt like I was stepping in some sort of mattress, not soft enough for me to fall in but not as hard as a floor. I could see fish swimming under us utterly unaware of what was going on.

I looked at the woman that was standing right in front of us, dressed in a beautiful gown in greyish tone. Her hands started moving in a different movement than usual, it took me a second or two to recognize she was speaking in sign language.

'Hello, Marcus. It's an honor to meet you finally. Will spoke quite highly about you,' I understood instantaneously what she was saying in signs. The sentence formed itself up in my head as it would usually do as if I were formulating my own thoughts.

'I understand this is quite all new to you but bear with me. I'll explain it all to you, little Natural.'

"My Queen," William bowed to her.

I followed.

'There's no need for formalities amongst us, Marcus. It doesn't matter how many centuries I've known William, he will always bow,' she bowed back in respect.

"This is Queen Angela Carey; she'll be taking care of you for the next few hours while I take Miles to Ms. Hills' house. Please behave nicely. I'll be with you before you can even say Exotic Matter."

Will jumped, and in midair, quickly transformed himself into the bluebird that I was getting used to seeing by now, all again in a matter of seconds. I guess it was somewhat normal for them to transform themselves at will, just as we would if we were to run, breathe, or even blink. It was just a matter of action.

'Trust me.' Will's voice spoke inside of my head as he flew upward grabbing Mileena before disappearing in the horizon. I wondered what would happen if anyone saw them flying in the middle of the evening. I could almost hear the anchorman on the local news channel, saying: 'Girl was seen taken by an unknown species of a giant blue bird, flying above the Charles River this evening. Officials are still on the lookout for them over the Cambridge area and its surroundings. If you have any information, please contact your local authorities.'

'They'll be alright, Marcus,' My own second voice inside of head brought me back to reality. I looked at her, and I almost lost balance on where I was standing. I thought I was going to fall into the river, but I

didn't. Instead, I just found my balance back again.

'Don't worry. While I'm around you, you'll never fall into the water,' she smiled at me proudly.

"So, you can walk on water, Your Majesty?" I asked very nervously, barely moving. I have never talked to a queen before, especially standing above water.

'You can lose the formalities, Marcus. My name is Angela Carey. I am the Porter of the Cancer Constellation, Wonderer of the Moon,' she introduced herself with the same authority I've heard before from Will, Allison, and every Porter I have met so far.

'Water manipulation is one of my abilities,' her voice echoed again in my head.

"How do you do this? I mean, William does this only when he doesn't want anyone to hear him but me, but now, I'm pretty sure it's just the two of us here." Who else would hang around under a bridge above water?

'I'm mute. I'm no longer capable of speaking with my mouth. I've been mute for a few hundred years now.' She explained, walking under the bridge.

"I'm sorry," I apologized.

'There's no need for an apology. It's a reminder of a war I once fought. It's my battle scar,' she held her hand up to her neck revealing her scar. Weird as it sounds, I could not see her as a warrior, especially fighting a battle in a war, but I guess I was wrong.

'And just like every Porter, I have the ability to send Thought Projections into a person's mind. T.P. for short, it can only be sent to one person at a time. All I

have to do is think of the person I want to communicate with and voilà, the other person gets the thought just like they would get a voice message on their cell phone. That's how William communicates with you sometimes, and that's how I communicate with everyone most of the time.'

"Yeah, but with William, I hear his voice in my head. With you, I hear my own voice. Is like if I was talking to myself."

"When you hear someone's Thought Projection, your mind "translates their vibrations into their voices in your head so you'll recognize the person's voice knowing where the Thought Projection was coming from," she gestured to me, "with me, however, you don't know my voice, so your body translates my thoughts into head into a default voice, your voice."

"That's pretty cool."

'And pretty soon you'll be able to do it just like the rest of us,' she assured me.

"I'm not so sure about that. I clearly have no control over any of this. Ouch!" Something hit the back of my head. I looked around expecting to see The Gemini Porters or even the big red scorpion, but I was surprised on what I saw: a little girl around five or six years of age crying, looking around for her ball. The same ball that had hit my head a few seconds ago.

'Watch this.'

With a gesture, the little girl stopped crying and started smiling again. She then stepped in the water and didn't sink as she ran for her ball. Once she grabbed the ball, her dad came along calling out her name, clearly not seeing her even though she was only a few feet away from him. She turned around and waved goodbye to us and surprised her dad by appearing right behind him.

'No one can see us or what we do inside of our Star-dust Dome, only those in it. Anyone who comes in it sees everything we do, but once they've stepped out of the dome's range controlled by the Porters themselves, they forget everything they saw, heard or experienced inside of it and keep on going with their own ordinary life.'

"Was that what happened to the people in the train?" I wondered curiously.

'I'm not entirely sure what happened in the train yet but most likely, yes. Naturally, the train's wreckage and everything damage inside of the dome will also go back to the way it used to be. Like nothing happened,'

"Naturally?" Apparently, I had a misconception of the word 'naturally' because that was nothing of natural about that to me.

'Shall we go to a different place?'

For a moment, I thought we were getting back to the firm ground above us, but I was wrong. Just like Allison did before in front of me, Angela put her right hand in the top of where her belly-button was, and a semi-sphere with a mini-universe trapped inside of it appeared above her shirt.

It was weird and curious at the same time; the fact that when a Porter transforms themselves, they get involved by this glittery dust coming out of their eyes seconds before it becomes a type of exoskeleton around all over their body taking the shape of their own Astrological Sign. When it's done, they return to their original body and clothes as nothing had happened. Just like now, her baseball size semi-sphere was stuck inside of her belly-button, yet it went right through her dress as if it was not there. Her eyes were shining just like Will's when he is about to become his bluebird self.

'*Shall we, Porter?*' She extended her left hand out as if inviting me for a walk. I hesitantly grabbed her hand, and everything was gone. I felt this tunnel sucking me in as if I was just aspirated by a vacuum cleaner and expelled right back out.

I opened my eyes, and we were no longer atop the river. We were in another place; a place I had never seen before. All around me was sand, a beach so white that it sparkled everywhere. On my left side, there was this beautiful river with shades of green and orange, calmer than I had ever thought a river could possibly be. It almost seemed like it was made out of colored glass.

To my right was a vast, open forest with beautiful tall trees of all different colors, shapes, and sizes, definitely not Earth-like. There was this particular one with a thick brown trunk, so thick that it would need fifteen people hand in hand to wrap their arms around it. Its branches went upward and turned downward in an upside-down-V-shape. The leaves were star-shaped, the size of my whole body, and in bright-purple color with yellow streams in its center, reminding me of the sunset on the horizon, too beautiful to describe. You had to be there to see it.

In front of me was a castle: a majestic white castle made out of stones, similar to marble. It shone so brightly with the Sun's rays reflecting that it was almost impossible to keep a steady eye. As I looked closer for more details, I saw there were huge pearls everywhere as if they were just mere accessories to the castle; pearls of every size, some of them bigger than me.

'How are you feeling?'

"It's beautiful!" I exclaimed.

'Can you breathe okay?' She looked at me somewhat curiously.

I took a deep breath.

"Yeah. Was I not supposed to?" I stare at her, afraid of the answer.

'Kent was right. You are a Natural,' she stared at me in amusement as if I were an exotic animal.

"And what does it mean?" I know I had this conversation before, but I wanted to get a 'second opinion' in that matter. I needed to know exactly what it meant.

'Porters can travel between worlds and all other planetary objects without the need of equipment. Their bodies adapt to any environment they are in, from the hottest point of the Sun to the coldest of our planets, Pluto,' she explained it to me as we walked passed the yellow leaf bushes with pink flowers with green dots on them, *'If you were just a regular boy, your body would probably give in for the lack of oxygen around*

the Moon, however since you're a Porter, your body ab-
sorbs whatever type of air around you making it possible for you to breathe.'

"Where am I?" I asked, amused by the view.

'Welcome to the Queendom of Luna, in the Moon,'
she gestured firmly, and now for the first time; I could
feel her tone of royalty.

"The Moon? As in the Moon that we see when we
look up to the sky at night? Or a place on Earth called
Moon that I don't know of?" I know it sounded foolish, but it was the best and reasonable explanation I
could find under the circumstances. We couldn't possibly be at the Moon.

'Look up there to your right,' she pointed to the
sky.

I could see it, but I couldn't believe it. Earth, our
planet was in the sky, half sphered like the Moon itself when looked up from Earth.

"It's beautiful!"

'We are on Moon. The Reason why you can't see my
queendom from there, it's because it is involved by a
Stardust Dome, where those who are inside can see out,
but those outside can't see in unless of course, you're a
Porter like ourselves.'

"Just like the dome you were talking about?"

"Exactly, except this one exists around every single
planet, with or without a Porter. It keeps humans from
finding alien life once they leave their home planets.'

"Home planets?" I know it shouldn't come as a
shock, but I was surprised even though I shouldn't be
since I was standing on Moon soil.

'There's so much you don't know yet, and I cannot understand why your dad has kept it away from you for so long. Let me take you to the castle, and I'll explain everything. Shall we?' She gestured toward the pearl castle.

I followed her down the path of white pearly sand with chocolate brown grass surrounding us all the way to the castle; it was weird. I could swear when I left Earth, the Sun was set entirely. And here the Sun was all the way up in the sky. How was that even possible? Then again, I recalled, I was on the Moon right now. I thought everything that was impossible was clearly becoming very possible.

The walk was short, giving me a little more time to acknowledge everything around me in this new place. There were birds of different sizes, colors, shapes; Some of them reminded me a lot of the birds on Earth, and a lot of them were completely different. Some with four wings, some with eight wings. The most beautiful one that caught my eye was this purple bird, not bigger than my hand, with two heads. It seemed like one beak was singing and the other beak was complementing the singing in a stunning duet.

'I heard you collect rocks?' Angela asked me just before we approached the doorway to her castle.

"I used to. Most of them got lost when our home got destroyed." The thought of not having my rocks gave me a little knot in my stomach.

'Why don't you start collecting them again?' Angela reached out to this pile of white rocks nearby and picked up this small rock. *'Here, your first rock*

from the Moon.'

"Thanks!" I gave a very good look at the rounded rock. Its look was very fragile and yet it was heavier than it looked, especially for its size; but not too heavy that I couldn't carry in my pocket, and that's where I put it.

'Pretty soon you'll have rocks from all over our Solar System in your collection.' Now that was one thing that I was looking forward to having.

Once inside the castle, we took a few stairs up to the tower, but not without passing through lots and lots of rooms; all of which were very simple and well decorated. The details of the wall pieces were made of pearls and silver. The floors were all in different types and colors of marbles, every room had a different shade. But one thing, in particular, caught my eyes: the tapestry on the main hall was made of what seemed to be the fur of an oversized hyena. But instead of the usual orange color, it was silvery green. The natural skin dots, instead of black, were dark-red. The rug took almost the whole room, which made it very clear to me that the animal that had that skin before was probably the size of my house, a three-story tall house. Oh, and eight legs.

Angela didn't step on the rug, and neither did I. Even though it was placed in the center of the room, we had enough space to go around it without making a lot of effort. The rest of the room was all white, with portraits of people in battle with weaponry never known to my knowledge and animals of different colors and types; animals so weird that they seemed to have come out of a science fiction movie. But that's pretty much how I felt right now: inside of a science fiction movie.

I wanted to ask so many questions, but I guess that's why I was here already, so I decided to be patient and wait until I had the opportunity. We then took a few more stairs up. This time, the stairs were narrower than the ones before and in spirals. It gave me the impression that we were going up to one of the towers, then in the middle of the stairway to its side was a door; a tiny door that only one person could pass through at a time, almost squeezing their way in.

The room was large and wide open, totally in contrast to the small door and the narrow staircase. It was very comfy and refined at the same time. We were in what seemed like a living room. Right in front of me was this vast balcony that took over almost the whole front wall. All around us were cushions, couches, and sofas. The entire decoration had this beige color, the walls and floor were once again in tons of white and silver, and pearls were hanging from the ceiling the same way Ms. Hills had the tiny lights resembling stars at her coffee shop. Between two of the couches was this nice chair, pretty much like a queen's throne, the only chair in the whole place that had purple upholstery, which was a big contrast against Angela's beige long dress. She took her seat majestically as I was sure she has done many times before.

'Have a seat, Marcus,' she gestured to one of the

many places available for me to sit. I took a seat on one of the lounge chairs by her right side, not too close, not too far from her. This way, I could see her and also appreciate the beautiful view in front of me.

'Would you like a refreshment, dear?' Before I could answer, she had one of the servants pour me an "O" shape glass of a purple drink that very much looked like one of my favorite drinks: grape juice.

"Thank you, Your Majesty." I took a sip of what I thought was grape juice.

'Call me Angela. I hope you like matiniki juice,' she said with a slight smile on her face.

"Mati-what?" The juice had a thin consistency, same as a grape juice. The taste, however, was light and refreshing, the same as a strawberry lemonade: bittersweet. It was the best juice I have ever had, and I had quite a few different types of juice in Brazil.

'Matiniki is a small brown fruit the size of a chicken egg from Earth. The outside has a few red dots as if it has chicken pox. Inside is purple as a grape, making the most refreshing juice known in the galaxy. But whatever you do, don't eat the fruit or you will become paralyzed for a long period of time,' she described it very casually.

I enjoyed a few more sips of matiniki juice, being very careful about it, hoping that there were no small pieces of fruits in it.

'Marcus, what do you know so far about us, the Porters?' Angela was serious again and yet as elegant as only a queen would be.

"To be honest, Your Ma..., I mean, Angela, I'm not

sure anymore. Mr. Hors, my father, and I can transform into bulls. Ms. Hills, into a ram. Then I met the Gemini Porters who, as far as I am concerned, don't transform into anything but can move pretty fast. Then there is this huge scorpion woman who tried to kill Will and me. Oh yeah, and William becomes this huge blue bird, lyrebird, who up to a few days ago, I didn't know was part of any astrological sign. Then I met you who, besides the fact that you walk on water, I have no idea what a Cancer does. Maybe transform into a crab?" The last came out with some tone of sarcasm, which I had not intended to, and of course, Angela didn't like my comment but decided to let it slide.

'I can understand your confusion, Marcus. I am going to try my best to clarify it for you.'

You see, the good thing about Angela was, that besides her whole queenly appearance, she was very approachable. It positively portrayed a contrast of power and kindness in one person. She got up and walked to the front window, gesturing for me to follow her, and I did.

'Marcus, look down outside my window. This is Luna, my Queendom. Everywhere you see belongs to me. Luna is under my jurisdiction. As you can see, everything down there is in peace, and I assure you that. Do you know why, Marcus?'

I couldn't even fathom that this all existed. Looking from her castle, the Moon looked like Earth in a parallel universe. I could see men and women on their way to work, taking care of their kids at home and fixing meals, just like Earth used to look like a few hundred years ago or how it should look now. The Moon had evolved as much, if not more, as Earth had, but also with a seventeenth-century look to it. There were plenty of trees everywhere. People were riding animals instead of cars; animals that I'd never seen before, seemed to beg their owners or strangers to take them where they needed to go. Farmers and executives were dressed differently for their duties, but all shared the same common sense and gratitude to one another. People were also herding their animals that didn't seem like they were caged at all. It was definitely a good, refreshing view of new and old worlds coexisting side by side harmoniously.

"I'm afraid I don't know the answer," I said, after analyzing the people for a bit.

'It's very simple. People have what they want. Therefore, they are happy. People here on the Moon do as they please. They respect each other's wishes. Parents help their kids achieve what they want based on one big factor; one common thing that rules every world in this galaxy. Something you've heard many times before Marcus: love. People of the Moon have nothing but compassion for one another, including animals and every living being in this place.'

"That doesn't make any sense. There's always one who wants more than the other, one that always wants what they don't have. Compassion, love is a beautiful thing on paper and all, but it is impossible that you could rule a world with love only."

'Yes, Marcus. At first, it seemed impossible to all of us, the Wonderers, to make sure that this goal could be

achieved. That's why we have queens and kings and Porters to protect each world to make sure that everyone on their planet is happy.'

"It all seems too good to be true. I mean, look at us on Earth. No matter what we do, there is always someone after something else. Nobody is ever truly happy with what they have."

'It seemed like that for all of us at first too, but now, Earth is the last planet in our Solar System at the moment who hasn't achieved this goal. Every planet ruled by our queen has found a way of living peacefully within itself. Earth is the last planet in our Solar System that compassion hasn't fully blossomed yet. Unfortunately, it got overruled instead by power and fear, just like a few remaining moons as well; and that's where we, the Wonderers, come along to help each planet in its own development,' she explained logically.

"You're telling me that Porters would come to Earth to help us?"

'No. We, the Wonderers, are chosen to protect our own planets in our Solar System. Also, we have Porters assigned to bigger and more important satellites and suns, like our Sun and where you're standing right now, Earth's moon.'

"Angela, I'm not following you. Why are there Wonderers in every planet, if every planet is at peace, besides Earth? Who are the Wonderers protecting their planets from?"

'Oh yes, I forgot to tell you the beginning. In our Solar System there are eight official planets as of now, plus the Moon and the Sun that if you look right now, *it's the same Sun shining throughout my queendom. Mariah Stars, the Queen of our Solar System, chose twelve Porters to protect each planet, plus the Moon and the Sun.'*

"But that equals ten Porters and not twelve?" I asked confused, trying to follow her train of thought.

'Yes, I'll get to that in a minute. First, let me show you clearly what I'm talking about. I'll ask Afirina to close the windows.' A woman standing behind us pressed a button by the narrow door that we had come in a moment ago and all the windows closed. It became dark as the night inside the room. *'Don't move, dear.'*

I was not even thinking of moving, but I guess it was a safe way to avoid me crashing into something expensive. I could hear the steps of a single person, and within seconds, the lights came back on. I had my back turned to the room, where before we were sitting. I was still gazing at the now-closed windows that showed the Moon Queendom.

'Turn around, Marcus. I'm sure you've seen one of these before.'

She was right, I have. All around us were the holograms of our Solar System, every planet, every moon. The Sun was right in front of me as if I could touch it and play ball with it. The projections were the same as what Mr. Hors had in his house, the same as what Ms. Hills had in her basement under Lulu's Coffee Shop. This was Angela's own G.O.L.

'This is our Solar System, home of your planet Earth and everything else you see here. As you know,

every planet is ruled by an Astrological Constellation, also known as Signs. All the planets could have many Porters but only one Wonderer. Let me show you what I mean.'

Angela touched what seemed to be just the plain thin air, and suddenly appeared a face inside of each planet with their names and signs and elements. I couldn't help noticing Earth's Wonderer, Mr. Kent Hors.

'Oh yes,' Angela began, noticing where I was looking to. *'Kent Hors, one of the most valuable Porters. He has been the Wonderer of your planet for quite some time. He, Margaret, and your dad, Roberto, have done an excellent job in keeping the peace on Earth.'*

"Peace on Earth?" I had to stop her, "unless you're talking about a Christmas carol, I don't think there has been peace on Earth for quite some time, Your Majesty."

'Angela, Marcus. You can call me Angela. We are all equal here, we are all Wonderers or Wonderers-to-be,' she smiled at me.

"I'm sorry, force of habit." Even though we were somewhat equal, she was still a queen, and I was just a boy. It was hard for me to just merely call her Angela.

'It's okay, you're young. Soon enough, you'll grow up to be just like the rest of us. As I was saying, Kent, Margaret, and Roberto have been doing a great job keeping peace on Earth, and before you roll your eyes, let me explain what I mean. They have kept Earth busi-

nesses on Earth and Universal businesses in the Universe. You see, as a Wonderer, your main job is not to let any other being from another planet interfere with your own planet, not even Mariah Stars, queen of our Solar System, would barge into your world without their knowledge. Even if you're allowing your one planet to destroy itself, no other Wonderer should interfere with your job, except the fact that your job is also to help Earth evolve in its own way to find peace within itself, to make sure Earthians live harmoniously with one another, including its animals and every single living being.'

"You've said Wonderers have their own planet to take care of, right? Then what exactly are we supposed to protect Earth from?"

'Now here is where things get interesting. Earth itself is a very well spotted planet in our Solar System. It's from Earth that we recruit Porters to all other planets. Earth was the first planet humans were first brought to from other galaxies, and from there, we divided, and still do, to the other planets in our Solar System. Every solar system has at least one Earth-like planet, a planet almost fully covered in water, and from there, we take the humans and divide them between the other planets.'

"So, you abduct humans?" I guess it was true after all those stories of aliens abducting humans to other planets.

'No, Marcus, we don't abduct humans. We approach humans, just like we've approached you and ask them for help in protecting our Solar System and *other sun systems and let them make a choice.'*

"And what if they say no?"

'Did you forget once they step out of the Stardust Dome, they'll forget everything they saw and heard? They'll go back to their normal lives like nothing happened and we'll look for another candidate.'

"Again, protect our Solar System from what?" I'm very persistent when I'm not getting my answers.

'Well, you see, as I mentioned before, every planet has a Wonderer, and pretty much every Wonderer live in peace with one another. But there are also the Porters of Constellations that don't have their own planet, moon or sun. The Wanderers. Even though they are still Porters, they just don't have a fixed place to stay, so they wander from planet to planet, helping and guiding whoever needs their help.'

"Wait a minute. So besides twelve Constellations that hold our Astrological Signs, there are also more?" I remembered vaguely what Mileena told me earlier at the Coffee & Books by Bella bookstore.

'Yes, the twelve Astrological Signs, simply known to us as the Wonderers, are Capricornus, the Mountain Sea-Goat; Aquarius, the Water-Bearer; Pisces, the Fishes; Aries, the Ram; Taurus, the Bull; Gemini, the Twins; Cancer, the Crab; Leo, the Lion; Virgo, the Virgin; Libra, the Scales; Scorpius, the Scorpion and Sagittarius, the Archer. Then we have the Wanderers, which add sixty-six more Porters on top of those twelve, equaling eighty-eight Porters of Constellations in our Solar System.'

"Wow, I never knew that there were so many

Constellations out there. I thought they were just stars."

'Every star is born with a purpose in the Universe, Marcus.'

"So, if there are twelve signs but only eight planets, the other four Wonderers are assigned to what?"

'Leo is assigned to the Sun, as you can see it there.' I looked at the Sun's hologram and saw a profile of a guy named Leonard Larkson. *"Mercury to Gemini, Venus to Libra, Earth to Taurus, Moon to Cancer, Mars to Aries, Jupiter to Sagittarius, Saturn to Capricornus, Uranus to Aquarius and Neptune to Pisces.'*

"What about Pluto? I see you still have it there as part of the Solar System." I touched Pluto's hologram, and Allison Prior's profile came up.

'Pluto, Pluto. The irony of Pluto. Mariah came with a new definition of Planets by the King of our Galaxy, The Milky Way. King Titus Vespasian decided that every object found outside of our Kuiper Belt was to be no longer considered part of our jurisdiction; therefore, Pluto not only was downsized to a Dwarf Planet, but it is now also no longer our concern.' She turned off Pluto's hologram.

"So, that's why Allison is pretty mad, huh? She's no longer a part of the Wonderers. What's a Kuiper Belt?" The more I learned, the less I realized I knew.

'Our Solar System is divided by two Belts, the Asteroid Belt, and the Kuiper Belt. Esther Bidden is the Porter of the Asteroid Belt, which is located between Mars and Jupiter, dividing the rocky planets from the big gassy planets. Esther prevents the Centaur Objects

from colliding with our planets. Todd Diaz is the Porter of the Kuiper Belt located after Neptune. He prevents any being from outside the Kuiper Belt from invading our jurisdiction.'

"I see. What about Virgo? I noticed it was never assigned to any planet."

'Good. I see you're paying attention. Virgo is, as of now, unassigned to any planet. Donna Saihtam is very good friends with Allison, so they still reside in Pluto till they are reassigned to a different world.'

"I hope it's soon. Virgo is Mileena's sign, and I don't think she would be pleased with this," I laughed.

'It is also your Ascendant,' she told me casually.

"Ascendant?" Again, the more I learned that less I realized I knew.

'Ascendant, or Rising Sign, is the sign that was rising on the Eastern horizon of the sky in the place and at the moment of your birth. Because the Ascendant sign changes every two hours all day long, you could have different types of Ascendants in the same day and month. That's why you have different types of Virgos, Leos, and so forth on. In your case, you were born in May, and the Constellation of Virgo was facing you in the sky at the time of your birth. That's why you're a Taurus with Virgo Ascendant.'

"Okay..." She completely lost me there. I've never even heard of Ascendants before, but I'm sure Miles had. I'll have to ask her once I was back on Earth again.

"So, these so-called Wanderers are the ones we are supposed to protect Earth from? They are the bad guys, huh?" I changed the subject.

'Not really. It's a theory that Kent has, but I can't possibly understand why they are after you. Lately, they've been wandering around the planets quite often. We don't know why anyone would want you not to become the next Wonderer of planet Earth.' Angela took a pause to reflect on that thought.

"Yeah, about that, I don't even know if I want to be the next Wonderer. I mean, I don't really think I'm Wonderer material." I lost my balance for a second, but I grabbed hold on to one of the couches nearby.

'Are you okay?' Angela moved a few steps closer to me, concerned.

"Yeah, I just got lightheaded for a minute. Look at my dad and Mr. Hors, they are built and strong. I'm just a boy," I continued.

'Marcus, honey, they were all boys once, and look what a fine job they have done so far. But then again, it's your call. We can't force you into anything, even though as you clearly noticed, it's in your blood, quite literally.'

Angela was right. Regardless if I wanted it or not, liked it or not. This, whatever 'it' is, is inside of me. I would have to find a way to learn how to control the bull inside of me.

"Yeah, you're right. I gotta think about all this. It's just a bit too much information to sink in right now. Besides, I have to learn how to protect myself from Ms. Allison Prior, right?" This time I sat down, reaching for the glass with a bit of matiniki juice left in it.

'You've met Allison Prior?' Angela, for the first

time, had a look of concern.

"Yes, I have. She almost killed William and me, I thought I had mentioned it."

'Marcus, sweetie, she didn't kill you or William because she didn't want to. Trust me, if she wanted you dead, you would be dead right now. I'm just wondering what the Wonderer from Pluto would want anything to do with you. Somebody like Allison must have a very good reason.'

"She is insane, Angela. Allison was talking about how my mom wanted me dead. She's definitely lost it, I—"

'Learn something from me, Marcus. People ruled by Scorpius can be anything, but if there's one thing that they are not, is liars. If she said your mom wants you dead, she has a powerful reason to believe so.' Angela's eyes were now leveled as same as mine.

"Angela, my mom loves me. Why would she want to kill me?"

'Where is Katherine right now, Marcus?'

"I don't know. My dad thinks she was kidnapped by one of the Wanderers." My head was spinning. I was getting dizzier and dizzier.

'Your mom is the wife of a Porter and mother of Earth's future Wonderer. I strongly doubt anyone would try anything with her. I'll keep an eye on all of this, myself,' she warned me.

I respect Angela very much. She had this whole motherly way of carrying herself. It was very doubtful that she would lie, but the thought of my mom wanting me dead was just not understandable, not

207

acceptable. But I decided to keep it to myself. There was something inside me, doubting my own feelings toward my mom, but I just couldn't wrap my head around it, so I just looked down.

She glanced at Afirina, and I'm sure she sent her a Thought Projection. The lights of G.O.L. were turned off, and all of the windows were open again. My eyes hurt with the sunlight making its way back in the room. We had been so long in the dark with dim lights that I almost forgot it was still day outside.

"May I ask you something?" I asked her as I looked out the window.

'I think we have established that you can ask me anything,' she looked at me with a granted wish face.

"Who's William Chase?"

'What a foolish question! William is the Porter of the Lyra Constellation. One of the most trustworthy creatures out there. Why do you ask?' The Queen of the Moon seemed very taken by my question.

"William seems like a good guy. Mysterious in some ways, but a cool guy. I was just wondering if he is a Wanderer, then why should I trust him" After all, our conversation about who were the good guys and who were the bad guys, it seemed pretty logical that William belonged to the bad guys' category.

'Not all Wanderers are bad. Not all Wonderers are good, remember that! That's why we have a system. Yes, it's not perfect, but it is the best we got. Remember when I told you every Wonderer was supposed to pro-tect their planet and no one else should interfere with that? Well, that wasn't always the case.'

I sat back in one of the lounge chairs close by, barely feeling my legs.

'Marcus, are you alright?'

"Yeah, I just feel funny, somehow."

'You must be exhausted, after all, Sun is already rising.'

"You mean dusk? The Sun has been up for hours." I glanced back at her pointing outside to the Sun in the horizon.

'Here at the Moon, as the Sun sets, it rises on Earth. You see, whenever it's day here, it's night there, and vice versa. That's why at night, you can see the Moon because the Sun reflects its light on us.'

"Of course." I guess I could have figured that one out by myself. After all, I'd been up for hours, and I was getting pretty tired, besides when I left Earth, it was dusk.

'Here, take this with you. It should help you fall asleep during the day on Earth,' she gave me a white fruit the size of a Ping-Pong ball. It definitely had a soft skin that reminded me of a peach.

"What is this?" I asked.

'Swayo. It's a sweet fruit that helps you fall asleep, almost like what passion fruit does to you on Earth,' she explained, as she gave me the fruit.

I got up and felt completely dizzy again. This time I couldn't breathe.

'Marcus, are you okay, what's wrong?' Angela got up, worried about me.

"Can't... breathe..." I was gasping for air that was not getting into my lungs.

'The air. We must bring you to Earth now.'

I saw her reaching out to me holding me up. Afirina was on my other side, both had their eyes shining bright-white like stars.

"But of course, my Queen. Hold on Marcus." For the first time, I heard Afirina's husky and sultry voice.

'Marcus, remember what I told you. Not everyone is who they seem to be, okay? Now be safe, and I'll see you soon, little Natural.' She bowed down to me just like Afirina did to Angela before. I then understood that they bow in a sign of respect for each other, just like in some Asian cultures.

"Are you ready, Marcus?" Afirina touched her stomach where her belly button was and, even though her blouse was covering it, a semi-sphere holding a mini-universe inside of it appeared through her shirt just like Allison and Angela have done before in front of me.

That was the last thing I saw.

XIV

THOUGHT PROJECTION
(T.P. FOR SHORT)

I woke up coughing, feeling the air inside of my lungs again. Regaining consciousness, I looked around and saw my dad, Mr. Hors, and Ms. Hills. Afirina was there too, standing close by with an apprehensive look.

"Son, are you okay?" My dad asked hugging me.

"Yeah Dad, let me breathe." I try to free myself of his strong hold.

"You got us all worried there, buddy." Mr. Hors sat next to me on the couch.

I got up and passed through them and stopped in front of Afirina, "are you a Porter, also?"

"I am Afirina Keeygee, Wanderer, Porter of the

Scutum Constellation, the Shield," she answered, with the same tone of authority that I heard before from every Porter I've met.

"What did you think, that I was just a servant?" She smiled handing me something: it was swayo, the little white fruit that Angela had given to me before I passed out. "You dropped this."

"Thanks," I grabbed the fruit, "I'm sorry, but it's good to know that I wasn't dreaming again."

"You're not fully a Porter yet. You may still be a Natural, but you need Stardust in your system to help you control your abilities, including breathing outside of Earth." She was right, I could do things, but I have no control over them.

"Thanks again."

"Now if you'll excuse me, my services here are no longer needed. See you soon, Natural." She disappeared inside of her Exotic Matter Sphere, leaving a trace of glittering dust in the air.

"Wormhole. A very neat and practical way to travel from planet to planet. You just think of where you wanna go, and the Exotic Matter Sphere in your belly button does the rest," Mr. Hors explained to me.

"It doesn't matter how many times I see it; I don't think I'll ever get used to it," I told them.

"You'll get used to it, son. How was the Moon?" My father asked.

"Oh no, not now, Roberto. Let the boy get some sleep. He's been up the whole night. It's barely seven in the morning. Go to your room upstairs Marcus and rest a little," Ms. Hills interrupted him.

"The Moon was beautiful, Dad, but Ms. Hills is right, I'm exhausted," I told him passing in front of the other rooms where I could see Mileena and Jacques still sleeping in the bunk-bed in the guest bedroom; Mileena on the bottom and Jacques on the top bed.

I got to my room; it was a smaller room, but I had it all to myself. I did have the balcony facing the backyard. I could see the Sun rising through the branches of the tree where William Chase came to visit me before in his blue lyrebird form. I wonder where he is now. If he had come to my place, if he had told Mileena to tell anyone about him or not, or if he had just vanished away like he always does. I didn't know, and right now all I could think about was my bed. I decided to take a shower before going to bed so I could relax. After all, I had been up the whole night.

As I took off my jacket, I remembered about swayo, the Ping-Pong-ball-size white colored fuzzy fruit that Afirina had just given to me. I took a bite out of it, not knowing what to expect. As my teeth clenched on the fruit, I realized the fruit reminded me a lot of pomegranates. Its flesh was thin and crunchy, but the inside was full of little thin green bubbles, kind of like tiny green grapes. And inside of it was this sweet orange-colored juice that tasted just like watermelon, but way sweeter and denser. I enjoyed it very much. I sat down on my bed, enjoying every single bite of that strange fruit, and then my body felt tired. I had to lie down; my eyes got heavy. I just needed to sleep.

***

"Marcus, honey, are you awake?" Ms. Hills asked, as she walked into the room with a tray full of food: scrambled eggs, toast, orange juice, a bowl of cereal, and a banana.

"Yes, I am. I dozed off for a minute, but I'm about to jump in the shower and try to I get some sleep." I sat up.

"A nap? Marcus, it's four in the afternoon, Cookie. I think you lost track of time when you were asleep." Ms. Hills laid the tray on the bedside.

"Four in the afternoon? Holy Cannoli, I feel like I've just fallen asleep, ha! I guess Angela was right," I said, remembering what she said about swayo.

"Let me guess, you had a few bites of swayo? Sweet and delicious little fruit, but it can put a bull to sleep, quite literally." Ms. Hills let out one of her high pitch laughs.

"Yeah, I've noticed," I agreed, "Ms. Hills, I have to apologize about my behavior. With all these Wonderer things going on all of a sudden, it sorta pushes me over the edge, and it doesn't help that my mom is gone; it's a lot to adjust myself to."

"I think you can start calling me by my name, we are family now, honey. You don't have to apologize. Trust me, I know what you're going through. We have all been there, Cookie, every single one of us."

"Still I wanted to say how sorry I am about it and thank you very much for letting us stay here at your place. You have been nothing but kind to me. Talking about that, is my dad around?" I didn't know why, but I felt like apologizing. All this nice treatment I was getting from Ms. Hills, and my dad was too much for me. I couldn't be more thankful to them for being there and protecting me from whatever it is out there after me.

"Yes, he's downstairs in the G.O.L, I'll let him know that you want to see him."

"Marcus, you're up!" Mileena said as she walked in the room with Jacques right behind her just before Ms. Hills left the room.

"Hey, guys, how are you? Are you okay?" I asked.

"We're fine! How are you? Tell us how everything on Moon was?" Jacques asked, excitedly.

"You know about that?"

"Yeah, *toqué*[29]. Your dad filled us in on all that's going on." Jacques said.

"Are you ready to take Mr. Hors' place as Earth's new Wonderer?" Mileena asked.

"Hmm, I don't know. There's still a lot of things that I don't know, and I'm gonna need to talk to my father first."

"I know if you don't wanna be, I'll become Earth's new Porter. I wonder how I would look like as centaur," Jacques wondered.

"Don't be silly, Jax," Miles interrupted his dream, "you can't be Earth's Wonderer, Marcus is."

"Ha-ha, thanks, Miles. I wish Mom was here so I could ask her opinion too." I went outside to the balcony.

"Marcus, son, did you sleep well?" My dad asked

---

[29] *Toqué:* Goofy (French)

as he walked in the room as Mileena and Jacques left, leaving us both alone to talk.

"Dad!" I rushed to give him a hug. I realized I hadn't really had a moment with my father ever since he came back from Brazil.

"Hey, it's okay. Are you alright?" He spoke through his smile. I could tell that he was waiting for this moment too.

"Yeah, Dad, I'm okay. I'm sorry I have been so stubborn about everything that's been happening. And with Mom not being here, I completely forgot about you. I really wish we could all go back home, you and I and Mom. You know, being a family like we used to be?"

"We are still a family. I'm sorry you're going through all of this, son. It's all my fault. I should have never accepted being a Porter back then when I had a choice. But I was young and hadn't met your mom yet, and I really thought I was doing something bigger for our planet. I just didn't have you in mind. I would never think that my son would genetically become a Porter."

"Dad, it's not your fault. You didn't know this was gonna turn out like this. You were only doing what you thought was best," I sat down on my bed followed by my dad.

"You're right, son. That's why I love you. You're the best son a dad can ask for, and I'm so proud of you." He proudly smiled at me.

"And you're the best dad, Dad." It felt nice to have closure with him again. I've missed this.

"Do you know where Mom is?"

"Somewhere on Earth, just not sure where. We have some places in mind that we think she might be, but nothing concrete yet. It seems like she just vanished into thin air." My dad's voice broke, and I could tell he was holding up his tears from falling down. The thought of losing Mom the same way we lost my sister was too much to bear.

"Do you have any idea who might have taken her?"

"We don't. I've asked other Porters from the other planets, but no one seemed even to know who she is, which is quite normal. They don't keep track of Unportables. Nevertheless, Kent and I are having a meeting with the council tomorrow in Jupiter, and hopefully, the queen will be able to have some Wanderers come here to Earth to help us look for her. At least, that's what I'm hoping for." His confident voice was back.

"Jupiter, huh? As in Jupiter, Florida, or the planet Jupiter?"

"You know it is the planet, silly." My dad messed up my hair with his hand.

"Just checking, Dad." I laughed.

"I got something for you." My dad gave me an envelope. I opened and inside were two tickets for a baseball game. Boston's Red Sox vs. Oakland's Athletics.

"I know it's not football tickets, but we are on baseball season now. Since we haven't had a chance to do anything for your birthday, what do you think of some father-son bonding time for ol' times' sake?"

"THIS IS AWESOME!" I hugged him. "Thanks, Dad, you're the best!"

"Oh, and there's one more thing," my dad got up and opened the closet doors. All of my clothes were there. Not everything but a lot of them.

"My clothes! How did you...?" I saw and grabbed my lucky dark-green t-shirt.

"I wouldn't have our home destroyed before grabbing some of your clothes out first."

"Awesome Dad, thank you."

"You're very welcome. Now get ready. We'll be leaving in an hour or so. Jacques and Mileena are dying to know how your trip to the Moon was."

"I'll be right down."

Dad was right, I'm pretty sure they must be dying to know all the details about the Moon. I forgot to ask Dad about William. I wonder where he is.

'I'm always close by, Marcus. Don't worry. If you need me, just call me.' I heard his musical voice inside my head. I wondered if he was a singer on his time off.

'I wanna talk to you, Will. See how you're doing.' I thought to myself, hoping that he could hear me.

Nothing.

I decided to take a shower. I knew I couldn't send Thought Projections yet, but I had to try.

I got out of the shower and heard music playing in my room; it was this classical tune almost Beethoven like. I hummed to it as I was dressing up.

"It's Mozart! Do you like it?" Will's voice echoed

in the room right behind me.

"Whoa, don't you ever knock?" I asked as I grabbed my towel back.

"What? You're somewhat decent," he smiled, making himself comfortable in the lounge chair, "and I've already seen you in your underwear before, remember?" As if I could have forgotten the night that both, Jacques and I had almost drowned by the Rowes Wharf.

"I'm never gonna get used to you appearing and disappearing like this. How are you?"

"I'm good. I heard you wanted to see me, so here I am."

"How do you do that?" I asked putting on my jeans and my lucky green t-shirt.

"It's called Thought-Projections. T.P. for—"

"T.P. for short, I know Angela explained it to me."

"When Porters want to communicate with each other, all they gotta do is think about the Porter who they want to send it and their thoughts go to them, and vice-versa. Think of it as a built-in cell phone," he explained casually as he looked through the pages of the Mirabilis comic book by a coffee table nearby not really reading it.

"So, you've been on my mind all this time?" I asked kind of annoyed at him.

"Nope! You're the one sending T.P.'s all the time. I just appear when I can."

His explanation made sense. Ever since I saw him in my dream with my grandma, I kept thinking about him all the time. Assuming that I was going crazy when in truth I was actually the one driving William crazy with my T.P.'s. I put on my sneakers.

"But, wait a minute. Didn't you say only Porters can do that?"

"Yup! Did you forget you're a Natural Porter? That you already possess all Porter's abilities inside of you?" He reminded me.

"Yeah, I did forget," I made my way to the mirror to fix my hair, "about that, do I really have to become a Wonderer?"

"You don't have to, but you're already a Porter. Like it or not. But only you can choose to become a Wonderer or a Wanderer," he explained to me.

"How so?"

"Let's go outside," William stepped out in the balcony and extended his hand out just like Angela had done before we had teleported inside her Exotic Matter Sphere

I grabbed it, shutting my eyes.

"Whoa Marcus, not too tight. We are only flying." Logically, before the word flying came out of his mouth, we were already flying. William's blue wings sprung open, and up in the air we went. We were higher than Margaret's tall tree in her backyard. Overlooking the whole city of Cambridge around us. "Pretty cool, huh?"

"Yeah, I—" Before I could finish my sentence, we were free-falling. William's wings were gone, but his eyes were still shining like stars. His hand still holding mine, but that didn't make me feel secure in any way.

"Will?" I looked down and saw Ms. Hills' backyard approaching faster and faster.

He smiled at me and let go of my hand.

William was gone.

My heart sank inside my chest. The sense of panic took over me, not leaving any space for me to scream. I was reaching the top of the tree, hoping that I would be able to catch a branch or something and not die.

Then I felt two hands holding my wrists.

"Missed me?" Will's voice came right from above.

I looked up and saw him with his body all covered in blue feathers and his matching blue wings sprung open again. "Will, you—"

PUFT

We were gone, inside of the hurricane vacuum that I had experienced a few times before and still wasn't used to.

I opened my eyes, and we were both under Ms. Hills tree, Will wearing such a proud smile on his face.

"DON'T YOU EVER DO THAT AGAIN!" I shouted.

"What? Didn't you always want to know what's like to fly?" He asked smiling at me.

"Flying, not falling!"

"Alright, I'm sorry," he apologized, "but it was pretty awesome, huh?"

"Yeah, it was," I laughed, "at least warn me next time, alright?" My anger was gone; the thrill was pretty fun.

"See, that's another thing that I don't get. How do you disappear and appear like that?"

"What, through Wormhole?" William asked surprised, clearly knowing that I've seen it before.

"Yeah, Wormhole. I thought it was just a theory."

"Obviously it's not just a theory," he had a logical look on him, "Wormhole is what Wonderers and Wanderers use to travel within worlds. Once you get your own tattoo," William rolled up his sleeve, revealing his Constellation Tattoo under his right arm similar to my father's, except the stars were positioned differently to resemble his Constellation, "you'll receive one of these." He pulled up his shirt, and where his belly button was, the semi-sphere with a mini-universe inside of it appeared.

"What's that, exactly?"

"That, my friend, is an Exotic Matter Sphere. Combined with your abilities, given by your tattoo, it allows you to travel between worlds. But only if you become one of us, not just a Porter."

"Not just a Porter?"

"Nope, anyone can be a Porter, but only a few can become Wonderers or Wanderers. It's all up to them."

"Can I choose to become one or the other?"

"Yes, but usually it chooses you. Once you go to C.H.E. P., they'll run tests on you to see what Constellation suits you best. Sometimes you become a Wonderer that does not match your birth-sign, and sometimes you fall into the Wanderers category. You, however, it's pretty clear that you're Wonderer. Porter of the Taurus Constellation," he explained proudly to me as if I had just graduated college.

"Hey, does my dad know of you helping me and all?"

"No, Angela had Afirina contact Kent and told him that she had found you wandering around town and decided to bring you to the Moon until the night was over. This way, they could rest a little bit while she kept you safe," William explained.

"Why didn't you let my Dad know about you? I'm sure he would be much more relieved if he knew that I was also being protected by you." I sat next to Will with my back leaned against the tree.

"Well, that's exactly the point. I'm not a Wonderer. I'm not one of the twelve chosen ones, handpicked by Mariah herself, I'm just a Wanderer. And some Wonderers don't really like having me around. They think I'm not trustworthy just because I don't have a fixed location."

"Angela seems to trust you..." I remembered how well she spoke of him.

"Well, Angela is a sweet woman and a powerful queen, but she is still one person. We have been friends for a long, long time, way before Kent was a Wonderer himself."

"I'm sure we could convince Dad as well." I tried.

"Everything in its right time, Marcus. Roberto has too much already on his plate as it is. We'll tell him at the right time, okay?"

"Yeah, you're right," I concurred.

"Marcus. I've been looking everywhere for you. How did you get down here?" Jacques came in the backyard, followed by Mileena and Jena.

"Oh, I'm talking to 'William."

"Who?" Miles looked around, not seeing anyone.

'They can't see me, Marcus.' William's voice echoed inside my head, a T.P.

I looked behind me, and William was still there. I was definitely confused.

'Call them closer.' William suggested.

"Come here." I gesture for them to get closer to us.

"What's up, Marks? Oh, hey William, where did you come from?" Jacques opened up a smile once he saw William right behind me.

"Porters have the ability to create an invisible dome around themselves and those within their range. However, all of those who are not Porter forget what they see inside of the dome once they step out of the range."

"That explains why Jacques and Mileena haven't been able to ask about you at all?" I asked him.

"Yup. Once I'm gone, they will not remember that I was here. Only you," he explained to me. "I thought Angela had shown you this."

"She did. It's just too many things to keep track of."

"Oh man, that sucks!" Jacques said very unhappily. "But I still remember you on the day you came and picked us up in the morning before we got attacked by the Gemini Porters."

"I have never left, Jacques. I stayed close by all night above your rooftop, just in case something would happen."

"Will, this is Jena Alvis, Jena meet William Chase."

I introduced them to each other.

"What good will this be? Once I step out of the dome, I will no longer remember him."

"Yes, but once you're back inside of the dome again, you'll recognize me. Just like Jacques and Mileena now have." Will extended out his hand.

"Nice to meet you, Willie," she extended out her hand to shake Will's, but he pulled back.

"If you wanna be my friend remember the number one rule: Don't call me Willie. Only Will or William okay?" He smiled at her.

"Will do." They all laughed after Jena's smart remark playing with Will's name.

XV

ATHLETICS

We sat under the tree, talked about me, my dad, and all the other Porters that I have met. I told them about Angela Carey, Queen of the Moon, swayo, and matiniki, about everything that had happened to me when either one of them was not around. Especially Jena, besides finding me passed out after my first encounter with the Wonderers of Mercury, she hasn't seen any of this on her own, besides now with William. Their curiosity was entertainment to William's ears, who was clearly enjoying every moment of this.

"Son, are you ready? We should get going. The game's about to start soon."

"Yeah, I'm ready." I looked around, and William

was gone, and so was all the memory of him in Jacques' and Mileena's minds.

"I'll see you guys tomorrow at school."

"Alright Marks, have fun," shouted Jacques, as I left with my dad. We got into my dad's car and headed to Fenway Park.

"Excited, son?"

"Most definitely. I'm excited just to be leaving the house, to take a break from everything that's going on."

"Yeah, I bet. I promise I'll do something about this tomorrow once I get to Jupiter."

"So, you and Mr. Hors are going to Jupiter tomorrow, huh?" I asked curiously.

"Yeah. The Queen Mariah Stars resides in Jupiter. Kent and I asked to be seen tomorrow in hopes she can help us find your mom."

"Do you think she will?" It was pretty presumptuous to think the Queen of the Solar System would stop what she was doing to help us.

"As you know, usually Wonderers don't interfere with each other's affairs; however, this is an out-worldly matter, so I'm hoping she will."

"What if she doesn't?"

"We'll cross that bridge once we get there," my dad said with a hard to read expression. He was hopeful that the queen would help us, but also, he knew that she could say no if she didn't feel like interfering in our business.

"Here we are." Dad parked the car a couple blocks away from the Fenway Park.

As we got closer and closer, the excitement grew even more. A lot of people were dressed in their Red Sox attire, hats, t-shirts, matching their favorite baseball team. I, on another hand, had my lucky dark-green t-shirt and jeans on. Then as soon as we got through the gates, my dad stopped surprised.

"Is everything alright, Dad?" I asked, looking around for any suspicious people around us. I wouldn't be surprised if the Gemini Porters were here trying to bring me to their king.

"No son, something's wrong," Dad stretched his neck up as if looking for someone, "Son, I need you to do something for me. Can you do that?"

"Yes, Dad, what's up?" I got closer to my dad, trying to see what he was looking for.

"Can you please go to that stand and get yourself a Red Sox jersey?"

"Huh?" I looked puzzled, wondering if I understood him right.

"You see, your t-shirt is the same tone of green of the Athletics' team color, we don't want everyone thinking we are rooting for them, do we?" My dad smiled at me, giving me his credit card. "While you're at it, grab me a hat. I'm gonna get us a couple of hot-dogs."

"Yes, Dad," I said relieved and not believing that my dad was joking with me. I haven't still recovered from all that's been happening.

I made my way to the stand and started looking for my favorite player's jersey.

"May I help you, young man?"

"Yes, hi, I'll take a hat, and a jersey number 14," I asked the attendant.

"Number 14, huh? I'm not so sure he's good, after all, he is somewhat new in the team." Someone behind me questioned my player's jersey choice.

"He's new to this team, but he's been playing ball since he was my age, William. What in the world are you doing here?" I asked him as I handed the card to the attendant.

"What? I came to watch the game." He smiled, putting my dad's hat on.

"Funny, I didn't picture you as a baseball fan." I took the hat off his midnight-blue hair.

"You're right, I'm not. I'm just here to keep an eye on you, if you need anything, just send a T.P. my way, okay?"

"Thanks, Will, but you shouldn't worry. I'm here with my dad, I'm sure if the Gemini Porters decide to show up, we'll be able to handle them." I put on my new jersey.

"You know, you're right. Roberto does have great skills. Let's meet up tomorrow in the afternoon?"

"Sure. We could also tell my dad you're on our side," I suggested.

"Talkin' 'bout him," William gestured to my dad, who was getting closer.

"Son, are you ready?"

"Yeah, let's do it."

I glanced behind me only to confirm what I suspected; William was gone, vanished, leaving a trace of glittering dust in the air. Stardust.

Dad had gotten good seats. Once the game started, I'd forgotten about everything that was happening to me. Maybe I wasn't going crazy after all. Perhaps everything was actually just fine. My mom was still missing, and that was still concerning me, but apparently, my dad had all this in control. He was going to Jupiter tomorrow to talk to the queen and then they will take over. I could go back to school and resume my normal life again.

The game ended and to my disbelief, the Red Sox lost by five points. I guess my lucky shirt was not very lucky anymore. Dad and I went to grab a few slices of cheese pizza before heading back to Ms. Hill's place.

When we got home, everyone was asleep. Jacques and Mileena were probably home; their bunk-bed was empty. I said good-night to my dad and went to my room.

I lay down on my bed and stared outside the window. I could see the small shining points in the sky, the stars. Something I have never paid any attention to was now part of my life. The stars, the planets, the Sun, and even the Moon had people living on it. Not aliens - people like us. Who could ever imagine it?

***

"Marcus, are you up? You're going to be late to school!" I heard my dad's voice on the other side of the door.

"Yeah, I'm up. I'll be right down."

I was relieved that I didn't have any weird

dreams last night. I looked around my room, and outside of the window, and noticed that William was not there. Not in his human self or his bluebird self. I took a shower, got dressed, and went downstairs for breakfast.

"G'morning, Marcus. Did you sleep well?" Ms. Hills handed me a glass of chocolate milk. "I ran out of regular milk. I hope you don't mind almond milk."

"Oh no, it's fine." I have never tasted almond milk, so I just took a sip out of it and to my surprise, it was delicious.

"Hey, son." My dad walked in the kitchen, pouring himself a cup of coffee.

"Hi, Dad." I grabbed a plate of scrambled eggs and toast.

"Good morning, Marcus. I heard about the game last night," Mr. Hors walked in, noticeably up for a while now, "so close, huh?"

"It's alright, it happens. It was a good game though."

"Son, Mr. Hors is going to drive you to school, okay?" I have to organize a few things before we go meet the queen this afternoon."

"That's fine Dad, but you know I could also take the T there too," I suggested.

"From Cambridge to Everett, you're gonna get there at noon." My dad laughed.

"And plus, I don't mind keeping an eye on you, just in case someone decides to interfere on our way there," Mr. Hors interjected.

"Thanks, but I don't think we should be living like

this. In a constant red alert status. I mean, do we re-ally think they are still after me?" It wasn't that I didn't agree with them, it was just that I didn't want my life to be like this. I just wanted things to go back to normal.

"Cookie, Mr. Hors will drop you off and pick you up from school later on so you can come over and help me at the coffee shop. Gingerbread is already here, and I gotta go help him soon before the morning rush starts." Ms. Hills kissed my forehead and made her way through the back door to Lulu's Coffee Shop.

"Here." Dad handed me my backpack.

"You couldn't've left this in the wreckage, could you?"

"Hilarious, young man, now go brush off your teeth and head off to school. We don't want you to get there late."

On the way to school, nothing uneventful hap-pened. Mr. Hors kept one eye on the road and the other on out for anything suspicious. We've talked about my mom, about being a Porter, about becoming a Wonderer and its responsibilities.

"Mr. Hors, what about William?" I finally asked.

"William Chase? Porter of the Lyre Constella-tion?"

"Yeah. He has been helping me, keeping an eye on me from day one. Why does he always disappear when either one of you is near?"

"Not us, your dad. He always disappears when Roberto is close by."

He was right, it just happens that every time Mr.

Hors or Ms. Hills was close, so was my dad.

"Why is that?"

"I think this is something you should ask your dad. He and William have known each other for a while but haven't spoken in years for reasons none of us really know. We're here."

Just then I noticed we were already in my school, Everett High School.

"See you later?"

"Right on the dot, Mr. Hors." I got out of his car and made my way inside.

The school-day was pretty standard. Jacques and Miles were there. We talked about the most random stuff, and also about serious stuff, including my mom, but nothing out of the ordinary really.

"Marcus, are you alright?" Mileena asked as we stepped outside once the school day had ended.

"Yeah, I'm just waiting for Mr. Hors to pick me up."

"That's not what I mean," she glanced at me.

"I'm just waiting for something to happen. Everything's been quite normal for the last twenty-four hours, and I'm not used to it. I keep waiting for someone with bright-white eyes to jump out of nowhere and kidnap me to their king or something."

"There you are, guys," Jacques approached us, "is everything okay?"

"Yeah, yeah. There's Mr. Hors. I'll talk to you later."

"Call me on my house phone, I still don't have a cell phone, you know," Jacques reminded me, which also reminded me that I don't have anyone's number memorized, but I'm pretty sure my dad had Jacques' house number on his cell phone.

"How was school? Any 'surprises'?" Mr. Hors asked me as I got in the car.

"Surprisingly enough, no."

"That's a good thing, right?"

I don't know. I didn't say anything, but maybe he was right. Perhaps it was a good thing that nothing had happened. Or maybe they already had accomplished what they wanted: kidnap my mom. Somehow, I was not relieved by this thought, if they had killed my mom, just like my sister, I don't know how I would react to this. Or my dad, for that matter.

We got to Ms. Hills' place, and I went straight to Lulu's Coffee Shop. The place was busy, so I decided to jump in and help Ms. Hills and Steve with the line. Also, to take my mind off of things.

Once the line died out, Ms. Hills came talking to me.

"Cookie, did you eat? You must be starving. Go take a break and eat something, 'kay? 'Kay. When you come back, Gingerbread will go on his break, and we can get this place clean."

I grabbed a bagel with tuna salad and headed to the kitchen.

"Son, how was school?" My dad, who was in the kitchen, grabbed some O.J. for the two of us out of the fridge.

"It was good, uneventful. Oddly enough." My dad stared at me as if waiting for me to say something else. "Is everything okay, Dad?"

"Yeah, yeah. Listen you know you can tell me anything, right? You can ask me anything."

He sat across from me. "Yeah, Dad, I do."

"With everything going on, I want us to be even closer than we are. Especially till we get your mom back, okay?"

"COOKIE, HURRY UP, GINGERBREAD IS TURNING SOUR." Ms. Hills shouted from the store.

"Of course, Dad, you're right. If anything happens, you'll be the first to know. Now, let me go back to work before Ms. Hills chops my head off," I said, heading back to the coffee shop.

"I'll see you later."

As soon as I made my way back, Ms. Hills handed me the broom. She and I cleaned up the place as Steve took his break.

The remainder of the afternoon went by quite smoothly with a few customers here and there. Steve and I put away the pastries in a box so Ms. Hills could take them to the Veteran Homeless Shelter later on. I went on to do the dishes. I stared out of the window, remembering my first day here and one of my first episodes when a girl drenched in the rain screamed at me and made me fall backward losing consciousness.

"Marcus, your gang is here," Steve told me as he woke me up from my daydream.

"My gang?" I left the kitchen back to the coffee shop.

"Hey, Marks," Jena greeted me as I walked in.

I saw Jacques devouring a muffin with Mileena sitting right next to him.

"MARKS," he shouted with his mouth still full, followed by Mileena's elbow on his stomach, "ouch."

"Manners, doofus."

"What's up, guys?"

"We came to see you. How are you feeling?" Mileena asked a bit concerned.

"I'm fine."

"Marcus, Cookie, let me close the store. Go play outside. I'll be back in a minute. I'm gonna take these pastries to the Veteran Homeless Shelter, and I'll be back, 'kay? 'Kay. If you need anything, your dad is upstairs, and Kent should be here soon. By-ey". Ms. Hills left the store, locking the door behind her, followed by Steve.

"Later, Marks."

"Bye, Steve."

"Alright guys let's go the backyard, it's so nice out," Jena suggested.

"Marcus, are you all done with work?" My dad walked in the kitchen as we were passing through.

"Yeah, we just closed. Ms. Hills just left to bring the leftover pastries to the shelter," I told him.

"Oh okay, Kent and I are off to Jupiter to speak with the queen. Are you guys gonna be okay on your own?"

"You know I'm not ten anymore, right?" I said, kind of embarrassed.

"Sometimes I wish you still were," my dad remarked. "We'll be back before dinner."

"Hi, kids," Mr. Hors waved, are you ready, Roberto? We don't wanna be late."

"Yeah. I'll see you later, Marks. If anything happens..."

"I know, I'll send a T.P."

"That's not what I was gonna say, but that works too. Bye kids."

He waved goodbye to us. Mr. Hors touched his belly button as my dad rested his hand on his shoulders and I knew exactly what was about to happen: Wormhole. Kent pressed his Exotic Matter sphere, and a small hurricane came from inside of it, engulfing him and my dad before disappearing back inside of it, leaving nothing but glittering dust in the air: Stardust. All that in a matter of seconds. I was getting used to it by now; however, Jacques and Jena had never seen it before, and it was clear by their expression how amazed they were.

"Your dad is going to Jupiter? The planet Jupiter?" Jacques asked, all excited.

"No, he is going to Florida, he just didn't feel like flying there. Of course, he is going to the planet, Jacques. Haven't you paid any attention?" Mileena rolled her eyes, looking at me as if she was stating the obvious to him, waiting for my agreement with my eyes, to which I just nodded.

"Yeah, he is going to talk to Mariah—" I began.

"Carey?" Mileena asked excitedly.

"No, Mariah Stars, the Queen of the Solar System!" I said, almost yelling and annoyed by her statement.

"Well, Mariah is the queen of music here in our

planet Earth, don't you know? A true legend." Mileena stated again as if I was oblivious to her statement.

"He is going to ask Mariah Stars to help us search for my mom,"

"That's great news, Marcus," Jena said.

"Yeah, but I have a strange feeling about this,"

"How so?"

"Miles, I think he tried the same thing when my sister disappeared, and that didn't work out," I remembered.

"How do you know?" Mileena asked.

"When I was little, after months and months searching for Daniella, I remember my dad coming home to Mom one day saying that there was nothing else they could do. She was gone for good. He hugged my mom, as she cried on his shoulders completely reluctant to the news."

"And they didn't tell you anything?" Jena was intrigued by it.

"No, Jena, I was only five. I barely remember all of this. I don't even think they know that I heard them in the living room from the staircase. My sister is still a sour subject in my house. It always brings them to tears, so I stopped asking questions."

"I'm sorry, buddy."

"It's okay, Jax. I barely even remember her. I just wish I had more time spent with her. She was gone too soon."

"This time around, they should be able to find your mom. With all the technology they have, I don't see why they can't."

"Mileena is right, Marcus. Didn't you see all the computers and holograms they have over Ms. Hills' basement? Imagine how many more resources they have at the queen's castle?" Jacques added.

"You guys are right. I'm gonna leave this to Dad. Between him, Kent, and Margaret, I'm sure they'll know what to do." I concluded.

"That's the spirit. Now, how about we go watch a mo-vie? Did you see the size of her T.V. in the living room?" Mileena suggested.

"I know, you think of all the technology they have, she would have a movie theater in her living room." Jacques was definitely not as impressed as Mileena was about the size of the television.

"Good idea, guys. You go to the living room and select a movie while I go to the kitchen to put some popcorn in the microwave and get us some soda.

"Alright, don't take forever. Otherwise, we'll start the movie without you," Jena said with her smiley face as they made their way to the living room and me to the kitchen.

"Can I talk to you first?" I turned around and saw William there, leaning against the tree, eating an apple. "Missed me, buddy?"

"Where have you been?" I approached him.

"I was waiting for your dad to leave so we could talk, you know, just us."

"I still think my dad would be okay knowing that you're around when he is not. I mean the more people on our side, the better, right?" I sat on one of the chairs around the backyard.

"True, but as we discussed before, all in its right time. Once your dad finds out what happened to your mom and figures out the connection with Jacques' unexplained quick kidnap, I'll come forward and prove to him that I'm trustworthy." Will sat across from me on a chair.

"Well, clearly you're more trustworthy than the Wonderers. Did you forget about Lee and Lynne? How about Allison? All of them are Wonderers who tried to kill me or bring me to their 'king,' whoever he might be. I mean, this all has to be connected somehow, right?"

"He doesn't know about Allison yet." Will reminded me.

"That's true. Everything is pretty weird, but I'm sure my dad will figure it out. I'm just curious to find out why and who would do this. I mean, what do they want with my mom?"

Will and I debated a few more times on who could have possibly taken my mom and the reason why. All without any clear answer to it. One thing was clear though, William was a friend. I can see now why Angela valued him, he could have been taking care of Wanderers issues or not even being here caring about anything that was going on with me, but he was. He was apprehensive about my mom and me. It was really nice to have a friend who I can trust and knows what I'm going through. Miles, Jax, and Jena are my best friends, but they are not dealing with what I'm dealing with right now. To Jacques all of this is fun, but to me, all this could become a matter of life and death in a blink of an eye, and I was really hoping for no more deaths in my life. Our conversation got interrupted by a crashing sound coming from the kitchen.

"Did you hear that?" Will's eyes turned bright-white like stars.

"It's okay Will, put those away. I'm sure Jacques got tired of waiting for me and went to the kitchen to get something to eat. He's always hungry. I better get back inside."

"Alright, Marcus. I'm gonna let you get back to your friends. If anything, just send a T.P., and I'll be right over, okay?" William got up and spread his wings open.

"They are beautiful, you know?" I touched his wings.

"Thank you," William said, very flattered and proud as if I was complimenting his brand-new car.

"I'll see you later, Will."

"Later, Marks." He flew away in his full lyrebird form.

I went inside the house, passing through the dining room, leading to the open kitchen, where I saw this woman with her back to me. She was at the stove cooking something, her long blonde locks down to her elbows. Her fair skin complexion and tiny posture looked somewhat familiar. It took me two long seconds to recognize who she was.

"Mom?"

XVI

REALITY

"Marcus, sweetie, did I scare you? I was looking for a frying pan when I knocked a glass to the floor. Hopefully, Margaret won't kill me," she said apologetically.

"Sit down, honey, I'm making cheeseburgers for everybody. They would've been done sooner, but I had to go buy some beef, you know Marge has no meat in the house being vegan and all. Have some macadamia nuts white chocolate chip cookies, for now. I know they're your favorites."

She gestured to a plate full of cookies on the table in a calm, normal voice without looking at me as if she had been there the whole day and not been missing for over a week.

I stayed where I was, standing right in the doorway with one hand on the countertop near the microwave and the other on the chair in front of me, exactly on the opposite side of my mom.

"Is everything okay? You look like you've seen a ghost," she asked me once she realized I hadn't moved.

I sat down.

"Do you want some milk?" She opened the refrigerator, knowing weirdly where everything was. She had been in Mrs. Hills' house before, without a doubt.

I nodded.

"I'm sorry honey, she only has almond milk. I should have bought milk also. I don't understand the point of someone being vegan. I mean what is—"

"Mom, where have you been?" I interrupted her, "what happened?"

"What do you mean, honey?" She sat down on the chair next to me, pouring me a glass of almond milk.

"Mom, you vanished without a trace, and now you are here in front of me like nothing happened, except that I haven't heard from you for over a week." I grabbed a cookie, but I didn't eat. Too much to process right now and eating was the last thing on my mind.

"What happened?" I asked, almost yelling at her.

"Son, calm down. I know that look of yours. I'll explain everything to you, everything you need to know from the beginning. Now have some cookies while I finish up the burgers."

I did bite the cookie.

I took a sip of the almond milk.

"So?" I asked, now staring at my mom as she slammed and crushed the meat for the cheeseburgers.

"All right, where do I begin? Oh yeah. On the night that your grandma Maria passed away, your dad called me, and we spoke about him coming back to Boston to get us for the funeral.

The next day I woke up and made some breakfast for us. When you came downstairs, I was on the phone with your dad, he was giving me all the details of his flight so I could pick him up that afternoon at the airport. I was going to tell you, but you left school before I could."

I nodded.

"Once I got back home from work, I realized you were not home yet, so I took a shower and was on my way to the airport when I heard on the radio about the little earthquake. I have never heard of such thing here in Boston. Next thing I know, we'll be dealing with hurricanes and tsunamis," she paused and let out a laugh of disbelief, expecting me to laugh too, but I didn't. She somehow was not the same as she has always been. I could tell when my mom was lying, but I decided to let her finish and see why she was keeping the truth away from me.

"Anyway, so I decided to turn around and make my way back home which was a good thing, your dad's arrival date got postponed till the next day because of the earthquake."

That was a lie. My dad did arrive that afternoon.

"I tried to call you on your cell, but it was off."

That was true. My phone got wet and damaged when I jumped out of Mr. Hors' place across from the Rowes Wharf building into the water.

"So, I called Margaret to see if you had gone to work, but she said she hadn't seen you at all that day."

Lies, Ms. Hills was with me pretty much until dusk.

"Yeah, I was out with Jacques." I joined in the lies.

"I finally got home only to find our house destroyed, so I called your dad and told him what happened. Called the insurance company and went to Alexia's house hoping that you may have shown up there and stayed the night. I left you a message on your cell phone, but again, no answer."

She didn't call my dad. I was with my dad. She didn't sleep at Jacques' house because I was there that night, and my mom's car was not parked in the driveway.

"And where have you been all this time?" I decided to see how far she would go with her lies.

"The next day, Alexia told me that Jacques called her saying that you had stayed over Mileena's and that later on, you would go meet up with Jena in the mall. Don't you remember, honey?" Mom asked as she put the patties down on the frying pan.

"Yes, I do," I lied.

"Yeah, so I went to pick up your dad at the airport, and we came here. I kept missing you. I've been busy at work as I'm sure you also have."

"Mom, how do you know Ms. Hills?"

"Sweetie, Margaret and I have been friends for a while. When I heard that you were working with her, I was delighted. She said only good things about you, you know?"

"What about Mr. Hors?"

"Oh, Kent is a very close friend of your dad. They've known each other since high school. He and Margaret have been together for a while, you know? Honey, can you help me with the buns?" My mom pointed out the bag of buns by the countertop.

I got the buns. I opened the bag and opened a few buns on the countertop. I approached my mom, reaching for the tomatoes on the other side of the countertop.

"Mom, why are you lying to me?"

She dropped a plate, letting it shatter on the floor.

"Marcus, why would you think that I'm lying to you?"

I walked away to grab a broom and a dustpan nearby.

"Marcus, leave it there and come with me," she turned off the stove and walked outside to the backyard where William and I were a few minutes ago.

I was expecting the truth from my mom. We never had any secrets in our family, so I was kind of sad and disappointed that my mom was lying to me. It was not like her at all.

We both sat on the chairs near the white roses' bushes, the opposite location where Will and I had sat before.

"Marcus, your father and I have always loved each other very much, so don't ever think otherwise. But ever since this whole 'Porter' thing came into our lives..."

"You know about that?" I asked, intrigued that even my mom knew about this and I didn't.

"Know about it? Honey, I lived through it. When I met your father in high school, he was always sick, or somebody else was sick, never showing up for classes, exams and all. Nobody seemed to notice that something was weird with him, but I knew. I knew that it was nothing related to sickness or anything that serious for that matter."

"I still can't believe you knew about all this and never told me, Mom. Why?"

"Marcus, you know very well about all the secrecy this is, and if I ever opened my mouth, they would make sure that I'd disappear somehow, either going to a new planet or worse, killing me if they had to."

"How did you find out about all this? Did Dad tell you?"

"Oh dear, no. Your dad never meant for me to know all this. You see, one day I was late for class, and I bumped into your dad when he was cutting class. Back then, we barely even knew each other, so he looked at me, apologized, and ran away to wherever he was going after. I saw in his face that expression that the world was ending or something like that, so I decided to follow him, without him seeing me.

He went on a few streets behind our school, your school, Everett High. He then met with a much younger Kent Hors and Margaret Hills, and this old bearded man. Then in a split of a second, they vanished. All four of them. I couldn't believe what I had just witnessed, so I decided to linger on a bit longer, hoping that your father would come back soon from wherever he was and tell me what was happening."

"Wait, I thought my dad grew up in Brazil..." The more I knew about my parents, the more I realized I was wrong.

"Your dad was born in Brazil, he came to America when he was five, he went to school here until he was nineteen. He and the rest of the family moved back to Brazil, but your dad could never stay there for long, he would come here for vacation and visit his old friends every time he could," she explained.

"So, what happened?"

"I stayed waiting all morning for your dad. The evening approached, and I didn't even notice when I fell asleep under a tree. And then I saw your dad alone, coming back with the happiest face I have ever seen. So, I had to ask what happened. Your dad at first was very skeptical about everything, but eventually, we became close friends, and he told me everything and how he became a Porter, Wonderer of Earth."

"But I thought Kent was," I was certain about this.

"He is and has always been. Your dad was a Wonderer in training to take over Kent's place one day."

"Mom, if everything is fine, then what do they want with me?"

"Well, son, time goes by and eventually they need replacements. You see, every so often Wonderers fall in love, and they no longer can assume two roles. They have to choose between being an immortal Wonderer or become a mortal Porter again to get married, have kids, and eventually die."

"But Mom, Dad is married and have kids. You know, me, right?"

"Yeah, but your dad never became a Wonderer. He decided not to be a part of it. His obligations with his family always came first. That's when he decided to move back to Brazil for good and forget about me and all this Porter stuff. Your dad could never have been a Wonderer. The whole idea of being immortal had always frightened him. After his dad passed away, your grandfather Rafael, he could no longer live with the idea of seeing all his family growing old and dying while he was going to be always young and immortal."

"So, all the Porters are immortals?" It was good to have my mom back and hear her opinion on all of this craziness.

"Only Wonderers and Wanderers. Take Mr. Hors for example. Kent is the Porter of the Taurus Constellation just like your dad. However, for them to become immortals, they have to get themselves tattooed with the ink of the Halley Comet every one-hundred years or so, if not, they will eventually grow old and that's what your dad didn't do. His Halley Tattoo."

"But I saw his tattoo," I remembered my dad's tattoo under his arm.

"That is his Constellation Tattoo made with the

ink of the Stardust of every single star that's part of his Constellation, Taurus. Every Porter has a tattoo to help them activate their powers and transform themselves into their Astrological Sign. Once they become a Wonderer or a Wanderer, they'd get a second tattoo within their existing tattoo. That's when they become immortal."

"I see. Why did they want my dad to become the next Wonderer?"

"Kent fell in love with Margaret a few years ago. At the time Margaret had just become a Porter. He knew that for Margaret to be immortal like him, she would have to become a Wonderer and take the place of Jennifer Lowell, the Wonderer of the Aries Constellation. And you know it's not easy like that. Only if Jennifer resigned her post or died, but as I mentioned, Wonderers can't die. Kent then decided to no longer be a Wonderer. He missed the last time Halley Comet passed us by, so once his ink wears off, he will grow old and die."

My mom's version of the story contradicted my dad's version that he told me yesterday in the living room. According to my dad, Kent is way older than two-hundred years. He couldn't possibly have gone to high school with my dad, only if my dad was just as old as Kent is. Also, Margaret was a Wonderer, and she gave it up to be with Kent. Someone was lying to me.

"So, I guess I should step into Kent's shoes and become a Porter, right, Mom?"

"Oh no, son, this is why I'm here. I'm here to tell

you not to become a Wonderer. You'll become immortal too, and you won't be able to have a normal life like your friends. You'll see them all grow old and die and you will still be in the body of a twenty-something-year-old man. Think of Jacques, think of Jena. Would you bear to see Mileena dying and you being all alone, unable to fall in love, get married, and have kids?"

"But, Mom, it's in my blood. What happens if I don't become a Wonderer?" I remembered William saying it was already in my blood.

"Marcus, I'm sure between your dad and Kent, they will be able to find a new Porter, right? I mean, how many kids are out there? You don't want to do this, son."

I couldn't bear when Mom had the pleading voice. It was almost impossible to deny any wish of hers.

'Marcus, listen to me. Remember the world needs your protection. You're unique. It is in your blood.' A very familiar voice spoke inside my head. It was a Thought Projection from Will.

"Son, what is it? Are you okay?" My mom's voice was shaken.

"Yeah, I'm okay. Give me just a sec, Mom. Why can't we talk to Dad when he gets here? He and William mentioned that they need me and couldn't be anyone else but me and—"

"WILLIAM? As in William Chase?" She grabbed hold of my arms with both hands in a frantic voice with her eyes wide open.

"Yeah, Mom. William Chase. He is a good friend of

mine, I—"

"HE IS NOT TO BE TRUSTED!" She screamed in my face. I had never seen my mom like that before.

"DROP THE KID!" I looked behind me, and William was there with his eyes shining like stars, his body in his usual midnight-blue color matching his hair and wings which were wide opened, flying in midair, ready to strike at any moment. "Do not harm the boy!" He warned her.

"William don't be stupid. This ends here and now." My mom then shielded herself with my body in front of her, took out a strange dagger and pointed to my neck. I couldn't believe what my mom was doing. My own mother.

"Fly any closer, and I will kill the boy," she said, getting the dagger very close to my skin making me bleed slightly.

"You should know that to kill you I only need to SCREEEEEEEEEEAM!"

I knew it was coming. Will let out a yell so high pitched, breaking all the windows around us, shattering them all in pieces, making my mom drop me and her dagger, to cover her own ears.

'Duck!' He sent me a T.P.

I did just in time, avoiding him by an inch. He dived straight to my mom, knocking her out in the white rose bushes that Ms. Hills had planted there.

He then landed on top of her with his two claws holding her arms while she was wrestling, trying to free herself, looking like a fish out of the water, trying to avoid the inescapable death approaching. William was too big of a bird in his full lyrebird form to try to free yourself from, and my mom knew that.

William let out one more bird-like squeal and darted at my mom's head, leaving a scratch in her left cheek.

"NO!" I yelled, "Will, she's still my mom, please don't!" I begged him.

She then saw the opportunity she needed. She kicked Will with one of her free legs and rolled on top of him, grabbing the dagger she once had pointed to my neck, now pointing it to his heart.

'I'm sorry, Marcus...' It was all I heard inside my head.

William then beaked my mom right through her neck, making her fall sideways, bleeding slowly from her throat.

"I'm sorry I failed you, son..." My mom whispered her last words, followed by a sigh just moments after she lost consciousness.

"NOOOOOOO!" I yelled, running toward my mom, but William was faster.

He took her by her the arms in a swift flight, with her neck dangling from one side to another, completely lifeless.

I stood there staring at the clouds where my mom had vanished in a few seconds before my eyes. I didn't even notice Jacques, Mileena, and Jena approaching.

"Marcus, are you okay?" Jacques asked me with a worried voice.

"We heard you scream. What happened?" Miles

spoke right after him.

"My mom, Miles, she was here..." I told her.

"What you mean, Marcus? She was here, here?" Jena asked, looking around for clues, but once William was gone all the windows reconstructed themselves, and in a matter of seconds everything was the same. Even the white roses bush that was destroyed by mom's impact.

"Yes, Jena, here. And then we started talking, and I mentioned William, she freaked out and was no longer herself and..."

The words and the tears became one in my speech. I wanted to get it all out, but I couldn't. I started sobbing like a baby, so I hid my face on Mileena's shoulders as she hugged me.

"Shhh, shhh, Marcus, it's okay. I'm sure she had reasons not to like William. Where did she go?"

"That's my point, Miles. She is dead. DEAD!" I freed myself from Mileena's hug to face Jacques, who was totally expressionless.

"What do you mean dead?" Jena asked from behind me.

"William killed her. She tried to kill me, so Will came and killed her and took her away before I could do or say anything..." I said falling to my knees.

"Marcus, are you sure it was William?" Jacques spoke for the first time, holding my elbows, looking into my eyes, trying to maybe hear another truth from me.

"YES, JACQUES, I AM SURE! OR PERHAPS YOU KNOW ANY OTHER FLYING, TALKING BLUE LYRE-BIRD LIKE THE ONE WE SAW WILL TRANSFORM HIMSELF INTO?" I yelled out at Jacques looking at him for some explanation, something that would make sense out of this.

"Marcus, we are your friends. We are here to help you and support you. You know that, right?" Mileena knelt on my right side.

"I know. I'm sorry, guys. It's just that so much is happening right now that I don't even know who to trust anymore," I gazed at the floor, "I thought he was my friend."

XVII

We went back to the kitchen.

Jacques picked up the pieces of the plate that my mom had dropped on the floor when I told her she was lying. Mileena grabbed four apple juices for us and put some sort of microwavable snack to heat up; no one was really in the mood for burgers.

I didn't eat.

Ms. Hills walked in the kitchen. She saw our expressions and eventually knew something was in the air. Then, just when I thought she was going to ask something, she turned around and left us there.

"What was that about?" Jena asked.

Mileena and I looked at each other and didn't say anything. Not long after, Mr. Hors walked in the kitchen, pulled up a chair next to me and sat down looking straight into my eyes. "Is it true, Marcus? Did William just kill Katherine?"

I nodded.

My dad walked in.

"Son, are you okay?" He hugged me, checking if I was hurt. Ms. Hills was right behind him with some gauze and some sort of liquid to clean the cut in my neck that up until now I had totally forgotten about.

"Dad, I'm okay," I said, pushing them both away from me, not before grabbing the gauze out of Ms. Hills' hand to wipe out the dried blood off my neck. I got up facing the door to the backyard where not less than a few minutes ago my mom was murdered right in front of my eyes by someone whom I thought was a friend.

Was it all my fault?

Maybe if I didn't have befriended William, none of this would have happened. Perhaps he would never even been able to find my mom.

My dad politely asked everyone to leave us alone.

Once they all left the room, he stood up next to me, facing the backyard.

"Son, do you wanna talk about it?"

"Talk about it, Dad? What is there to talk about? Mom just got killed in front of my eyes!" I said, trying to keep my tears from falling. I didn't like crying, but in this case, it was impossible not to.

"Marcus, I know, I understand, but Porters are completely forbidden to kill humans. Do you have any idea why William would break a Universal Law to kill your mom?" My dad asked me with a sad but also icy voice.

"Dad, I don't know. Mom said Will was not to be trusted, and that was the only thing she told me before he showed up, then she threatened to kill me. He tricked her and killed her right before my eyes." This time the tears did start to fall. I couldn't hold them in any longer.

"Come inside son, let's get you a glass of water."

I sat again at the chair where once I was facing my mom. My dad grabbed a glass of water and placed it in front of me.

I took a sip out of it.

"Son look at me. Did your mom threaten to kill you?"

"She had a knife, a dagger of some sort held on to my neck; hence the cut I have right now."

"Something is not right, son. Your mom is your mom. She would never have a reason to kill you, you're her only son," my dad stepped outside in the backyard.

"Actually, she might have had a reason, Dad," I followed him outside.

"What do you mean?"

"Dad, she said she didn't want me to become a Porter, that it wasn't the best choice for you back then and it isn't for me now either."

"Nonsense. Being a Porter is in your blood. I am a Porter! I mean, you can transform yourself into your own Astrological Sign at will. That was never possible before, not without Stardust in your bloodstream and the tattoo that helps activate it all."

I nodded, remembering what my mom had just told me about their tattoos.

"Dad, how did you know about all this? I mean, Ms. Hills never asked anything, and she knew, same with you and Kent. How is that possible?"

"Porters can project thoughts in other Porters' minds at will. It's one of the fastest ways to communicate with one another. We call it—"

"T.P., I know. Queen Angela Carey explained it to me when I met her. She said it was the only way she had to communicate with people."

"Truthfully so, as Angela is no longer capable of speaking. When Margaret walked in the kitchen, you involuntarily sent her a T.P., a Thought Projection that was playing in your head over and over again until I saw you."

William just killed my mom. A thought that I just couldn't shake it off. "I wish Will had taught me how to control this ability before."

"Have you and Will spoke before?"

I remembered never telling my father about my encounters with William.

"Marcus, did you know William before tonight?" He insisted asked again.

"Yes Dad, I did. I met him on my birthday. He's been watching over me ever since."

"William is not trustworthy. He is a Wanderer, son." He interrupted me.

"He was afraid you'd play that card. Dad, William saved my life countless times. If wasn't for him, the

Gemini Porters, even Allison, would have gotten to me. I thought I could trust him."

"Allison as in Allison Prior, Porter of the Scorpius Constellation, Pluto's Wonderer?" What was up with every Porter that they had to say their whole title?

"Yes Dad, Allison Prior, Porter of the Scorpius Constellation. Pluto's Wonderer." I repeated after him.

"That doesn't make any sense, son. Why would anyone like Allison, Lee, and Lynne be after you? They are all Wonderers!" I sat down in one of the chairs nearby in complete disbelief. My dad faced me in silence. His eyes were gone. They were bright-white, just like the ones I've seen on Will's face many times before.

"Dad?"

My father got up and a few long seconds he replied: "I don't know, son."

"Roberto, I'm sorry to interrupt, but the Queen and the Wonderers are all on their way here. They want to talk to you and, of course, Marcus." Ms. Hills stepped outside followed by Mr. Hors.

My dad and I looked at each other, and even though we didn't say anything, I heard his voice inside my head, just like William did before.

'You and I need to talk later. I have a feeling we are on our own for now, we shouldn't trust anyone till we uncovered the truth, even if it's only us two, son.'

My eyes almost gave away that I heard my father's T.P. inside of my head, but I knew better. If my theory was right, my dad and I couldn't show any

'

emotions or let anyone know what we were suspecting. Someone among us was a traitor, and we couldn't risk letting anyone know.

"Margaret, we are ready." My dad's eyes were back to normal, from bright-white like stars, to brown.

Ms. Hills gave a look to Mr. Hors, who disappeared inside his Exotic Matter Sphere.

"Did you get my T.P.?" My dad asked casually in a tone only I could hear just like when you ask your friend if they got your text message.

"Yes. Wasn't I supposed to?" I said a bit uncomfortable, unsure if I should have read my father's T.P. or not.

"No, I mean, yeah. I wanted to send you a T.P. but didn't know if you would receive it or not, son. You truly are a Natural, Marcus. Being a Porter is in your blood!" My dad said, all proud of me.

"Dad wait a second. What do they want with me? What do I say?" I asked, a little bit nervous.

"Just tell them the truth, son. And if you get lost, I'll send a T.P. in your way, or you can send one to me too. Now that I know you can do that, we'll be inseparable. Are you ready?"

"As ready as I can be."

"Good, because here they come."

I was right behind my dad when we reached the middle of the backyard with Ms. Hills' big tree right behind us. First to appear was Mr. Hors, followed by all the other Wonderers, each one of them out of their own Exotic Matter Sphere.

There must have been about fifteen people out there, all of them dressed so nicely that I was actually embarrassed for being in my jeans and T-shirt.

"Hello, Marcus, how do you do?" This woman sitting at the center of all those people stood up, as everybody bowed down on one knee, and with that, and her beautiful, silvery dress and crown, I knew she was Mariah Stars, Queen of the Solar System.

I looked at my dad and he send me a T.P.: *'Bow, son.'*

I did.

"Marcus, do you know who I am?" She made her way toward me.

"Mariah Stars, Queen of the Solar System, Your Majesty," I said, without glancing at her.

"That's right, Marcus. I am indeed Mariah Stars, Porter and Queen of the Solar System!" She touched my chin and lifted me back up to my feet. She spoke with authority much more prominent than all of the other Porters when they introduce themselves. Now I knew where they got all the authority in their speech from.

"I'm here because it was brought to my attention that one of the Wanderers has killed a human, your mom, Mrs. Katherine Mathias, is that true?" She asked as she went back to her seat, as everybody got back to their feet again.

"Yes, Your Majesty, it is true," I said, followed by everyone's gasps of disbelief.

"Do you know by whom?" She asked me as she and everybody else were looking at me.

"Yes, Your Majesty." My voice came out shakier than firm. She was stunning, but her tone of authority made me feel like a bug that she could crush before I could even think of moving.

"I'm waiting for a name, young one," she said quite impatiently.

"Your Majesty, I might be wrong. Maybe she is not really dead, William couldn't—"

"William as in William Chase, Marcus? Porter of the Lyra Constellation?" She interrupted me.

"Yes, Your Majesty." Suddenly I started feeling bad for William, but at the same time, he did kill my mom.

"Marcus, I want you to look around me. Do you know who all these people are? Do you know why they are all here?

I shook my head. I had no clue who these people were.

"Well, let me introduce to you to the twelve Wonderers of the Solar System, my Chosen Ones. All the way down to my right, Leonard Larkson, the Lion. Wonderer of Sun, Porter of the Leo Constellation. To his left, the Porters of the Gemini Constellation, Wonderers of Mercury, Lynne and Lee Yang, the Twins."

They waved hi to me with a smirk on their face as if they were hiding something that no one but my dad and I knew.

"Next," Mariah continued, "we have Patrick Cobain, Libra's Porter, the Scales, and Venus' Wonderer. I'm sure you've met Kent Hors before, the Bull. Wonderer of Earth, Constellation of Taurus." Mr.

Hors nodded with a half-smile on his face. He also could also tell that something was up with the Gemini Porters.

"I believe you've also met The Queen of The Moon, Ms. Angela Carey. Porter of the Cancer Constellation, the Crab."

I just then noticed Angela. She gave me a friendly smile and a single nod. It was amazing how her queenly appearance from before was now clearly diminished in comparison to Mariah's.

"Jennifer Lowell, Porter of the Aries Constellation, the Ram, Wonderer of Mars; the Archer Josh Rogers, Wonderer of Jupiter, Sagittarius; on my left, Claire Flowers, the Mountain Sea-Goat, Wonderer of Saturn, Porter of the Capricornus Constellation; Mr. Ben Cruise, the Water-Bearer, Aquarius from Uranus. Michelle and Adam Ford, the Fishes. Porter of the Pisces Constellation, Wonderer of Neptune; Pluto's Wonderers are Donna Saihtam, Virgo the Virgin; and Allison Prior, Scorpius' Porter, the Scorpion."

As she spoke the name of every Wonderer, they all made eye contact with me to make sure I knew who they were. And there, standing last in the line was Allison. Allison's face was as if she had never met me. She actually couldn't care less about everything that was going on around her. I wondered what would happen if I said in front of everybody that she had tried to kill me in the subway station?

"These are my Wonderers, Marcus, handpicked by me to become the most important Porters of the Solar System. However, we still have other Porters who aren't so happy with this. Some of them are wandering around planet to planet wondering why I chose these people and not them." Mariah's tone of authority made everyone look out on the horizon, just as if they were soldiers with their general speaking in front of them.

"The answer is simple: They weren't just simply chosen by me. Their choices made them who they are today. And that's why I chose them." Every single Wonderer had a proud look on their face. It was something beautiful to see and yet frightening since I could tell all of them could do wonders to protect their Queen, even kill.

"Some Wanderers have tendencies of breaking the law, and breaking the Universal law is punishable by Oblivion." Something told me that she did not mean it as in just making them forget about something but more like to be obliviated to the world, as in a jail planet or something.

"With that said, I'm here to ask you, Marcus Donovan Mathias: In front of all the Wonderers, including your future mentor if you choose so, do you confirm that William Chase is accused of killing your mom, Mrs. Katherine Mathias?"

'If you say anything about that day on the train, I will kill you with my own two hands, you little brat.' I heard Allison's Thought Projection in my head.

"Marcus, I asked you a question," Mariah spoke again.

'Marcus, say something.' My dad sent me a T.P.

"MARCUS!" The Queen spoke getting up.

"I'm sorry, Your Majesty, but I have something that I need to say before if you would please allow me," I said, bowing down to one knee.

"This better be relevant to my question, young man. Do speak."

"I'm sure it's a foolish question, Your Majesty, but I have to know." I walked closer to the Queen followed by everyone's curious eyes.

'What are you doing, son?' I ignored my dad's Thought Projection.

"Very well, go on then." The Queen demanded as she sat back down.

"I want to know why Ms. Allison Prior tried to kill me on the subway a few days ago?"

There was a moment of silence followed by people's gasps and murmurs.

"Is that so?" She got up, facing Allison. "Silence, everyone! Ms. Prior, would you please come closer?"

Allison passed through everyone and stopped right in front of the queen.

"Your Majesty," She spoke, down on one knee.

"Allison, would you please address this court and tell us if this accusation is false or not."

"It would be my pleasure, Your Grace." She got up to her feet. "When I heard that Marcus was in some sort of danger and being associated with that Wanderer, William, I immediately contacted Ms. Margaret Hills, asking for her permission to interfere and rescue Marcus out of Will's hands. Margaret was busy protecting the other kid, Jax I think is his name, while Kent was taking care of business with Roberto. Since

Margaret and I have been close friends, she allowed me to do so, and that's what I did. I went after the boy to rescue him from the grip of that blue bird. Once I got there, William, of course, put up a fight, not wanting to surrender Marcus to me. I then used some force on him, but the little Dogie there interfered and almost got me killed. If there's someone here who should be upset, it is I, Your Majesty." She concluded.

"Do you confirm that, Ms. Hills?" Mariah now turned her attention to Ms. Hills.

"Yes, Your Majesty. Once I learned that Marcus was hanging around with William, I told Allison to do so," Ms. Hills told the Wonderers, who seemed all to agree with her, to my disbelief.

My dad and I exchanged looks, but no T.P.'s this time.

"Very well, if this is all you have, Mr. Mathias, would you mind answering my question?"

"Yes, Your Majesty. It was William Chase who killed my mom." I was so embarrassed about my accusation. How was I to know that Margaret and Allison were close friends?

"William Chase, from this day forward, is being wanted for judgment. Anyone who finds him must immediately bring him to me alive. No questions asked. Court dismissed." Almost immediately, everyone started disappearing inside of their Exotic Matter Sphere. Except for Kent and the Queen, everyone else had disappeared out of there.

"May I have a word with you, Marcus?" Mariah approached me.

"Yes, Your Majesty."

"Call me Mariah. I am your Queen but ultimately someone I want you to trust first. If there's any problem, don't hesitate to contact me. Kent knows exactly how. Trust your mentor. He knows what's best for you." Her voice was so friendly and warm that it took me a couple of seconds to realize that it was really the queen of the Solar System talking to me.

"Yes, Your Majesty," I answered awkwardly.

"And, Marcus, one more thing. Do you really want to find your mother's killer?"

I looked up meeting her eyes, surprised by her question, "Of course, I do."

"Then what are you waiting for? We could use someone with your talents to join this court. As centuries passes, it gets harder and harder to find trustworthy people these days, if you know what I mean." She then winked at me followed by a smile.

She went on to say goodbye to my dad, Kent, and Margaret right after disappearing inside of her own E.M.S.

I looked up to the balcony of my room and saw Jena, Jacques, and Mileena there looking down at me. I knew the expression they were wearing, concern.

Dad asked me one question that I wasn't sure if I was ready to answer: "Are you ready to become what you are meant to be, son? A Wonderer?"

I looked into my dad's eyes and saw the pain and grief he was feeling. The weight of having lost his baby girl, my sister Daniella, and now my mom, Katherine, was about to take a tool on him. If I remember right, my father didn't handle losing my sister well, and he just came back from his mother's funeral to his wife's funeral. I really have to do something about this. I need to help my dad avenge my mom.

"I'm not quite sure if this is the life for me, Dad, but one thing I am sure. I'm going to make Will pay for what he did to my mom. Make me a Wonderer."

"But first, we must make you a real Porter, son."

"Wasn't I born a Natural Porter?"

"Yes, but you still need training, you need to learn to control your abilities and not pass out after using it. You need to get your Constellation Tattoo. With the Stardust flowing in your veins, you'll have control over your powers, transmutations and all of your abilities, including your element, earth," Dad explained it to me. "Once we'll get you to Venus, Kyle Ptorn will be able to explain everything to you and how exactly all this works. But for now, go to your room and try to get some sleep."

I left the kitchen and went up to my room. Jena, Miles, and Jacques were all standing in the living room. None of them moved or said anything. Mileena's eyes were all full of water, she had undoubtedly shared her tears. Jacques was sitting by the window staring with a blank face as if he was not even there. I don't think he had processed all that had just happened. Jena had a serious look, sad but something told me that she was the only one who truly understood my pain. She had also lost her mom not long ago.

I shut the door behind me, kicked off my shoes to the side, and lied down on my bed. I couldn't sleep. I got back up again and out to the balcony. I looked down to the backyard and couldn't believe what had just happened. My mom couldn't be dead. I know I just saw William kill her, but it couldn't be possible. William had shown to be such a great guy, a spectacular friend; he even saved Jacques and me from drowning, why? Just so we can stay alive to see him kill my mom?

"WILLIAM!" I shouted out of the balcony on the top of my lungs. "I DON'T CARE WHERE YOU RAN OFF TO, BUT I'LL GO ALL THE WAY TO PLUTO TO FIND YOU IF I HAVE TO, DO YOU HEAR ME? AND WHEN I DO, YOU BETTER RUN BECAUSE I WILL MAKE YOU PAY, WILL. YOU WILL PAY FOR WHAT YOU DID!"

XVIII

MOONIAN

I woke up later than my usual time.

Took a shower and got dressed. I passed by the guest room where Jacques and Mileena were staying, and no one was there. Went to the living room, empty as well. I made my way downstairs into the kitchen and saw no one. I was too late to go to school this morning but not late to help in the coffee shop.

"May I help the next person in line, please?" I heard Steve's voice coming from the coffee shop.

I passed through the kitchen into the shop. Steve was handing a cup of coffee to a line of customers. Ms. Hills was getting some pastries for a group of college kids.

"Next person in line?" I jumped in to help.

Steve and Ms. Hills stopped for a couple of seconds to glance at me and at each other. They shared a half smile and continued what they were doing. I stayed at the register taking orders and payments. Steve was making coffees, cappuccinos, and all other types of fancy coffee beverages while Ms. Hills was handling the pastries, bagels, and other edible goodies.

"Are you okay, buddy? I heard what happened," Steve asked me between an order of a large non-fat latte with three sugars and a blueberry bagel toasted with butter.

"Yeah, thanks," I managed to say.

Truth is, I would rather not think about that right now. My dad is probably out there with Mr. Hors figuring out a way to find Will, and I was better off just staying out of it. I've already done enough by befriending a traitor and getting my mom killed.

"Good Morning, did you sleep well?" Ms. Hills asked me once the everlasting line of customers came to an end.

"Yeah, I did." I honestly didn't remember falling asleep. When I opened my eyes, it was already morning.

"Go grab something to eat while there aren't many people in the store," Ms. Hills told me.

"Alright. Where is everyone else?" I asked.

"Your dad and Kent are downstairs at G.O.L making arrangements on how to find William. Jacques and Miles are in school and Jena—"

"Good morning, Ms. Hills," Jena greeted as she opened the door of Lulu's Coffee Shop allowing herself in.

"...is right on time." Ms. Hills finished her sentence. "How are you, sweetie?"

"I came to check on Marks," she looked at me with a hard to read expression, "how is it going, buddy?"

"I'm alright. About to have breakfast. Care to join me?"

I helped myself with a cup of chocolate milk and a bagel toasted with cream cheese. Jena had already her breakfast, so she only grabbed a bottle of orange juice.

"What are your plans for today?" Jena opened her bottle of O.J. as we both sat on a booth.

"Not sure. I missed school today, so I was planning on staying here and help Ms. Hills in the store. I still have to work, you know?"

"I'm sure Ms. Hills could give you the afternoon off if you want."

"Jena, I think is best for me to stay focused on my job. It helps me get my mind off of things. I keep reliving what happened last night over and over again in my head."

"I was only five when I lost my mom, Marcus. I barely remember anything about her except one thing: She used to smile a lot, I remember her laughter, her happiness. That's what I hold on to. I know you, and your mom, have great memories together, and that's what you should hold on to as well. Don't let what happened to your mom get in the way of who you are." Jena was full of sadness. I could tell she had never truly recovered from losing her mom.

"I won't lose sight of who I am, Jena, but I will avenge my mom. I will not rest until William pays for what he did. For lying to me, betraying my trust, and killing my mom."

"He also saved you and Jacques, remember?"

Jena was right. Will did save us. A thought that I did not want to be reminded of.

"Good morning, son." My dad walked in from the basement followed by Mr. Hors right behind him.

"Dad!" I hugged him. "Good morning, Mr. Hors."

"I think it's time we lose formalities, kid. Call me Kent."

"Kent and I were downstairs discussing about your mother's situation."

"And?" I moved back in the booth allowing my dad and Kent to join us in it.

"Nothing. If my memory serves me well, William is not working alone. Remember the car chase on your way to the airport?" My dad began, "Well, we think it might have been the Gemini Porters. Also, Allison Prior, Porter of Scorpius, attacked you before you met up with Angela Carey, Wonderer of Moon, who swore to you and us all that William was a great and trustworthy guy."

"So, what does that mean, Dad?"

"Your dad and I have decided that the people we thought were trustworthy, may not be after all. William could very well be working with Lynne, Lee, Angela, and Allison," Kent concluded.

"That makes no sense! What would they all want with my mom?"

"Son, that's the thing that doesn't make sense. Your mom didn't know much about the Porters, she never truly wanted to know anything about them. She didn't seem to care for any of this at all."

"What about the Queen, Mariah Stars? Why don't we ask her?"

"Jena, your idea is viable, except that the Queen was here in the backyard and seemed completely unaware of what's going on in our Solar System. Besides, she believed Allison blindly when Marcus accused her of trying to kill him in the subway." Mr. Hors remarked.

"On that note, how come we haven't heard of any of that in the news?" Jena asked completely astoundded by all of this.

"It all comes down to one thing: Stardust. When Porters are around, a Stardust Dome forms protecting the humans and the surroundings. Once Porters leave, the Stardust Dome vanishes, everything goes back to its original state before being destructed or affected in any way by Porters. Just like Margaret's house went back to the way it was right after Will attacked my wife," My dad explained.

"Just like the exoskeleton that revolves all the Porters, right?"

"It's made out of Stardust as well, Marcus. Good job."

"That explains why it can inflict everything around us, but it can't be inflicted by everything around us."

"That's right, Jena."

"So, what do we do now, Dad?" I asked trying to get us back to our conversation.

"We will carry on and pretend nothing has happened. We'll arrange your mother's funeral—"

"MY MOTHER'S FUNERAL?" I got up to my feet. "How are we going to hold a funeral without a body?"

"Son, it's symbolic. Only so they'd think we are not going after Will. Then we'll send you to Venus for training."

"Venus? VENUS? I'M NOT GOING TO VENUS! I'm going after William. I want my mother's body."

"Marcus, please,"

"No, Dad. I will not sit still while my mother's body and killer are somewhere out there. You know what? Why don't we go to the Moon? Yeah. Let's go talk to Angela, I'm sure she would have a perfect excuse that I'm dying to hear."

"Marcus, we can't just go the Moon and accuse the Queen of allying herself to a killer. She would have us killed before we could disappear out of there."

"Of course we can't, Dad. What can we do?"

"Son, I—"

"You know what? I have to get back to work. If you'll excuse me,"

I stormed out of the booth, passing through Steve behind the counter who was standing there with his jaw dropped.

"Marcus," Ms. Hills came in through the kitchen.

"We are all out of cookies," I grabbed a tray and

headed through the door into the kitchen.

A strong, thick wisp of air engulfed me, throwing me in every direction. I lost sight of where I was or where I was going. It felt like I was being trapped inside of hamster ball. And just when I thought I was gonna faint for the lack of air in my lungs, everything came to a halt.

I opened my eyes and could not believe what I was seeing. It was in the middle of the night, in a forest, not your typical forest but one made out of trees in shapes of a 'W', trunks in the color of lilac, others in the shade of cyan blue.

The leaves were also in random colors of orange, green, blue and red. Some of the trees were just as tall as I am, some were towering me like a skyscraper.

Birds with two, three, four and five heads. Some with two pairs of wings, some with four. Some tiny as a chick and others bigger than an elephant. The color scheme was varied in all of them. A few were quite similar to the ones we have on Earth, but the majority of these were weirdly beautiful. A fantasy-feeling I had only once before when I visited the Moon a few days ago.

But this couldn't possibly be real. I couldn't be on the Moon; I didn't have an Exotic-Matter Sphere on my belly button. How can this be?

"There. There is he." A man's voice came through the forest approaching very quickly. "See he I can."

A group of at least fifteen people or so was coming my way. They all seemed like they've been out in the wild for a long time. Their appearance was that of a tribal people, full of pearls and shining metals. Their weapons were drawn, and it was clear that they were made out of tree branches that resemble spears, axes, swords, bows, and arrows. A few were carrying some sort of a shield. As a people they looked very diverse in skin tones, heights, and weights; however, their intercorrelation was there. Some had feathers on their head for embellishment others as a disguise. Their clothes were minimal, covering only their private parts, reminding me of a lot of people in the Carnival in Rio de Janeiro, which always made me somewhat uncomfortable.

"Who you is? Why you is on land my?" The man spoke spoke from atop of this enormous animal. The beast had six legs, white and dark purple color fur. More massive than two elephants put on the top of each other it had two long necks just like those of giraffes, its heads, however, were very similar to those of a ferret. And no tail.

"I once say who you is, boy?" The man looked like the tribe's chief.

"Marcus. My name is Marcus Mathias. I'm from Earth." I replied.

"Name, boy?"

"What? I'm uh—"

"Alright, Wha-ta'um. The why you is on land my?" He asked loudly again.

"My name is Marcus. I'm from Earth. Where am I?"

"Mock I you, Wha-ta'um?"

"No, I... I'm..."

"What? Forgot the how speak Moonian?" He lowered the front portion of his animal's body to get a closer look at me with both of its necks wrapping around me as if they were about to squeeze me like a snake.

"Moonian?" I thought to myself, I was right, I was in the Moon. "The Queen. Bring me to your Queen!" I pleaded as the animal's neck was wrapping around my body tighter and tighter.

"Speak Moonian, boy or no?"

"Angela. Take me to Angela Carey." I said with the little air that I had before his animal had completely squashed me to death.

"Angela Carey? The Queen?" With a pull of his rope, the beast dropped me on the floor.

"Yes, that's what I've been trying to—" I got up, massaging my neck trying to alleviate the struggle.

"MOONIAN! Speak Moonian! Zad'iria, glastunia on he." He interrupted me again.

A woman holding a necklace with a glistening black rock of the size and weight of billiard's ball approached me and placed the necklace around my neck making me fall to the floor on my knees.

"Hands, boy." She demanded.

I put my hands backward as if I was getting handcuffed, but she put my arms up and around my neck tying both of my hands behind my neck.

"Walk!"

I got up and fell instantaneously backward.

Everyone laughed.

"Up, boy. The day whole I not have," The same

woman spoke again.

"Zad'iria, the boy. I bring he to Carey Queen.

"Sir, yes."

She grabbed me by my hair and pulled me back up, "Walk!"

I followed her and the rest of the people with the chief in its two-headed beast right behind us.

We walked for miles and miles until the Sun was up. If it weren't for the conditions I was in, I would have enjoyed the walk and especially the view. It amazes me that no one on Earth has any idea of how truly beautiful the Moon actually is.

They sat camp in the middle of the forest nearby the river with shades of green and orange.

Once everything and everyone was all set, Zad'iria brought me to this wooden cage. She untied my hands, and I instantly fell to my knees. She then removed my necklace and hung it outside in the front of the gate, right before locking me in it.

"Rest, Wha-ta'um. More walk later." She walked away.

"Marcus..." I spoke with the last bit of strength I had, "My name is Marcus..." But those words barely came out, I fell flat face on the floor and fell asleep. The weight of the necklace, plus my arms around my neck made me very tired, so I just collapsed.

***

"Wake, boy." A bucket of cold, orange colored water splashed all over my face making me jump awake.

"Release him. By the orders of the Queen, I demand you to release him."

A man made his way through the forest and stopped a few feet away from the cage I was locked in. His appearance was also that of an indigenous native, but his rigid posture and walk seemed that of a royal.

"But, Your Grace—"

"Do you dare defy your Queen's order, Chief Hazur'Al-Hur?"

"No, I—"

"That's enough, Indio."

I knew that voice. Afirina and the Queen finally made their way through the forest. Angela was dressed in a beautiful gown as always, while Afirina had her battle clothes on, a silver armor. At the sight of the Queen, everyone bowed including Chief Hazur'Al-Hur, who was still in front of the cage with his tribe right next to him.

"YOU!"

'Bow, Marcus.' I heard my own voice speaking in my head. Didn't take long to realize it was Angela's T.P. Her Thought Projection is the only one that comes into my head as my own voice, since she doesn't have a voice due to an injury she had in a battlefield.

"I'm not bowing to you, YOU'RE A TRAITOR!" I shouted from the top of my lungs.

"BOW DOWN TO YOUR QUEEN, BOY." Indio, the man who demanded my release a few seconds ago, had a spear drown out of thin air into his hand and almost reaching my neck inside the cage. One look at his eyes and I knew he was a Porter himself; they glowed like stars, even though was daytime.

"Open the cage, your Majesty? But—" Indio began, but clearly got interrupted by Angela's demanding Thought Projection in his own head.

"If you dare to do anything stupid, I'll kill you myself, boy," he warned me as he removed the necklace hanging around the cage and opening it, setting me free.

"YOU! QUEEN ANGELA CAREY, YOU BETRAYED ME," I sprinted out of the cage, pushing the Porter out of the way, and ran towards the Queen.

I could feel my whole body tingling. My upper body weighing more and more by the second and, truly in a matter of seconds, I was running in all fours fully transformed in a bull.

The last time I felt like this was when Allison was about to kill William, looking back now, I should have allowed. The Queen and I knew I was gonna strike her, but she didn't care, and I neither did I.

In a split of a second Afirina standing a couple of feet in front of the Queen, opened up her arms above her head as if she was in prayer or something like that, allowing some sort of round, metal wings to sprout under her arms. Her eyes were shining bright like stars just like Angela's and, I'm pretty sure like mine as well.

I saw Afirina in front of me, protecting her Queen and I knew I was gonna strike her, and she just stood there, not moving. I went for it. I was mad and I didn't care, they both lied to me about William and, for that reason, now my mother is dead.

BANG

I fell backward in so much pain as I had never felt before, entirely back in my human form, incapable of barely any movements, followed by everyone around us laughter, besides Indio, Afirina and the Queen herself.

"What happened?"

'Afirina is a Wanderer herself, Porter the Scutum Constellation, the Shield. You would know more about her and the rest of the Porters if you actually consider going to C.H.E.P., as your father suggested.'

"Get up, boy." Indio had his spear drawn out to my neck. "No one can touch the Queen while Afirina is around, her shield protects the Queen from everything, including stupid Porters like yourself."

'Excuse their manners, Marcus, but as the reigning Queen of the Moon, they will do everything in their power to stop anyone from harming me. Let's go to my castle. Can you teleport over there?'

"No. I don't know how. I'm—"

'It's okay, Indio will take you.'

Just as her T.P. finished in my head, Indio grabbed my arm and, with one hand he lifted me back up to my feet. He was definitely much stronger than he looked.

The same vacuuming feeling that I felt before, came over my body. I felt like I was sucked inside of something and expelled right out again in a blink of an eye and just as I opened my eyes, we were all back again where I was once before. We were inside of the Queen's castle, on her main tower overlooking the Moon Queendom, Luna.

"Please forgive my manners, young Porter," Indio let go of my arm and bowed to me as in a sign of respect like I've seen Afirina and Angela do to each other last time I was here in the Moon.

"What in the world is going on?" I asked Queen Carey.

'The people of the Moon, the Moonians, do not know of you. You're not supposed to be here, especially by yourself. You're not a Porter yet, you're not allowed to travel within worlds, Marcus.' The most interesting thing to see is Angela Carey gesturing in sign language and have my brain translate it naturally as if I somehow understood every sign. As so did every Porter around her by the looks of Indio and Afirina.

"I tried to explain to them who I was and what I was doing here, but they didn't seem to understand me."

'Of course not, they do not speak Earthian languages, especially English,' Angela sat in her throne as she explained it to me.

"But how was I able to understand them?"

'You're a Natural Porter, Marcus. Every Porter is able to understand any language in the Universe, their ears translate it naturally to their own native language. That's why you understand them, but they don't understand you.'

"Wait, so are you speaking English right now?" I stand across from her.

'I'm afraid I actually haven't literally spoken in quite a few centuries. At least not the way you do,' she pointed to her throat reminding she can't actually speak.

"Oh…" I sat on a couch in front of her, embarrassed by my stupid remark.

'It's okay, Marcus. Dealing with languages right now is the least of your worries,' she stopped for a second as Afirina handed me the same 'U' shape glass filled with the same color juice I've tasted before, matiniki.

I took a sip out of it.

'I know you have a lot of questions and I also know how aggravated you are about William—'

"About William," I interrupted her, "you told me he was a good guy, you told me he was trustworthy, you told me I was lucky to have a friend like him and yet he murders my mom in front of my eyes! Care to elaborate on that?" I got up on my feet again.

'Marcus, I'm just as surprised as you are. William has never murdered anyone else before, it's not like him. Or at least I thought it wasn't. I'm truly sorry, Marcus.' It was weird to hear my own thoughts with Angela's feelings. Even though she was gesturing, I could "hear" her tone of defeated inside of my head.

She made her way to the balcony, staring out at her Queendom.

"You're sorry? SORRY? Well, sorry won't bring my mom back, will it?"

'Marcus, we can't change the past, we can only prevent something like that to happen again in the future.'

Her tone of voice was apologetic but firm. *'He fooled us all,'*

"I'm going after him, Angela. I don't know how I'm gonna do it, but I am doing it!"

'How about by going to Venus for starters?' She asked casually as if she was just making conversation.

"Well, I wasn't planning on moving, especially to a different world for the remaining years of high school."

'Marcus, the Center of Higher Education for Porters in Venus, has everything you can dream of—'

"I know, I know I heard it all before," I interrupted her remembering Mr. Hors' exact same words.

'Did you know you'll have classes outside about all different types of soil and rocks, throughout the Solar System?'

Angela knew of my love for rocks, all different types, colors, and sizes. I approached her in the balcony looking outside over her Kingdom.

'Marcus, there is so much that you don't know yet, and it would be great for you if you go to a school that can teach you everything that has to do with being a Porter.'

"I know, and it probably would be the best for me, but I really don't want to become a Porter. I just wanna go after William and avenge my mother."

'Doing the right thing for the wrong reason isn't a smart move. You might be a Natural Porter, as rare as it is, but you're still lifetimes younger than William. He will kill you if he has to, before you could even get to him.'

"I have to try. Even if it means the death of me,"

'Okay, so you'll need all the help you can get. How about if you go home, talk to your dad, and come up with a plan? Once you become fully a Porter then you could go after William, and Marcus, sometimes things might not be what you want at first, but it could become something you could truly enjoy.' She insisted.

"Sounds like a good plan, for now. I'm sure Dad would be happy with that," I said as we made our way back in the big room.

'And Marcus, whatever was the reason that William did what he did, I'm sure it was a very strong one. Think about it, we know him. It doesn't seem like William at all.'

I nodded.

I didn't wanna agree with her, but she was right, William didn't seem like the murderer type. I never had any doubt that he could kill anyone, not even when Allison tried to kill me on the train a few weeks ago.

'Should we take you home now before you start losing oxygen again?'

"Yeah, everyone must be wondering what happened to me."

'How did you get here anyway?'

"I have no idea. I was so angry with you, all I was thinking about was how could I get to the Moon and, boom. Next thing I knew I was here, in the wild, surrounded by the Moonians."

"Are you ready, Marcus?" Indio approached me.

"Just a second," I faced Angela again, "I'm sorry

for being rude to you earlier and thanks for not killing me."

'Remember Marcus, my Queendom is ruled by love not hate. I'll see you soon, young Natural.'

I looked at Indio, as he stretches out his hand as if to give me a handshake. I shook it and boom. I opened my eyes again, and we were all back in Ms. Hills' backyard.

"Thank you, Indio," I thanked him, "for not killing me like I know you could."

"I would if you were truly a problem, little Porter. You're really brave, but if I may give you a tip, I'm pretty sure you're not always gonna run into nice Wanderers like myself. They will kill you before you can even scream for help. Take my advice and become a Porter as soon as you can. It's the only way to protect you and those around you from all the other Porters."

"Thanks, again and what Constellation are you a Porter of?" I wondered.

"Indus. The Indian." He smiled and vanished inside of his Exotic Matter Sphere.

I stayed there looking at the tree and its surroundings. Visions of my mom's death poured into my mind. That alone was a good reminder for me to become a Porter, even if it was something I didn't wanna be but if I wanted to play with the big guys, I would have to learn how to handle the big guns.

"There you are, I've been looking everywhere for you." Jacques came out in the backyard.

"Hey, Jax."

"We haven't had a chance to talk about what happened a couple nights ago. How are you?"

"I'm alright, man. I'm just trying to figure out what to do next, you know?"

"I think we should do what your father told us, go to your mom's funeral this weekend and get you started on becoming a Porter. Only then I think you'll be able to avenge your mom." He suggested.

"What about her body, Jacques? How can we have a funeral without a body?"

"We'll do it to honor her memory, Marks. If we ever find her body, we'll bury it and make it a proper funeral."

"I think you're right. I'm gonna head to bed, I'm pretty tired."

"Long day?"

"Long night actually," I responded to Jacques who clearly didn't understand my comment. "I'll explain it later."

"That's alright, *pote*[30]. Go get some rest."

I went upstairs. I could hear Mr. Hors and Ms. Hills in the living room talking with my dad. I decided to just go straight to my room. Had spent the whole day on Earth, a whole night on Moon, dragged by Chief Hazur'Al-Hur made me completely exhausted.

"Hey, son? I know you want to be left alone and all, but I just wanted to see how you're doing," Dad spoke from behind the close door of my room.

"Come in, Dad."

---

[30] *Pote*: Buddy (French)

"How are you feeling? Angela told me about your little encounter with the Moonians." He sat next to me.

"Yeah, luckily I'm fine."

"You know, the people from the "dark side of the Moon" are very dangerous. They are not like the people from Luna." My dad told to me.

"But I thought the Moon was all reigned by love,"

"Son, everything is in peace in the Moon because the Moonians don't interfere with the Lunaians. The two people don't ever cross each other's paths. One side is evolved and reigned by compassion, but the other side is still ruled by people attached to their animalistic instinct."

"That's interesting," I remarked.

"Not all planets are safe for you to wander around, you know?"

"I didn't mean to, plus I'm a Wonderer, not a Wanderer." I laughed.

"Technically you're just a boy having a hard time controlling your soon-to-be Porter abilities and far from becoming Earth's new Wonderer, young man."

"I know, Dad, I know."

"But hey! That's the spirit," he got up with a proud smile on his face. "Have a good night son."

"Good night, Dad."

XIX

MAJESTY

I got up way past the time to go to school. I was getting used to being woken up by either my dad or Ms. Hills to go to school since I no longer had a cell phone, but I guess they had forgotten it too.

I got out of the bed, grabbed the little white stone that Angela gave to me on my first trip to Moon, and head out to the balcony and stared at the white rose bushes, the place that my mom was killed by my so-called friend.

What was I thinking?

I barely even knew him, and I trusted him. I befriended him, and he betrayed me. He not only betrayed me, but he killed my mom, right here in front of my eyes.

I decided to take a shower and go downstairs for breakfast.

Once I got in the kitchen, I was very much surprised in what I saw. My dad was sitting on his regular chair on the left side of the table, Mr. Hors was across from him. Ms. Hills was grabbing a jar of orange juice out of the fridge, and Mariah Stars was sitting at the head of the table on the opposite side of me, helping herself to a couple of wheat toast on her plate of scrambled eggs and bacon.

"Good morning, Marcus," she spoke as soon as she noticed my face in awe.

"Huh, good morning, Your Majesty." I bowed.

"No need for formalities, we are just having breakfast, honey. Now, have a seat before the eggs get cold." She gestured for me to sit down on the chair in front of me, across from her as my dad handed me a plate of scrambled eggs.

"Oh, just in time, Cookie. I got your toast right here for you." Ms. Hills gave me another plate with a couple slices of toast on it, taking her seat next to Mr. Hors.

"Thanks," I replied automatically, "so, what's going on?" I asked, still surprised by having the Queen of the Solar System sitting across from me, enjoying her breakfast.

"Well, Marcus I didn't wake you up earlier because Mariah wants to talk to you, so no school for you today, buddy," my dad told me between sips of coffee.

"Thanks, I guess," I mumbled under my breath.

Not that I was not excited to not go to school, but only because I was curious to hear what the queen wanted to talk to me about. Have I done something wrong? Was I in some sort of trouble?

"Curiosity killed the cat, don't you know, young Porter?" Mariah winked at me. *'You should be more careful with your thoughts,'* She spoke in my head through a T.P.

"When I was invited to become a Porter a while ago, Mariah herself brought me on a trip, the same trip you're going on in a couple of minutes, that helped me decide if I wanted or not to become a Porter and even a Wonderer later on," Mr. Hors told me.

"And where exactly are we going?" I asked more annoyed than happy about it.

"Oh Cookie, that's a surprise. Go upstairs brush off your teeth, put on your shoes and get ready because this is a trip you won't forget, hehe." Ms. Hills said so excitedly that her high-pitch candied voice almost came out again, making everyone on the table smile.

"Alright, then. I'll be right back." I excused myself from the table and went upstairs to do precisely was Ms. Hills told me, brush my teeth.

I sat on the bed to put my shoes on and started to think on what place on Earth could the queen have interest in bringing me to. I guess the only way to find out is just getting this over with and heading downstairs. At least I didn't have to go to school today.

"Are you ready, Marcus?" Queen Mariah asked me with a very bright smile on her face, completely the opposite of when she was here with the rest of the Wonderers a couple of days ago.

"As ready as I can be," I told her making my way outside to the driveway.

"Marcus where are you going?" My dad asked before I could leave the kitchen.

"To the driveway?" I asked puzzled.

"Marcus, we won't be doing any driving today." Mariah showed her Exotic Matter Sphere in place of her belly button was.

"We're gonna disappear out of here?" I asked.

"Precisely. Inside of my Exotic—"

"Matter Sphere?" I asked.

"Your dad was right, you are learning fast," she smiled at me proudly.

"Son have fun. There's no one safer that I trust you with, after all, you are with the queen. While you're away, Kent and I will be out looking for William to find out if he has been spotted in any other planet, okay? We'll see you soon."

"And I have a store to run, you know Gingerbread can't handle the morning rush by himself," Ms. Hills spoke as she left to her coffee shop. "Have a good time, Cookie."

"We'll see you before dinner." My dad hugged me.

"Later, Dad. Bye, Mr. Hors."

"Bye, Marcus, keep an eye open up there," Mr. Hors said looking at the ceiling, but I did not understand what he meant by that.

"Alright, Marcus, here we go." Queen Mariah put her left hand on my shoulder and pressed her Exotic

Matter Sphere with her right hand, and we disappeared out of there.

The feeling was pretty much the same as when I went both times to the Moon, except this time it felt more controlled and less rushed, I wasn't being tossed side to side, and the feeling of asphyxiation was almost non-existent. Just as usual, everything was done in less than a couple of seconds.

I opened my eyes and almost fell backward. I was standing on a big floating rock, a bit bigger than William's blue S.U.V.

"Look around you, Marcus. Tell me, what do you see?" The Queen of the Solar System spoke with a very soft and friendly tone.

"Stars, stars everywhere." I couldn't grasp the intensity of what I was seeing. There was no horizon; nothing concrete just stars in front of me. Some of them small, apparently too far out and some of them so big that I could almost walk to it and touch it as if there was actually a bridge connecting us.

"We're standing on a dark, frozen asteroid located at the Kuiper Belt. Everywhere you look is out of my jurisdiction. Outside of this protective asteroid belt, there are many other galaxies ruled by different kings and queens," Mariah explained as she pointed out to a few clusters out in the Universe.

"How many more are out there?" I asked curiously, still in awe.

"Even I don't have the answer. However, if you looked behind us..."

We faced the opposite direction and saw the most

beautiful thing I had ever seen. All around the asteroid where we were standing, were many more, hun-
dreds of thousands more, asteroids all around us,
forming what I now know, the Kuiper Belt. I could see
the Sun's rays touching every single one of them, at
least the ones near us. I tried to look for the Sun, and
it was right there in front of us. About thirty times
smaller than what we see from Earth, but unmista-
kably the Sun. Next to us, I saw this gigantic icy-blue
ball floating in the Universe with its rings circling
around it in a very harmonic way, five or six distinct
rings that I could count.

"It's HUGE!" I exclaimed in awe.

"About four times bigger than Earth in diameter.
If it was hollow, you could fit about fifty-eight Earths
inside of it. I remember the first time I saw Neptune
out here; I couldn't speak either," Mariah told me. "Its
beautiful icy rings make a pretty sight to see in contrast to the deep blue planet."

"I didn't know Neptune had rings." I was still gazing at the massive blue planet.

"All Outer Planets have them." Mariah injected.

"Outer Planets?"

"I divided the Solar System into two sectors: The
Inner Planets and the Outer Planets. The Sun, as you
can see from here, is in the center of the System followed by Mercury, Venus, Earth, and Mars; these are
the Inner Planets or the Rocky Planets. Between Mars
and Jupiter, we have the Asteroid Belt or Main Belt,
which divides the Rocky Planets from The Big Gassy
Planets. Everything inside the Asteroid Belt is known

as Inner Objects, everything outside of it is the Outer Objects. Jupiter, Saturn, Uranus, and Neptune are the Outer Planets." The queen explained it.

"Is that Pluto?" I pointed out to this smaller than Neptune white sphere next to it.

"That's Triton, Neptune's biggest moon out of the fourteen he has," she told me.

"What about Pluto?" I remembered seeing Pluto over Ms. Hill's G.O.L.

"Pluto is right over there." She pointed to the right side of Neptune.

From afar I could see the tiny icy planet known as Pluto. "It's so tiny," I analyzed.

"Smaller than every other planet in the Solar System yes, but Pluto is almost half of the size of the Moon; about 1,430 miles in diameter and 6,427,806 square miles in surface, it could hold almost 24 states of the size of Texas."

"Too bad it's no longer considered a planet, I remarked.

"That was a decision made by the King of the Milky Way Galaxy, Titus Vespasian that I have to enforce." Mariah Stars spoke with her queenly authority tone again, implying that this particular subject was not open for discussion.

"Once you go to the Center of High Education for Porters you will understand more about it."

I couldn't help relating to Allison Prior's anger toward her home planet being completely dismissed just because a king said so. It made me wonder about King Titus' motives. I guess the never-ending Pluto saga of being a planet or not was over.

"But enough about Pluto," Mariah's voice interrupted my train of thoughts. "What do you think about those planets over there?"

The Queen pointed out to the left side of Neptune, and I could see three more big planets to which I could recognize the remaining Outer Planets: Uranus, Saturn, and Jupiter. All of them with their rings just like she mentioned before. One thing caught my eyes though: Uranus' rings were vertical instead of horizontal like the other planets.

"What's up with Uranus?" I asked.

"Why don't we look closer?" Mariah Stars touched my shoulder, and I got sucked inside of her Exotic Matter Sphere again, transporting us from the asteroid we were standing on to anywhere she thought about. In the blink of an eye we were standing in a very dark, frozen rock.

"I thought if I could bring you to one Uranus' closest moon you could see the planet better." Mariah wore a very proud smile. "Welcome to Miranda."

I looked around me and saw a very rocky moon, with big craters everywhere and all covered in thick ice.

"Still amazes me that I'm standing on a moon able to breathe and not feel a tiny bit cold, wearing nothing but jeans, sneakers, and a t-shirt," I stated.

"It amazes me too. I haven't ever seen a Natural Porter before you." She looked amazed for the first time.

"Do people live here?" I looked around for signs

of civilization.

"Down south of here there's a small country, but we are not here for that. Uranus is right behind you," she showed the planet to me.

The pale-blue planet was about the same size of Neptune with rings much farther out but yet much thinner and lighter, and just like I observed before, it circles the planet sideway instead of horizontally.

"Why are the rings different than Neptune's?"

"Uranus is tilted over ninety-eight degrees, its south pole faces the Sun. The planet rotates not only sideway but also backward, the opposite direction than most of the planets in the Solar System."

"That is interesting." I stepped closer to analyze the large beautiful planet and its rings, almost falling to my knees after tripping on one of the little icy rocks.

"Are you alright?" Mariah approached me, helping me up again.

"Yeah, I just tripped on one of those rocks. By the way, they are pretty cool." I pointed out to the estranged elliptical black ice rock close by.

"If it wouldn't melt on Earth, I would say for you to take it." Mariah smiled. "Now let's get out of here, we got a lot to see." She touched my shoulder again, and we got dragged inside her E.M.S.

This time took longer than the previous times. The air was getting thinner and thinner, making it almost impossible to breath. We finally came to a halt. Once I could feel my feet on a solid floor, I collapsed to my knees, coughing as I was gasping for air.

"What's wrong, Marcus?" The queen kneeled in front of me, clearly worried.

"I just lost air for a second there, not used to this transportation system, you know? I'm fine now." I said standing up again.

"Are you sure you're alright?"

"Yeah, yeah. Where are we?" I asked looking around the very similar soil we have on Earth, except it was dark-grey. Everything around had a very gloomy feeling, just like Boston can sometimes have in the middle of cold February snow storms. The sky, however, had a more purplish tone to it than Earth did.

"We are on Titan, Saturn's Moon," Mariah answered, still not convinced about my earlier statement.

"It looks, in a sense, just like Earth." I saw an incredible vast ocean nearby.

"Titan's soil and the atmosphere is very similar to Earth. Except that what you see is not what you think it is; for instance, that ocean you see over there is mostly composed of methane. If you were not a Porter, you couldn't drink it without avoiding certain death."

I turned a bit to my left, and for the first time, I saw Saturn. The planet was smaller than Neptune and Uranus combined, its rings spread out for thousands of miles in its bright-white and gray colors, I had to sit down to observe it all.

"Unbelievable!" That was the only word I could come up with to express something of such a majestic feature.

"Saturn's rings go for over 40,500 miles wide. It is definitely a sight to see." The queen sat next to me.

She pointed out to a few moons in Saturn's rings and outside the ring all around us; she also mentioned Saturn's beautiful auroras and something about a great white storm that frequently happens on its atmosphere and that even though we couldn't get killed, we could get hurt if caught in one of those.

"Saturn's purple color is beautiful." I interrupted the queen's teaching.

"Purple? Where do you see purple? Saturn is pale-yellow, Marcus." Her face was in totally surprised by my statement.

"What you mean, 'pale-yellow'? The whole planet is purple like a grape," I told her, getting up to my feet kind of annoyed with the fact that she couldn't see it. However, this common feat was not possible. As soon as I got up, I lost balance and fell to my knees again.

"Marcus, what's wrong? Are you alright?" Mariah rushed, kneeling in front of me, looking inside of my eyes.

"Dizzy. I feel dizzy." I let the words out barely making any sound.

"Take a deep breath, Marcus. Try to breathe."

"Can't!" I managed to say before losing consciousness and falling sideways.

***

I opened my eyes, trying to make sense of my surroundings. A royal purple lounge chair was where I was laying down.

"Marcus, how are you feeling?" Mariah sat down next to me.

"What happened?"

"You fainted. Your ability to breathe air that is not oxygen must have worn out," The queen explained to me.

"Where am I?" I glanced around and saw this big high ceiling room that I was in. Everything seemed to be made out of dark-grey stone, some sort of granite.

"You're in the castle I reside in, in Jupiter." She got up to her feet, walking toward this ancient man. His beard was snowy white all the way down to his belt, compensating the lack of hair on his head; his spectacles were half-moon shaped, hiding his tiny blue eyes, matching the also delicate features of the pale-white complexioned old man.

"I think he's ready," the queen told him.

The old man was barely able to walk, but he managed to come five steps closer. "Drink this," his soft, raspy voice told me.

I met Mariah's eyes. She nodded to me as in approval of his command. He then drove the goblet close to my mouth, feeding me the drink. I couldn't see anything in it, the liquid was clear like water but had a silvery tone to it, I closed my eyes and drank it. To my surprise, it had no flavor, no consistency, nothing, just like drinking water.

"What's this?" I asked once the old man took his

goblet out of my mouth, making it disappear leaving a trace of glittering dust in the air.

"That was Stardust dissolved in water," Mariah began. "We give Stardust Water for Porters in training before they can get their Constellation Tattoo, it helps you breathe in any environment."

"Oh!" Was all I said. I was still staring at the weird old man behind the queen.

"Marcus, meet the Porter of the Crater Constellation, Alfred Stars." She introduced me to him once she noticed my curious face for him. "He's the only one capable of creating the Stardust Water you just drank; he is also known as the Goblet."

I got up to my feet to greet him, but he didn't bother waiting, he disappeared inside of his Exotic Matter Sphere leaving a trace of Stardust in the air just like the goblet has done before not even a few seconds ago.

"Alfred Stars?" I emphasized on the Stars.

"Yes. My dad became a Wanderer right after I became a Porter myself. He chose to wander by my side since we no longer had anyone."

Mariah Stars never shows her soft side. She has a very strong personality, very fitting for a queen. Her skin complexion was similar to her dad's, her eyes were also blue, her hair was straight and down to her elbows in tones of dark-brown.

"I'm so sorry." I managed to say.

"It's alright Marcus, my mom passed away thousands of years ago."

"Mariah!" A little girl wearing a white flowery

dress with her brown hair up in a ponytail walked in the room, interrupting our conversation.

"Gia!" The queen greeted her, embracing her in a warm hug. "What are you doing here?"

"My cousin told me you were here, so I had to stop everything I was doing to see you." The little girl's brown eyes were shining with happiness. She must not be older than seven years old.

"Your Majesty, I'm truly sorry to interrupt," a guy in his 30's walked in the room. His skin was the same tone as mine, his eyes were black matching his shoulder-length hair. "I told you not to interrupt the queen, especially when she has visitors, Gia." The guy kneed in front of the little girl in a reprehensive tone.

"Oh, it's no trouble whatsoever, Josh. By the way, I believe you have met Marcus Mathias future Porter of the Taurus Constellation, Wonderer of Earth," the queen reintroduced us.

"Mr. Mathias, it is a pleasure to meet you officially, we didn't have a chance to talk the other day when we were in the backyard discussing the mysterious reason why William Chase murdered your mom, Mrs. Katherine Mathias." Josh clearly didn't mean to upset me, but his words clearly pierced right through me like a sharp arrow.

"Forgive me, Josh, you are?"

"Oh, I'm sorry, I'm Josh Rogers, the Archer, Porter of the Sagittarius Constellation, Wonderer of Jupiter, also the queen's advisor. The day I came to Margaret's backyard I had my hair pulled back, remember?" Josh pulled his hair back as if to put on a ponytail, and just then I recognized him.

"Oh yeah, I remember you now." I shook his hand.

"Marcus this is my cousin Gia Lea," Porter of the Sagitta Constellation, the Arrow." He introduced me to the beautiful little girl.

"Hello, Marcus is very nice to meet you." She said extending out her hand.

I shook it back. "Nice to meet you too, Gia."

I looked around the room, and I couldn't help but feel underdressed for the occasion. I was standing in a place much bigger than the whole house of Ms. Hills, backyard and all; there must have been ten windows around us standing at least twenty-foot-high, with ordained, beautiful white silk curtains. Besides the royal purple lounge-chair I woke up on, there were not many other chairs in the room. It also didn't help that Mariah was wearing a pale-yellow gown, her short blonde hair was up in a hairdo. Gia had a flowery dress perfect for her age and location; Josh had a very stylish brown suit and expensive shoes, whereas I was wearing a brown t-shirt with jeans and sneakers.

Definitely underdressed.

"My queen, I hate to do this but King Aether and Queen Aithra wanted to see you, they said they might have a lead on Marcus' mom case." Josh's words reminded me of the reason why I wanted to become a Porter: to avenge my mom's killer, William Chase.

"Your Majesty, if I may—"

"Go back to Earth? Yes, of course, Marcus. Josh will do the honors of escorting Marcus back safe and sound?" Mariah spoke with her authority, reminding me why she was the Queen of our Solar System.

"But I—"

Before I could finish my sentence, I felt Josh's hands on my shoulders, and I had less than a second to comprehend what was about to happen. I felt my body being sucked right into Josh's Exotic Matter Sphere and expelling right out again in a matter of seconds.

"Why did you do that for?" I asked him furiously once we were all out of the Wormhole.

"When queens and kings get together the best thing to do is let them do what they do best: monarch. We are better off staying away from it. Plus look around you, I thought you wouldn't mind if we stopped in a few places before heading to Earth."

I looked around and couldn't believe what I was seeing. We were standing on a much rockier rock than before, with Jupiter right in front of me followed by Saturn, Uranus, and Neptune. Pluto was nowhere to be seen. Behind me was a much smaller planet than the ones I saw before; first was the red planet Mars, followed by our big blue marble Earth, then Venus and Mercury. The Sun was to my right, much closer than I last saw it when I was by the Kuiper Belt.

"You're standing on an asteroid on the Main Belt, or Asteroid Belt, the belt that divides the Big Gassy Planets from the Rocky Planets. Earth looks beautiful from here, doesn't it?"

Josh was right, even though I could see all the four

Rocky Planets, Earth was definitely the most beautiful of them all from out here. "Yes, it is."

"Come on, let's look closer." Josh's lower body kicked out of himself, transforming entirely into a centaur; half man, half horse with his suit completely gone and his hair wilder than was before.

"Jump on." He gestured for me to jump on his horse-like body. "I usually don't let people ride on me, but it's my honor to show the future Wonderer of Earth around," he said proudly as I began to get onto his back.

"Alright, I'm ready," I told him once I was secure on his back.

"Let's do this, then."

Josh took off just like a racehorse sprinting for the finish line. He jumped between asteroids throughout the Asteroid Belt; it was an exhilarating adventure. Then, when I was least expecting, we disappeared out of there, reappearing on the Moon. He strutted all the way up a mountain where we could see Earth perfectly from there.

"How are you holding up, buddy?" He asked as I got off his back.

"I'm fine, actually much better than before. I can see things more clearly. The stars are brighter, the planets more colorful and I can breathe much more easily," I responded as Josh returned to his human form again.

"That's good. Stardust Water can do wonders in your body, it heightens your senses. Wait till after you get your tattoo."

I looked ahead to Earth and got to thinking that it wouldn't be a bad idea to become a Porter after all. I was enjoying this trip through the planets quite a lot.

"Was it always like this?" I asked sitting down.

"Like what?" Josh sat next to me.

"Earth from up here looks very peaceful, you cannot even see the wars, the people, nothing. This perspective changes how I feel about myself, you know?"

"I do, actually. You know, when I was debating on becoming a Wonderer myself, my mentor, Larry Coupe, brought me here. At the time the Moon had barely been formed, and Angela was not a queen yet. This made me realize how little I am, and also how much I can do to change the world, or better, the worlds."

"So, you've been around much?"

"About a couple of billion years." He let out a joyful laugh.

I couldn't wrap my head on the fact that Porters could live for a very long time. It just seems like a science fiction movie, but then again, I was having this conversation on the Moon, wasn't I?

"How were things back then?"

"Well, I was actually born on Thea, the first planet that humans were brought to in our Solar System. When I was in the middle of my training something very tragic happened to all of the Theaians. Our planet was destroyed by our Queen, Mariah Stars."

"What do you mean, destroyed?" I got up to my feet, outraged by his statement.

"Whoa, calm down, Dogie."

"What does Dogie even mean?" I asked even more furious than before.

"An orphan strayed calf," he responded surprised with my burst of emotions. "It's an endearment term."

"I heard a few times before from other Porters who didn't mean it like an endearment term." I reciprocated.

"Are you certain about that?"

To be fair, I wasn't sure of anything. The Gemini Porters had called me Dogie before, as had William and Allison.

"But why did Mariah destroy your home planet, Thea?" I returned to the subject.

"You see, Thea was ruled by Regina Khales, Porter of the Virgo Constellation, the Maiden. Her reign wasn't one of the best. Regina let everyone do whatever they wanted. Little by little the small green planet was becoming dark, consumed by all types of narcotics and hallucinogens. All people on Thea were consumed by power, wars, and death. There were a few people like me who were saved per se, but everyone was gone."

"What about your family?" I kneed next to him.

"My mom died giving birth to me. My dad died when I was fifteen, of overdose. That's when my mentor found me and took me under his jurisdiction, and we moved to Jupiter, to start my training." A tear fell down his left cheek.

"I'm sorry." I felt somewhat bad asking about it. "And where is Mr. Coupe?"

N.M. BOBOK

"Dead. When Mariah asked for few of the Wonderers to go to Thea to help gain control of the planet back, Larry volunteered to go with her, but he never came back."

"Are you SERIOUS? Are you okay with that? Doesn't she feel any remorse?" I was still outraged by her actions.

"Oh, but if there's someone who feels any remorse every single day, it is Mariah. You see, she and Regina were terrific friends, Mariah took it upon herself to train her. She introduced Regina to the King of our Galaxy herself. When Queen Stars realized that her friend was beyond repair, she sent a T.P. to every single Porter that went down with her to go someplace safe. Some did, and some didn't. Once Mariah was safe in Venus, she threw Thea against Earth, completely destroying Thea and almost Earth in the process. If it wasn't for Angela Carey helping from Venus, Earth, who had no humans in it yet, would have been annihilated also."

"Oh wow. It must have been horrible." This time we both got up.

"From what I could see from Jupiter, it was. Once Mariah realized what she'd done, she formed the Moon from the remains of Thea and the debris that flew from Earth; so technically speaking, the Moon is Earth's and Thea's daughter." He kinda smiled.

We made our way down the white mountain where we were.

"Do you ever miss it, you know, Thea?"

"Sometimes. But life in Jupiter has kept me busy

training other Porters."

"Are there others?" I asked curiously. Maybe this is what I needed to know to help me decide to either become a Porter or let someone else be.

"A few here and there. A handful are being trained on different campuses throughout our Solar System," he explained.

"Campuses?"

"The Center of Higher Education for Porters, commonly known as C.H.E.P., is all over our Solar System, five locations to be more specific." He told me. "Let's go see it?"

Before I could even say yes or no, Josh's eyes lit up like stars, and again we went in his Exotic Matter Sphere. As soon as I could feel my feet back on the floor again, I opened my eyes to see where we had disappeared to. This time we weren't on an icy, rocky asteroid, but instead a very orange sandy place; no trees, lakes, rivers around us, just sand everywhere. I knew we weren't on Earth since I could see Earth in the horizon, just like we can see the Moon back home at evening.

"Marcus, welcome to Venus," Josh said, kind of excited.

"Uh, thanks," I said, a bit disappointed. Unlike every other planet I've been to so far, there was nothing here, just a very long desert all around us. Even Moon had a castle, a kingdom of its own.

"Don't look so disappointed. I just wanted you to see Earth from here. Let me bring you to C.H.E.P. campus here on Venus."

Josh was about to lay his hand again on my shoulder so we could disappear out of there, but I stopped him just in time.

"Can we just walk over there?" I was tired of being tossed from side to side just like I was thermite sucked inside of a vacuum cleaner and expelled right out.

"How about we run over there?" Josh transformed himself back in the centaur form with an excited face, just as if we were to race for some sort of prize or something.

"Sure..." I approached him as if to mount on his horse back again, but he pulled back neighing just like a horse does if you approach him unexpectedly.

"Whoa Nelly, who said anything about you mounting on me?" He straightened himself up.

"How am I supposed to keep up with you?" I asked, surprised by his reaction. Nobody can keep up with a regular size horse; imagine a ten-foot-tall centaur.

"Bulls are not as a fast as centaurs, but you can definitely keep up."

"Except that I have no control of it yet," I said, a bit ashamed.

"Now you do. You have Stardust water in your system. All you gotta do is think about it and go. Trust your instincts," he said sprinting in front of me. "Let's go!"

I saw him running so I ran right behind him, but nothing happened. I could only run as a boy, and after a few minutes, I was getting pretty tired and hot. Did

PORTER: MARCUS MATHIAS

I mention is pretty hot in Venus? It reminded me when I went to the dunes in Brazil in the summer. Pretty hot.

"I can't! I just can't." Words came out as I was trying to gasp for air. "Josh, man, I'm sorry but I can't. I don't know how to transform into a bull, and I can't keep running like this, not here at least."

When I heard nothing back from Josh, I decided to gain my strength back and look up for him, but he was nowhere to be found.

"Josh? JOSH? I shouted. Great! Now I'm exhausted, lost, and in the top of that, I am in Venus. What am I gonna do?

'You shouldn't give up so easily, Porter.'

Josh appeared out of the thin air right behind me, and with one swift move of his hand, his slapped me across the face, making me almost fall backward.

"WHAT DID YOU DO THAT FOR?" My rage was back, and I didn't care who heard me. I shouted with every strength that I had left.

"There he is." He smiled proudly at me. "You feel that tingling sensation inside of you? That adrenaline kicking in? That, my friend, activates your Stardust. Let it run through you."

"Are you nuts?"

"Come and get me, Dogie." He pushed me again. This time I didn't care, I was going for it. And I did. I ran right after him. I let the tingling sensation dominate my whole body, and in a couple of seconds, I had totally transformed into a bull again, running on all fours.

315

"There you go, Marcus, I knew you had in ya!" He shouted running in front of me.

It wasn't so bad to run entirely free in my bull form. I could breathe better, I could see better, and I could definitely run much faster. Josh was right in front of me only by a few feet; he was clearly pacing his struts. If he was strutting as I was running, I can only imagine how much faster he could actually run.

"You can stop now, Marcus." He told me as soon as we approached a village, transforming himself back into his human self.

"I don't think I know how," I said, slowing my steps but still somewhat running.

"This will help."

I turned around to face Josh, and a bow and arrow appeared on his hands out the thin air, he pulled it back, and the arrow's head was now on fire.

"Josh?" I asked, afraid of what he was gonna do with it. He fully ignored me, and I could see his lit eyes were aiming at me. He let the arrow go and shot me. I saw the arrow on fire reaching me and setting me on fire, making me fall on the floor. I rolled side to side, trying to extinguish the fire.

"Marcus, you're alright. You can stop rolling now." I stopped by the sound of his voice only to realize I was laying down on the floor fully back to my usual self and besides sand all over my body, I was fine.

"What in hell?" I asked, surprised and furious.

"Language young man. Self-defense helps ignite your powers; same thing happens when you're angry.

My arrows, however, can either pierce through you or dissolve into Stardust by the touch of your Stardust skin. The latter is the one I used on you to scare you and bring you back to your human form." He explained to me.

"Sorry." I got up.

"Nonsense. That's why you gotta go over there, and they'll teach you how to control your abilities." Josh was pointing out to a house a bit smaller than the one Ms. Hills had but much bigger than the houses around us. The front of it had a little sign that read C.H.E.P.

"It's just a house."

"I was gonna take you inside, but I think you had enough for one day, plus it's getting late so we should get you home before dinner," Josh suggested.

"Dinner?" I looked at him as if he had lost his marbles. "It's still day out." He just looked at me, waiting for me to realize.

"Wait, this is one of those things that not just because it's a day here, it's day everywhere, isn't it?" I remembered the same thing that happened on the Moon was happening here. We were on opposite side of the same Sun.

"Yes, it is. Are you ready?" He moved closer so we could disappear out of there.

"Wait, wait," I told him.

"What now?"

"I collect rocks." I grabbed one of the rocks nearby. It was the same size and color of an orange.

"You know, there's no point on collecting rocks

317

when you can literally travel to anywhere you want in the Solar system to see as many rocks as you want to."

"But I'm still gonna take this one." I held the somewhat heavy rock on my hand.

"Alright, if there isn't anything else..."

"No, I'm—" But I couldn't finish my sentence. Josh's hand was already on my shoulder, and we had already disappeared out of there. No matter how many times we had done it, I still didn't like being tossed inside of the Wormhole. There has to be a better way of traveling between planets.

"Son, welcome back." I heard my dad's voice as soon as I opened my eyes.

"Hi, Dad, this is Earth, right?" I said, checking my surroundings.

"Wow, you already forgot what Ms. Hills backyard looks like? Plus look up there." I did, and I saw the big full Moon, just like I did a couple of times before here on Earth.

"You did good today, little Porter. I'll see you again soon," Josh told me waving goodbye.

"Mr. Mathias," he greeted my dad before pressing his Exotic Matter Sphere and disappearing again with just a trace of Stardust left in the air.

"Mr. Rogers," My dad replied. "Did you have fun?" He turned his attention to me now.

"Yeah. I'm exhausted," I told my dad as we made our way back into Ms. Hills' kitchen where she and Mr. Hors were putting the table together for dinner.

"I hope you're hungry," Ms. Hills spoke as she saw

me, "I made rice, blacks beans with mashed potatoes, and roasted chicken."

"I wish I could eat, but I'm not really hungry." Interestingly enough I honestly wasn't.

"Is it the food? Your dad told me it was your favorite," Ms. Hills said, a bit disappointed.

"Let me guess, Stardust Water?" Mr. Hors asked.

"How did you know?"

"It provides everything you need for a couple of days, no wonder why you're not hungry. Porters can go without food or water for weeks if they are fully transformed in their forms. You'll be hungry in the morning, though." He explained it.

"Is it okay if I just go to bed? I'm really exhausted."

"Oh yes, Cookie, I'll save something for you in case you wake up hungry later." Ms. Hills removed one of the plates from the table.

"Have a good night, son." My dad kissed me on my forehead.

"'Night dad. Good night everyone. Once again, I'm sorry Ms. Hills."

"Don't be silly, you can have some tomorrow for lunch." I heard before I went upstairs to my room.

I took a shower and went straight to bed.

XX

WANDERER

It was the middle of the night, sometime between two and three o'clock in the morning.

> *'Marcus Mathias, where are you?*
> *I know you're here somewhere,*
> *I bring you wondrous news,*
> *News to tell you that no one dares.*
> *Where are you Marcus, where?'*

I heard that song before.

I remember distinctly when he sang this song for the first time before I even knew who he was. I was at a beach when my late grandma Maria appeared to me as a lion, her Astrological Sign. Little did I know then what she was trying to tell me; I was too awestruck by her beauty. Come to think of it now, she did try to warn me about people coming after me.

'A lot of people will try to get close to you, to gain your trust. A lot of them are not your friends, and they will do whatever they can to destroy you, and there will be a time when you'll have no one but yourself to trust in, only then you'll have the strength to become who you are meant to be.'

Those were her exact words, and she was right. She was warning me about a danger I didn't even know existed. A danger who befriended and betrayed me only to kill my mother in front of my eyes: William Chase.

"Have you gone completely crazy? Did you come here to kill me or perhaps to get killed by me, William?" I could hear him, but he was nowhere to be seen.

'What's up with the anger? I'm here to help you.'

"Are you here TO KILL ME, TOO? SHOW YOUR-SELF!" I got up, demanding to see the traitor's face.

'If you insist.'

Before William's words were even projected in my mind, a huge wave of air came rushing through the doors of the balcony, bursting them wide open. I fell backward with the impact of the wind. Will was there flying in midair, not entirely in his bird shape but only with his blue wings spread open, and tail. His whole body was blue, featherless but in the same midnight-blue he has always been, except his eyes, which were bright-white shining like stars.

"The nerve..."

"Now, now Marcus, I AM your friend, and I'm not here to harm you. I'm here be—"

I couldn't hear him any longer. I was deaf with anger, so I ran toward him.

"That's bullsh—"

"Language, young man." With a swift movement of his wings, William flew over me like if I were a kitten playing with a hawk.

"I like your spirit, but you're coming at the wrong guy. I'm not the bad guy here."

"You KILLED my mother! How can you not be the bad guy? Please enlighten me."

"Marcus, I was only trying to protect—"

I ran against him again, this time he flew around me and out of the window, landing on the parapet.

"I'll be back to talk to you once you have calmed down."

"NO! Come back here." I ran and jumped out of the balcony in an attempt to get him, but William spiraled out of my reach, and I fell out of the balcony, all the way down to Ms. Hills' backyard.

"Marcus, are you alright?" William landed next to me looking exactly how I met him a few weeks ago, in his full human form with only his eyes in the shade of midnight-blue.

"Leave me alone." A mix of anger and embarrassment stamped in my voice.

"Marcus, I—"

"I said, leave me ALONE!" I could barely move; my whole body was hurting.

"Oh my gosh, Marcus, what happened?" Ms. Hills rushed in the backyard to my aid.

"William," I said trying to get up, noticing that William was nowhere to be found.

"Stay still I'm gonna go call your dad. You might need to see a doctor."

"Marcus," My dad said as he saw me laying down on the floor, "can you get up?"

"No, I think I broke my leg."

"We should get you to a hospital, son." My dad picked me up and carried me to Ms. Hills' car, who joined us on the way to the hospital.

We got to the Cambridge Hospital's E.R. about ten minutes later. The doctor saw us right away. He took some X-Rays and just like I had predicted, I'd broken my right leg.

"Marcus, the doctor would like to keep you till morning, just to make sure you're okay," Ms. Hills told my Dad and me.

"Oh man, I don't wanna stay overnight."

"Actually, it's almost four in the morning, so you'll only stay here for about four more hours or so." Jena walked in the room with her tablet and a few extra blankets.

"Jena! What are you doing here?" I asked surprised at the sight of one of my best friends.

"My mom is working the overnight shift, whenever that happens, I like to come here to spend the night with her, keep her company," she sat next to me, "I figure if you're staying here overnight, I'll stay here with you."

"No Jena, I'm okay, I—"

"Nonsense. Ms. Hills and Mr. Mathias can go home to get some sleep, I'll stay here with you. We can play some games, watch some silly cat videos till you fall asleep." She insisted.

"Thanks, Jena. But what about you? Where are you gonna sleep?"

"The couch. It's not so bad once you get used to."

"You're gonna be okay, son?"

"Dad, I'll probably fall asleep as soon as you leave through that door, I'm still quite exhausted."

"Jena, if there's anything you need please don't hesitate to call, 'kay? 'Kay." Ms. Hills told her before leaving the room with my dad.

"So, what do you wanna do first? Play Angry Donkeys or watch silly cat videos?" Jena made herself comfortable next to me in the bed.

"Actually, I wasn't lying when I said I would go to sleep as soon as my Dad left. I am pretty tired from yesterday's trip throughout the Solar System."

"It's okay, Marks. Go get some sleep. You can tell me all about it in the morning once we are out of here." Jena got off the bed and made herself comfortable in the sofa. She pretty much fell asleep right away.

I was looking outside of the window from my bed waiting to fall asleep, thinking where possibly William could have gone. I was still pretty mad at him, and the more I thought about him, the angrier I got.

"Be careful, too much anger can give you cancer, don't you know that?" I looked to my right, and there he was standing just a few feet from the door.

"You little piece o—"

"You and your dirty mouth. One of these days I'm gonna bring some soap and wash it off, young man."

"We are roughly the same age, William..." I told him off.

"Yeah, give or take a few hundred years." He laughed as he sat by the bed next to me. "How are you doing?"

"You came to break the rest of my bones?" I asked angrily.

"Having trouble sleeping?" A nurse standing in the doorway peeked inside the room.

"Don't forget she can't see me or hear me, Marcus." William reminded me.

"No, I'm fine. An obnoxious bird woke me up, but I'm okay." I told her.

"Birds are beautiful creatures, darling. Try to get some rest." She walked out of the room, not before closing the blinds and the door behind her.

"See, birds are beautiful creatures, Marcus." William clearly loved the nurse's remark.

"What do you want, Will?"

"Gee, alright. I'm here to prove to you that I'm still your friend. I want you to meet a friend of mine. Dr. Octavio Ruer."

Right after William finish his sentence, a wisp of glittering air burst in the middle of the room revealing a man, around his 60's with barely any white hair left.

"Let's make this quick, shall we? I still have to check a few things in Uranus..." He was wearing a knee-long white coat atop of his regular clothes, if it wasn't for his walking staff almost as tall as he, with two snakes intertwined on top of it, I would have mistakenly taken him for a real doctor.

"Uh, Doctor, I broke my leg. What does that have to do with my an—"

"You weren't joking, William, he does have a great sense of humor. Just like his mom."

"My mom? Do you know my mom?"

"Shhh. Not now, young boy. Let me look at that head of yours." He was staring so close to my face that made somewhat awkward to look at him, but then, through behind his small spectacles I could see also his tiny eyes, shiny like a Porter's eyes do when they are using their abilities.

"And you are?"

"Dr. Octavio Ruer, Porter of the Ophiuchus Constellation. Now lay still." Dr. Ruer lifted his staff above, and both of snakes came to life, untwining themselves off the staff and on to the top of my body. One just sat right there on my chest while the other one wrapped itself around my broken leg.

"Uh, Doctor?"

"Shh, Marcus. You don't want the wrong snake to bite you." He warned me.

"To bite me?"

And it did.

I felt the snake on my leg bite me exactly above the cast. I could feel a cooling sensation inside my veins and taking over my whole body.

"There. Let's go girls." Both snakes jumped out of

my body and wrapped themselves again around his staff.

"William?" I said to William with the last breath I had before falling unconscious. I could still see them both vanishing inside of their own Exotic Matter Sphere.

And that was that.

"Marcus?" Mrs. Alvis, Jena's Mom, woke me up. "Honey, I take you had no problem falling sleeping at all?"

I looked around the room and Mileena, Jacques, Jena, Mr. Kent, Ms. Hills, my dad, Mrs. Alvis and the nurse, were right there staring at me with half-smiles on their faces.

"Gee, everybody. What time is it?"

"It's almost noon," Jena answered, "you slept all morning."

"Yeah, I guess I did."

"You're alright, son?" My dad sat next to me.

"Yeah. Yeah, I guess. Weird dream. That's all. Can I go home now?"

"Not so fast. We still have to get you a new cast." Mrs. Alvis told me.

"A new cast?" I looked at my leg, and the cast was destroyed to pieces all over my bed and the floor. "What happened?"

"I was hoping you'd tell me?" Mrs. Alvis was looking at me rather curiously.

"I don't know, actually."

"It's alright, honey. Let's get some X-Rays done to see how bad everything is and put a new cast on you, okay?" Mrs. Alvis said, getting a wheelchair close by.

"Here, son. Let me help you." My dad put his arms around me and helped me get up and into the wheel-chair.

"Wait, wait. STOP!" I shouted.

"I'm sorry, son. What is it?"

"My leg. I don't feel anything!" I said standing on my own with my two feet on the floor.

"It's alright, honey. The pain must have made your leg temporarily numb."

"No, Mrs. Alvis. I don't feel anything broken. I can feel my leg alright, and I don't feel anything broken. I can walk, heck I can even run."

"Marcus, sit down on the chair. Your leg was frac-tured in three places last night. It couldn't have pos-sibly been healed overnight," Mrs. Alvis told me.

"She is right Marcus, that is impossible, even for you." My dad was looking at me slightly scared than surprised.

"Yeah, maybe you're right Mrs. Alvis. Let's get some X-Rays done. I'm sure the pain will come back soon." I sat on the wheelchair as the nurse wheeled me out of the room.

After the X-Rays, I sat on the waiting room with my Dad and Mr. Hors. Everybody else had left to Ms. Hills' place.

"Dad, do you think it's possible I could have healed myself?" I asked when no one was around.

"Son, even for a Natural it's very much impossi-ble."

"Marcus, a Porter cannot be harmed only if he is

somewhat transformed into his Constellation, only then he won't break any bones or get killed. But you did break your leg last night." Mr. Hors explained it to me.

"Yes, you did. I was there. Porters don't simply heal themselves up. They just don't get hurt ever in their Porter form." My dad assured me.

"And if you do, you have to heal just like everyone else does, in casts, surgeries, things of that nature." Mr. Hors told me.

"Or maybe if you can schedule an appointment with Dr. Octavio Ruer, Porter of Ophiuchus Constellation." My dad mentioned to Mr. Hors.

"Except he hasn't been seen in centuries. He's gone crazy after the loss of his son. Last we heard of him, he was searching for him in the moons of Uranus."

"Dad, I—"

"Marcus, I have your results, shall we go in?" Mrs. Alvis interrupted us.

My dad wheeled me into her office.

"I looked at your X-Rays and no sign of any fractured bones."

"How's that possible, Marisa?" My dad asked Mrs. Alvis.

"I don't know, Roberto. All I can think of is his X-Rays got switched last night. I know it's something hard to understand, but mistakes happen..."

"It's okay, Doctor, I understand. Are you sure this is his, though?"

"When Marcus woke up and didn't feel any pain

on his leg, I suspected something like this might have happened, so I took matters in my own hands and took care of his X-Rays myself. So yeah, no one but me handled them today." Mrs. Alvis assured us.

"Are you okay, buddy?" My dad asked, concerned.

"Yeah, I feel fine." I was still thinking about the conversation my dad and Mr. Hors had in front of me in the waiting room. Suddenly the dream that I thought I had was no longer feeling like a dream anymore.

"Alright, let's get you home. You must be starving. Care to join us, Marisa?" My dad invited Mrs. Alvis to have lunch with us.

"I wish I could but after pulling an all-nighter I'm looking forward to going home to my own bed, and besides Jamal is bringing me lunch in a few minutes." Mrs. Alvis thanked him.

"Alright, let's go then. Tell Jamal that we miss him on soccer Sundays." My dad told her before we left.

***

We left the hospital in Mr. Hors' car and went straight to Ms. Hills' place where everyone was eating already. I sat in between Jacques and Jena. Mileena had left to go to work. Mr. Hors helped himself with a plate of mashed potatoes and broccoli while my dad went for the steak with mashed potatoes as well. Ms. Hills gave me a plate of mashed potatoes with gravy, steak, and broccoli. Jacques was already halfway through with his plate, with only broccoli left in it, while Jena only had broccoli on her plate.

"How are you feeling, Cookie?" Ms. Hills asked as she sat across from me next to Mr. Hors.

"I'm good. Like nothing happened."

"Dr. Alvis thinks they may have mistakenly switched Marcus' X-Rays from the night before. His leg is fine, no broken bones." My dad interceded.

"That's awesome, Cookie."

"Yup," I said, thinking if I should tell them about the visit I had from Will and Dr. Ruer.

"Now that we took care of that, we can focus on your mother's funeral, son."

"Again, with that story? I told you I don't think it's right to have a funeral without a body. Am I the only one who thinks this is all weird?"

"But Marcus, you yourself saw William killing your mom. The fact that we don't have a body doesn't mean she's not dead."

"I understand, Mr. Hors, but I truly think we could give a few more weeks..."

"Son, Kent is right. We—"

"NO, DAD. WE ARE NOT HAVING A FUNERAL WITHOUT MY MOTHER'S BODY!" I shouted getting up on my feet, to everyone's surprise.

"MARCUS!" My dad shouted back at me.

"I'm sorry." I sat back down again.

"Son, I know you're grieving your mom's death but—"

"I saw William last night, Dad." I finally said it.

"You what?"

"At least I think I saw him," I corrected myself, "I

had just fallen asleep, at least I thought I did. Then, Will appeared with a man, Dr. Octavio Ruer if I'm not mistaken. He had one of his snakes bite my broken leg, and after that, they both disappeared."

"Are you sure about that, Marcus?" Mr. Hors seemed more puzzled than ever before.

"I think I am. I mean, it was all very fast, and I was tired. Could have been a dream but it was all very real to me."

"That's very weird. Why would William bring Dr. Ruer to heal you?" Ms. Hills asked.

"I don't know. He also mentioned my mom."

"What do you mean, son? Did he mention Katherine by name?"

"Not by name, but he said that I had the same sense of humor that my mom does. How could he know that, Dad?"

"He couldn't. Your mom had never met Dr. Ruer, even I have never seen him. He has been gone for centuries, way long before I became a Porter."

"Marcus, I think now it's clearer than ever that we should take you to Venus." Mr. Hors suggested.

"True, Cookie. The Center of Higher Education for Porters has everything you can think of, they can help you control your abilities." Ms. Hills added.

"Angela has mentioned it before to me, but now I'm not so sure if it's the right way to go with this."

"Why do you think that?" Jena asked.

"Well, for starters she's friends with Will."

"Will betrayed us all, Marcus, not just Angela. Besides, we all went to C.H.E.P. and turned out just fine.

In order for you to become a true Porter, you need to enroll." Mr. Hors advised.

"Dad?"

"It's your call, son, but I think they are right."

I looked over to Jacques who still hadn't eaten the broccoli, looking for some sort of help from him but he just nodded in agreement with everyone else.

"Marcus, how about this, we'll give you till the end of the afternoon to think things through and then we'll talk. What do you say?" Mr. Hors suggested.

"I think it's a great idea, Mr. Hors. Now let's go, Marcus, I wanna talk to you." Jacques responded to him in my place.

"Don't go too far, Marcus still have to work in a couple of hours." Ms. Hills reminded me of my displeasure.

We went outside to Ms. Hills' backyard, and Jacques didn't waste any time.

"What's going on Marcus, why are you so against becoming a Porter? Anyone in your shoes would jump at this opportunity in a heartbeat."

"But I'm not everyone. I didn't sign up for this. I just wanna go to school like everyone else and not have to worry if I'm gonna have a vision between periods. I wanna be able to play football, soccer and not transform myself into a bull unwillingly in the middle of a final match. I just want my normal life back, with my mom alive baking cookies for me in the afternoon and playing soccer on the weekends with my dad and my best friend. Is that too much to ask?"

"I think I can help you with what you're going

through right now, Marcus." I didn't even hear Jena and Mileena approaching us in the backyard. "I know I'm the youngest one of the group, but I know a thing or two about grief."

"I'm fine, I'm not grieving. I just want my life back the way it used to be."

"When I lost my mom, my life was never the same again. Yes, I was too little to remember her—"

"Jena, you're still, uh, *petite, ma chère*[31]."

"Thanks for the remark, Jacques. Anyways, what I was trying to say is, when I was much younger than I am now, my mom was taken from me, I will never forget the brief moments we shared together. As short as they were, I will always remember my mom as a happy woman who always loved to cook, to see the house full of people eating and having a good time. Don't get me wrong, Marisa is like a mom to me, and I couldn't be happier, but the point is, be thankful for every moment you had with your mom, hold on to the good memories and let her go. Let's give her the proper goodbye she deserves. Let us say goodbye to her. Don't hold on to something that can never come back."

"That's exactly my point, Jena. I want to give my mom a proper funeral, I really do, but I'm not doing that without her body. I'm not giving up just yet."

"If you're planning on going after Will yourself, you will need to become a Porter, Marcus. There's no way you can survive all of this on your own."

---

[31] *Petite, ma chère:* Small, my darling (French)

"I know, Jacques. I will become a Porter, and once all this is over, I will find someone to replace me just like Mr. Hors is doing right now."

"You know that Mr. Hors is only doing this so he can be with—"

"Ms. Hills, I know, Jena. She is growing old, and he wants to grow old with her." I sighed. "Guys, I know how all of this sound, but this is my choice. I will become a Porter, I will avenge my mom, I'll get her body back, we'll have a proper funeral, and then my dad and I can find a new Porter for the Taurus Constellation."

"Alright, but if you're looking for a Sagittarius Wonderer, let me know." Jacques decided to just insert that.

"Alright buddy, it does work like that." My tone of sarcasm was well received by the both of them.

"Marcus, Steve has to take his break. Can you clock in, please?" Ms. Hills head popped out of the window.

"Be right there," I told her. "I gotta go to work. I'll text you guys later. And Jena, thank you." I gave the three of them a group hug before going back in to work.

I made my way through the kitchen to Lulu's Coffee Shop and almost as instantaneously Steve left to take his break with a 'thanks, buddy' as he passed right through me. I put on my hat and name tag as I heard Ms. Hills' voice:

"Now that is just us, Porters," she locked the front door of the coffee shop.

"What's going on, Ms. Hills?" I asked unsure of what was going on.

"Give it a second, Cookie." Before she was even done talking, two people appeared in the middle of the coffee shop right in front of Ms. Hills.

"Oh, you're finally here." Mr. Hors came in the coffee shop from the basement followed by my dad. "Marcus, there are two people that I'd like you to meet: Mr. Kyle Ptorn and Ms. Maisha Thompson."

"Hello Marcush, I'm Kyle Ptorn, Porter of the Caelum Conshtellation, the Chishel. Is nice finally meeting you." Mr. Ptorn said stretching out his hand for me to shake.

"He means, the Chisel, you'll get used to his lisp. I'm Maisha Thompson, Porter of the Sculptor Constellation," She barely moved a muscle.

I shook Kyle's hand and nodded back to Maisha, meeting her small meaningful brown eyes. She was a woman in her mid-twenties, with an olive complexion like mine, definitely Sun-exposed. Her body was very well defined, toned, slim and muscular but not significant, she could definitely be a gymnast. In contrast, Kyle Ptorn was an older man around his 50's, the semi-bald head and wrinkled face definitely gave it away. He was slightly hunchback, his eyes were light blue, his skin was very pale and fragile, and unlike Maisha, he was wearing a smile from ear to ear, not caring that some of his teeth were missing.

"Is nice meeting you too." I managed to say with a half-smile, wondering why these people where here.

"Marcus, Maisha, and Kyle are here to help you become a Porter. They are two of the teachers over C.H.E.P." my Dad said, putting an arm around my shoulder with a proud smile.

"Dad, I—"

"Son, before you say anything let me tell you something," he lowered himself a bit, meeting my eyes, "I know how reluctant you are about going to Venus to become a Porter so, I've spoken to Mariah and she has allowed you to go to Venus twice a week, maybe on the weekends, only to study science and all you need to know about Wonderers and Wanderers."

"That's awesome, Dad!" I said, thrilled knowing that I didn't have to go full time to Venus for my school year.

"With one little request, young man," Ms. Hills interjected, "you'd still be working here at Lulu's Coffee Shop three times a week after school, okay Cookie?"

"Yeah, sure, I can do that," I agreed, still very happy about my dad's decision.

"So, it's settled then," I said, relieved that I didn't have to compromise my high school years by going to Venus. Now I only had to go twice a week, I couldn't be happier.

'Marcus, there's no need for you to go to Venus.' I received a very familiar Thought Projection.

"Can I be excused for one second, Dad?" I said as I walked out of Lulu's Coffee Shop, through her kitchen and up the stairs. I've heard his voice before too many times to know that William Chase was sending Thought Projections in my head. Once inside my room, I closed the door behind me and pretty much shouted out:

"Where are you, Will? Why don't you show yourself? FACE ME!" I pretty much demanded.

'Marcus, I don't wanna fight you, I don't have much time to talk but know that you don't need to learn how to become a Porter, you are one already. A Natural Porter.' He sent me another T.P.

"You have no right to tell me what to do, not after what you did to my mom and me!" I said, holding back my voice so my father and all the other Porters wouldn't hear me from downstairs.

'Listen I gotta go, but don't forget I'll always be looking after you, I'll see you soon, buddy.' He concluded our Thought Projection conversation.

I was infuriated! The nerve of Will telling me what to do and where to go, he had no right, no right whatsoever! I left my room and went back downstairs where everybody was still talking about my journey to Venus.

"So, when am I going to Venus?" I asked, to everyone's surprise.

"What was that, son?" My dad said a bit shocked almost not believing what he had just heard.

"Yeah. I mean, I was thinking, if I have to go to Venus to learn how to become a Porter, I just might as well begin this weekend, you know, tomorrow," I told everyone around me. If that was something William did not want me to do, I was going to do it. I'm going to do everything I can to get him, especially now that I knew he was watching every move I make

"I say now," Maisha spoke. Besides her first initial 'Marcus' greeting, that was all I heard her say since she got here.

"Yesh, yesh, yesh, that soundsh great. We shall take you to Venush at onshe and show you around and begin your training right away, you are right young man, we have no time to loshe." Mr. Kyle Ptorn said getting up and hugging me, messing with my hair.

"Huh, Kyle aren't you forgetting anything?" Ms. Hills asked him.

"Oh yesh, yesh, yesh, how wash I to forget such a thing like that. Mr. Mathiash, may I pleashe take your shon to Venush for schooling purposhes only?" It took me a minute to realize what he was talking about, and not because of his lisp, but for the some-what serious and at the same time, mocking voice that he was talking to my dad.

"Mr. Kyle Ptorn you may take Marcus to Venus for schooling purposes only," my dad said with a very much serious voice, which made me realize that it was not a joking matter.

"Cool, I'm gonna go upstairs, pack up some stuff for the weekend, and dad, when I come back, we'll schedule a proper funeral for my mom, okay?"

I figured by then we will be able to recover my mom's body.

"If that's okay with you then it's okay with me." My dad smiled.

I went upstairs to my room and packed a couple of shirts and shorts. If I remember anything about my trip to Venus with Josh Rogers, Sagittarius' Porter, is the hot weather there.

I came downstairs, and everyone was in the kitchen waiting for me.

"Son, I just want to know that,"

"Dad, I'm only spending the weekend on Venus. I'll be back before you know it." I hugged him.

"Alright son, now go and have fun."

"Bye, everyone."

"Shall we?" Mr. Ptorn said as he put his hand on my shoulder. I wasn't looking forward to being sucked in and tossed side to side inside of Mr. Ptorn's Exotic Matter Sphere, but I know I'll be in Venus in a blink of an eye. I took a deep breath.

"We shall."

EPILOGUE

"So, how did it go, William?"

"How do you think it went, Camille? Marcus doesn't believe me. He thinks I've killed his mother when I was saving him from you."

"Well, honey, I guess you and I both know you shouldn't have interfered with my plans, I had everything under control." Camille's tone of arrogance was almost as intolerable as the sound coming from the chains wrapped around her ankles and wrists.

"What you and I both know is that you're not doing this on your own. Who hired you? Who are you working for?"

"I'm working for myself. I'm a Wanderer just like you, but unlike you, I don't want that stupid boy becoming the next Wonderer of Earth. His family has disgraced our reputation for way too long, William.

343

Don't you see?"

"All I see is how lunatic you are! Marcus is the Natural Porter of the Taurus Constellation, regardless of what you think. But sooner or later, you're gonna have to tell me who you're working for, Ms. Liam."

"Will, buddy, it's me, Marcus. Let me out of here so I can help you." The voice was of Marcus and even the looks, if I didn't know better, I would have been totally confused by the abilities of Ms. Camille Liam, Porter of the Chameleon Constellation.

"You're not the only one with the ability to mimic someone's voice, Camille." Even though she could change her looks and voice, I could also mimic voices, and hers was the voice I've just spoken.

"Willie, come on, let me out of these chains. You know they can't hold me forever." She begged me as I turned and walked out of the cave.

"It's involved in Antimatter; it should hold you long enough."

"Willie—"

"WILLIAM! My name's William. I should've truly killed you in front of Marcus when I had the chance." I stepped out of the room locking the gate behind me.

"Now if you'll excuse me, I gotta go find the real Katherine Mathias."

ACKNOWLEDGEMENTS

Porter: Marcus Mathias, Book I wouldn't exist without the support of my friends and family, thank you! Special thanks to my sister Marcela Miranda for designing the cover, to Daniel Bandeira for taking my picture for the back-cover, to Alma Gabriela Alvarez and Bailey Nascimento for editing it for me, and to Jonathan Hanson-Pereira for revising it. You guys are the best!

Thank You,

-N.M. Bobok

Made in the USA
Lexington, KY
27 November 2019